Ross took another drink of the whiskey that was dulling the pain of the wound in his head, and set the bottle behind him in the brush. He heard Blade's horse approaching the top of the ridge. He studied his Colt, as if he were buying it, and rocked the hammer back. It was a rifle shot—*but maybe,* Ross thought, *if I can stop my hand shaking, I can settle the Pacheco claim right here . . . .*

FRANK BONHAM

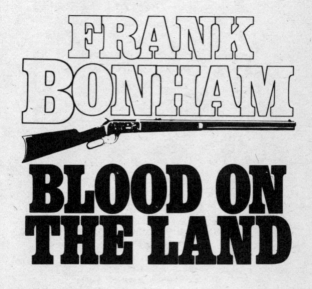

BLOOD ON THE LAND

BERKLEY BOOKS, NEW YORK

BLOOD ON THE LAND

A Berkley Book / published by arrangement with
the author

PRINTING HISTORY
Berkley edition / April 1978
Second printing / December 1980
Third printing / October 1982

ISBN: 0-425-05756-9

1

CHANCE CROUCHED IN the smoke of a piñon fire, a cigarette lax in his lips as he sliced potatoes into a Dutch oven. His eyes were half-closed against the bite of the smoke. As a clatter of chain hobbles came from the stream below the horse camp, he glanced down and saw his Mexican wranglers bringing the horse herd back to the tufted grass of the bench. The herd moved briskly up the slope, its dust pierced with sparks where the shod hoofs of the wranglers' ponies struck stone. Ross Chance stood up, a large, dark-skinned man in his middle twenties, slender but with the hard-shouldered look and whittled hips of a horseman. His black hair was roached like the mane of a mule.

Chance placed the lid on the kettle, muting the sound of the frying food. Shirtless, he moved back from the heat of the fire and looked up as a second man came through the dusk into the efficient disorder of the trail camp. He saw Blade Ramsey trip over a crossbuck and heard him swear under his breath. Ramsey encountered a bedroll on the ground and kicked this aside, and Ross Chance smiled to himself.

Ramsey, who was blond, tough of jaw and in his early twenties, tilted his Stetson over his face as he came up. He was deeply burned by nine months of mountain horse-trapping.

"God damn' Mexicans," he said, "would leave bear traps in the way if we carried 'em."

"Watch where you're going, then," Chance suggested cheerfully.

Blade Ramsey grunted and inclined his head toward the Dutch oven. "Spuds again?" he asked.

"They've been good enough for nine months," Ross Chance said. "Why change over the last night?"

Without replying, Ramsey stared down the slope, where the horses were clattering up through the withered highland trees. "Them damned greasers," he said, "will break half the horses' legs, running them with chain hobbles!"

1

Chance set two tin cups on the ground and poured coffee from a large blue-enamel pot. As he handed a cup to his partner, he smiled. "Hang on, kid. Tomorrow night we'll be in Las Truchas. If we get a quick sale for the horses, maybe you can have a drink."

"*Tomorrow* night!" Ramsey exclaimed. He took the coffee, continuing to stare at Chance. "That's forty miles, ain't it?"

"Give or take a few."

"Then why the hell-sweat to make it in a day?"

"Well, for one thing we're not driving cattle, so we don't have to worry about weight loss. And for another, this is the first week in October. Every stock buyer in New Mexico will be in town. They're paying the good prices now. They'll begin to slide soon."

Ramsey sipped some of the coffee. "It seems to me," he complained, "that we've been working like it was the first week in October ever since we teamed up to trap horses last winter. What's the rush? Are horses going out of style or something?"

Ross gazed off across the dark ranks of desert hills stepping down into the east. His face was serious as he drew on the cigarette.

"You see, Blade," he said, "I don't know how much time we've got left on that deal I told you about. Death and taxes; two things that won't wait for anybody. And we're bucking both."

"Two more things I didn't know," said Ramsey stiffly.

Ross shrugged. "I told you. I've told you the whole deal. Not all at once, maybe..."

"That's the truth! A word here and a word there. I ain't quite sure whether we've been trapping horses to pay somebody else's taxes, or just to work up the biggest bunch of the worst horses in New Mexico."

"Both," said Ross. "The horses will pay the man's taxes. The man happens to be my father. Now, here it is," he said. "Just so you'll know why I took your whiskey away and put you to work—"

He gazed thoughtfully at the tip of his cigarette, and he was aware that Blade Ramsey watched him closely.

"It's a little involved," said Ross. "The ranch I mentioned belongs to my father. It's down on the Mexican border. Just before I met you, I got word from his lawyer that the old man was going under for taxes. But if I could raise a couple of thousand within a year, I could cut in for half the ranch. Otherwise," he concluded, "he might leave it to the Society for People with Five Thumbs, or something."

Blade Ramsey grinned. "He sounds kind of crusty."

"He is. Well, that's the taxes part of it," Ross told him. "The death part—the lawyer said my father had had a couple of heart attacks. You figure out for yourself why we've been working on the double. If he dies before the taxes are paid, the whole works goes at auction."

They drank their coffee and smoked, and Ross shredded a quantity of jerked venison into the Dutch oven. Blade asked how long he had been gone from home, and Ross said:

"Five years. I wouldn't exactly call it home. It's just a place I grew up in. And a nice place to grow up, by the way, as far as country goes."

"What've you been doing all this time?"

"What's anybody do who doesn't know anything but horses and cattle? Breaks horses and punches cattle. I've been doing it all over central New Mexico. And I found out one thing I never knew before."

"What's that?"

"It's a hell of a lot different working for somebody else than working for yourself. It's the difference between working as a guard in a jail and being a prisoner. Take it from me, I'll never work as a prisoner again, if I can help it!"

Through the dust and smoke he gazed in satisfaction at the horse herd being bedded on the bench north of camp. On the hillsides, the darkness was thickening. Here in the camp the firelight ate a ragged pattern in the encroaching night. Both men glanced around as a rider jogged in through the litter of harness. He was a thin-faced Mexican with a frayed black mustache, one of the wranglers.

"*Ya vienen caballeros, patrón,*" he said to Ross.

"*Quién?*" Ross asked him.

"*Parece que—*" The Mexican made a gesture of balance. "*—Que viene Señor Hackley,*" he finished.

"Okay," Ross said. "Let 'im come."

"What's he say?" Blade asked. "Think the stupid Spik would learn a little English, wouldn't you?" he added truculently.

"He says Tom Hackley's coming," Ross told him. He put the cigarette in his mouth and pensively rolled it with his tongue. Hackley was the rancher on whose ranch they had been mustanging.

"Well, let 'im come," Blade repeated. But in a moment he asked uneasily: "What do you figure he wants? The deal with him's all buttoned up, ain't it? We're all done mustanging his range."

"Sure."

"We cleaned out the mustangs for him and done some fencing, didn't we? What more does he want?"

Ross grinned. "I'm not arguing with you, Blade. Maybe he doesn't want anything. Give the man a chance. It did seem, though," he admitted, "that he looked kind of hungry last week, when he rode up and saw how many broncs we'd trapped out."

Blade snorted. "Well, that's just too bad! The culls were eating his graze down to bedrock. If he's going to try to bluff us out of any of these horses, he'd better go slow. You know, all that stands between being prisoners in that jail again, instead of guards, is these broncs."

Ross raised the lid of the Dutch oven and stirred the potatoes. "I think he said he was taking some cattle to town this week. Maybe he's camped near here and he's just riding over for a cup of coffee."

"That's fine," Blade said stiffly. "That's just about what I'd spare Mr. Hackley, after the tricks he's pulled. The son-of-a-bitch."

2

THE SUN WAS off the ridges, now. In the late dusk, Ross Chance and his partner watched Tom Hackley and three of his riders ride past the herd which the Mexicans were shaping up for the night. He observed Hackley draw rein beside a line of horses tied to a rope stretched between two stakes.

Blade began to swear under his breath. "And don't think you're going to trade us out of any of those saddle horses, either," he growled.

Ross chuckled, big-shouldered and swarthy. "You've had it in for Hackley," he said, "ever since he charged us twenty dollars for that steer of his we butchered."

"Why, hell, it had a broken leg!" Blade argued. "The pumas would have eat' it if we hadn't."

"I'll tell you what I think about Tom Hackley," Ross said thoughtfully. "He can part easy with something he owns but hasn't ever seen, like wild horses that are eating him poor. But once he sees it, he can't let go of it. Suppose you keep quiet and let me handle him? I know the breed."

"We aren't going to knuckle down to him, if that's what you mean."

Ross rubbed one fist against his palm, watching the riders come on now. He noted the blanket rolls behind their saddles, and knew then that they were on their way to the railroad town of Las Truchas. He said, "No, that's not what I mean. If he once gets the idea that we're going to knuckle down, we're licked. He could slap a lien on the herd at the railroad pens. It might be two months before we cleared ourselves. By that time the horses would have eaten up all our profits. Don't think he doesn't know that, either.... Now, keep quiet," he told Blade quickly.

Blade was staring hostilely at the oncoming rancher. "He looks like an old graze bull that's about due for a whippin', to me."

5

Hackley and his men halted at the rim of the firelight. Tom Hackley raised his hand in a brief salute. He was a big man with a look of blunt strength. His sleeves were rolled and his wrists looked heavy-boned.

"We've got a gallon of coffee going to waste here, boys," Ross greeted them.

"We'll be making camp soon," Hackley said. "I've got a herd coming down that we're going to meet."

"Unload and rest, anyway."

He thought Hackley's men looked uneasy. They were merely run-of-the-mill cowboys, but they had the appearance of hoarding some secret they were not proud of. Hackley spoke suddenly, with a nod at the horses.

"Well, it won't be long now, eh? You boys will be stinking rich."

"We've still got to sell them," Ross pointed out.

Hackley glanced at the herd with a bitter grin. "That won't be hard," he said with heavy irony. "You've got some pretty nice-looking horses in that outfit."

Ross bent to touch the tip of his cold cigarette to an ember. "We've got a few the canners won't turn down," he conceded.

"A few!" Hackley laughed shortly. "A few, the man says! Mister, it looks to me like you've got about fifty percent saddlers in there. I thought you men were hunting culls," he added stiffly.

Blade came in impatiently. "If we've got anything that doesn't look like a cull, it's because Ross can take anything with a mane, and four legs hanging down at the corners, and make a horse out of it."

"Jesus, I'd like to have about two hundred culls like that myself!" Hackley said harshly.

Ross braced a foot on a crossbuck. Though his mouth and eyes were young, they were weathered and mature. "What are you working up to?" he asked.

Hackley placed one hand on the pommel and dismounted. He hitched up his heavy bullhide chaps.

"I thought maybe we ought to clean up the rest of our deal before you sell those mustangs."

"We have cleaned it up. You checked the herd for loose brands the other day. What's left?"

"What's left is squaring for the saddle stock of mine in that herd. I had thirty-odd colts ranging in Chloride Canyon when you started your work. I didn't bother moving them because I thought you knew a blooded horse from a bronc. But when I went looking for them last week, they were gone."

Chance threw his cigarette away with a snap. "Get out of here," he said.

Hackley looked surprised. Then he pointed his finger at Ross. "You'll damn' well explain where you got them ponies! Or else you'll pay me ten dollars a head for them."

Chance smiled, now. There was something barbarous in the shine of his teeth. "Why should we pay you for something we were to have free?"

Hackley's hand clenched the buckle of his chaps. There was a tinge of yellow in his eyes and the pugnacious expression of his mouth soured a little.

"I don't bluff worth a damn," he stated. "I'll settle for ten dollars a head on those horses, or you won't ship them." Then he added, almost defensively, "You baling-wire operators seem to figure that because a man's got a little land, he's an easy mark. By God, if I range bigger than you, it's because I watch things. And I've been watching you!"

Chance winked at Hackley's riders. "Yes, you're a smart rancher," he smiled. "Like hell! You're just a damned bull who needs a belt across the nose once in a while. Now, get out of here."

Hackley's nostrils frosted faintly. He came straight up as though he had been slapped. "If I don't get the money," he said, "I'll slap a lien on your herd. You won't sell a horse until you've answered in court."

Blade started past Ross to get at Hackley, but Ross's arm stayed him. "Listen to me!" he told Hackley. "I never paid off on marked cards before, and I won't start now. Your lien would fall apart the first time a judge looked at it. But it could wreck us just as well as if you had a sound case against us. I'm not telling you anything; you've been working on this one all summer, I expect. But what may be news to you is that it won't work."

"No?" Hackley said. "Why not?"

"Because you're not going to serve us with any liens. The only way you're going to hold us up is with a gun, and I'll kill you if you try that. And if you come at me with a lien in Las Truchas, I'll whip you so your own horse won't recognize you. We need every cent this herd's worth!" He kept his eyes on Hackley's as he added bluntly: "Now, get out."

Hackley appraised him. Ross was outweighed by forty pounds, though he stood nearly as tall as Hackley; but the rancher's eyes seemed to recall old brawls in which he stood triumphant with a beer bottle in his hand, and at last, with a tight smile, he asked Ross:

"Why don't you make me?"

Chance hit without warning. His fist smashed Hackley's mouth. He saw him falling back, astonished and hurt, and he followed with a ripping left. He jolted Hackley in the belly and the man went down on his rump. In a moment Hackley rolled onto his hands and knees and came up. His face was yellow as suet.

"You dirty horse-stealing squaw-raper!" he shouted.

He came back with a wild swing which Ross took on the shoulder. The rancher swung a left and another right, snorting through his nose like a bull. Ross kept backing, aware that if he stopped one of Hackley's swings he was finished. Hackley's ponderous strength corded his forehead when he swung. As he backed, Ross tripped over a packsaddle, but recovered as Hackley lunged upon him, and for an instant Hackley's face was an open target. Ross stabbed at it. His fist split Hackley's upper lip. While the rancher was off-balance, Ross stabbed him again in the face and then slugged him in the belly. Hackley gasped and bent over, and Ross's lips stetched across his teeth in a vicious smile as he brought a clean, sweet blow up into the man's face.

Hackley was on his hands and knees, shaking his head. Then his face turned up and he looked at Ross dully. Ross Chance's grin was tight as rawhide.

"How about that lien?" he said.

Slow and hurt, Tom Hackley rose, staggered a bit, and said, "Damn you, Chance!" He plunged with desperation at the mustanger. Ross stood his ground, firing short, savage hooks into the bloody face. At each blow Hackley's hair shook. Hackley stumbled and went down again.

He was beaten; every man there could see it, but Ross seemed possessed by some cold savagery that would not release him. He heard himself saying:

"Come on! You don't do all your fighting with a bankbook, do you?" and Hackley with a great and weary force got to his feet. But he was only able to stand there as Chance measured him, his eyes narrow; then a hand gripped Ross's wrist, and Ross heard Blade saying gruffly:

"You don't have to kill the son-of-a-bitch."

The rage drained out of Ross. He felt shaken and yet elated. One of Hackley's men came to his side and supported him.

"I meant that, about the lien," Ross said. "Thought maybe I'd better show you first that I can whip you, if I have to—in case there was any doubt in your mind."

Someone produced a canvas water bag. Hackley drank deeply, then poured a quantity into his Stetson, which he put on his head, letting the water spill over his head and shoulders. Looking dazed and ill, he mounted without help and rode before his men into the thickening dusk.

When the hoofbeats had died, the gentle autumn night lying over the hills, Blade said: "Christ, you didn't have to kill him! If I hadn't stopped you—"

Chance gazed wonderingly at Blade, this big, blond, good-looking ruffian with the weak mouth and reckless eyes. He was surprised, somehow, that Blade had not seen the inescapable logic of what had happened.

"I had to whip him," he said. "I had to knock any idea out of his head of slapping a lien on us. That'd finish us, don't you know that? And this money we're after is earmarked for something I'm damned well going to have."

"He was licked before you stood him up again."

"Maybe. But believe me, I know his stripe. Anything he sees on its knees, he'll kick in the face. And that ranch—by George, Blade, I think I'd kill a man before I'd let him blow that deal. I feel like my cord was tied to that land when I was born, instead of to my mother. If I lose it, I reckon I'd just about bleed to death."

Without comment, Blade walked off.

When night watches had been set, the men found level spots and unrolled their beds. As he had done every night within Ross's memory, Blade Ramsey pulled off one boot and sat there with it on his lap, musing fondly. "Man, what I'd give for a jug of whiskey and a little ol' yella-haired gal!"

And Ross made the answer he customarily made when his partner's spirit flagged. "Hang on, kid. If this deal works out, I can personally guarantee the whiskey. But you'll have to find the girl yourself."

3

THEY TRAVELED HARD from dawn to late afternoon. An hour before they reached the railroad town of Las Truchas, on the Rio Grande, Ross rode ahead to find pen space for the horses. But the pens rocked with cattle, the whole town throbbed with fall shipping. Ross rode back and they camped that night on the bank of the river.

In the morning, while the horses nuzzled the fat ripples of the stream, Ross saddled again. Blade had not argued when Ross suggested that Blade stay with the horses while he went ahead to find a buyer: both men knew that when Blade hit town, business with Chance and Ramsey would stand still for a time.

"Anybody in particular you're looking for?" Blade asked him.

Ross hesitated. "You remember when I came down here for supplies last spring? Well, I ran into this fellow, Gunlock—George Gunlock. He used to ramrod for my father. He's working for the new owner now. A man named Lamar Shelton."

Blade stared at him. "The *new* owner! Then what the hell are we buying into, if the old man's sold the ranch?"

"There's forty thousand acres left—could you make out on that without getting cramped? You see, my father sold half his place last year. Don't ask me why. I wish I knew.... Anyway, Gunlock was up here to prospect for beef when I ran into him. I told him about the horses we were trapping, and he said Shelton would probably buy them. He sells quite a few to some mine, for pit animals."

"There's a hell of a lot I don't know about this deal, ain't there?" Blade suggested.

"Not so much," Ross shrugged.

"For one thing, what makes you think you can make the ranch pay if your father couldn't?"

"He's sick. The lawyer figures the hands have been robbing

10

him blind because he doesn't get around enough. There's nothing more to tell you," he said, "except that I left because he and I never hit it off. I left when I was seventeen. Now he's in trouble. So I'm going to try to help him, and help myself, too. I had to have a partner if I was going to make a killing in horses. It was just a gamble. We might have come out with twenty-five broomtails, instead of a hundred and eighty. As far as you're concerned," he said shortly, "all you need to know is that you're about to go into ranching—for a year's work. You're not going to cry over that, are you?"

Blade examined the stubborn, calm eyes under the black brows, and began to smile. "Okay," he grinned. "Don't get excited. Find your buyer and let's get rid of these nags."

Ross rode down the river.

Las Truchas lay in an elbow of the Rio Grande, the stony desert hills on the west blocking it from a view of the mountains. The buildings followed the curve of the river. At the north end of town was the railroad station, where an alkali-crusted yard engine labored and cattle bawled, and cowboys half-visible in sorrel dust shouted profanely at steers jamming the loading chutes. Drawn by a light breeze, the dust sifted through the cottonwoods into the sand hills across the river.

Ross had to swing from the road to avoid a small herd of steers being driven toward the station. Sitting his pony there, he watched the punchers jogging past, and suddenly recognized one of them as a man of Tom Hackley's. Just after this, Hackley himself appeared from the dust. He saw Ross, and Ross stared with a twist of guilt at the cut and swollen face. One of Hackley's eyes was completely closed, blue as a mouse, and his lips were puffy. For an instant in the dust their glances touched, and a muscle ridged in the rancher's face. The compressed viciousness of his glance startled Ross. A moment later Hackley had gone on with the herd, and Ross, shrugging, wondered how else you could tell a man like that that you meant something. He jogged into the town.

More Mexican than American, Las Truchas was a gaunt-looking village of whitewashed adobe buildings and dirt sidewalks. There were a few two-story structures, a blunt church spire in the distance, and more street traffic than three towns its size were entitled to. Outside every store, wagons were being loaded with supplies. Red-necked men with rough country haircuts drifted awkwardly past chattering girls on the walks, and women in heavy black gowns with leg-of-mutton sleeves gossiped beneath the trees. Everywhere were dogs and boys and strutting blackbirds.

For the last few years Ross had got his mail at the Rio Grande House, a small hotel where he stayed on his infrequent visits from the ranches he happened to be working on. While the proprietor fingered through the pigeonholes, he suddenly recaptured the tension of that day, nearly a year ago, when he had had the letter telling him his father was ill and the ranch might go for taxes. It was a complex excitement made up of apprehension, but also of anticipation—of knowing that there was an opening for him to go back. And for the first time he had known how much he needed to return to Amargosa, to its easy border ways and the not-all-bitter memories it had for him.

"Nothin' for you, Chance," the old proprietor in his paper collar said. "It seemed to me like they was, but—"

"Try 'Ross,'" Chance said. "You might have posted it wrong."

The old man pulled with thumb and forefinger at a whiskery wattle under his chin. "I remember, now. There was a letter not long after you were in last spring. We held it three months. Then my wife sent it back. She didn't know you wanted us to hold your mail any more. Thought you'd moved."

"Where was it from?"

The old man did not know. A keen disappointment rubbed at Ross. He was momentarily irritated, feeling that through an old woman's forgetfulness he may have missed something important.

"All right," he said, finally. "Thanks."

As he went out, a man and a girl moved into his path. Blinded by the sunlight, Ross had a soft and agreeable collision with the girl. He caught a scent of lavender before he stepped back. He received a smile from the girl's gray eyes—they were the lightest of grays under hair that was lustrous black.

"Excuse me," Ross said.

The man said, "It's all right," without glancing at Ross. He was tall and dark-skinned. He wore a gray business suit, well cut, and a black Stetson with a beaded band. Probably the girl's father, he looked about forty-five, aggressive, capable, and vigorous. Holding the girl's arm, he went on.

Ross watched them stop at a green buggy. He caught a glimpse of lace petticoats when the man helped the girl up. The throb of a long-suppressed hunger rose strongly in him. He breathed deeply and crossed the street to the first saloon on his list.

There was a spirit of autumn and season's end in the saloons of Las Truchas. Ross shared the feeling. Cowboys who had not tasted liquor in six months were getting a good start on a spree. There appeared to be enough girls and gamblers on hand to insure that they did not spend all their money on liquor. His eye found a few of the respected foreigners to whom the town was host—the packing-house representatives, feed-lot men, and drummers.

In the first three saloons where he asked about Lamar Shelton, the man did not seem to be known. He took the names of other men who might be interested in buying horses, but he did not look them up. What George Gunlock had told him last spring indicated that Shelton might be able to pay more than the ordinary buyer of horses. Yet Ross knew his interest in Shelton had deeper roots than this. He wanted to see the man who had taken over the better part of the ranch which had been the only home he had ever known.

A bartender in the Cloverleaf recalled having sold Shelton a drink a couple of days ago. "And I seen his foreman last night," he mentioned. "So maybe Shelton's still in town."

"Do you know where he stays?"

"Probably the National Exchange. It's the best. Shelton looks heeled."

Ross walked through cool, lemon sunlight to the National Exchange, crossed the porch to the lobby and asked about Shelton. "Yes, sir, he's registered here," the clerk told him. "Do you want to leave a message?"

"He's not in?"

"No, he left for the station a half-hour ago. He's shipping cattle this morning."

"How will I know him?" Ross asked.

"He wears a black Stetson—dented crown. I saw him leave in a rented buggy—green cut-under with a fringe top."

"Did he have a girl with him?"

"That was him," the clerk smiled.

Ross jogged up the road toward the station, thinking less about Lamar Shelton than the girl into whom he had bumped. He came into the dusty turbulence of the cattle pens. He did not see Shelton nor the buggy at the first chutes, but as he rode past the low-eaved station the green buggy flashed from behind it, making for the road. He recognized it, but now only the girl was in it. He waited at the edge of the road until she came up to him. Then he raised his hand.

"Excuse me, Miss—is this Mr. Shelton's buggy?"

"We've rented it—yes," the girl told him. She smiled straight into his eyes. He felt stiff and awkward and excited, and thought, *What's the matter with you? Haven't you ever seen a woman before?* What was it about this woman that was different? Her slow voice seemed to have a sheen. Her hair was black and her skin tawny and her eyes light gray, and her teeth were so white and even that he could not look away from them while she smiled.

He moved on the saddle. "Maybe you can tell me whether Mr. Shelton's in the market for some horses."

"He might be." Again she smiled, the faintest touch of a smile, but it seemed to Ross that when her eyes went over him, hesitantly, they had an almost physical impact. It was time he had returned to town, he decided....

The girl told him Shelton was with the cattle train which was preparing to leave, and Ross said, "I'm obliged." Yet he did not ride away. He seemed unable to take his eyes from her.

"How—how many horses have you?" she asked him.

He turned back. "About two hundred."

"You didn't raise them all yourself?"

"No, we trapped them. We've been in the mountains the best part of a year—or the worst, depending on how you like being kicked by horses."

She laughed. Then there was a silence of a few seconds, and it seemed to make plain the fact that they had been merely making conversation. Ross sat soberly staring at her with his hat hanging from one hand. She was incredibly neat and dainty, her white blouse crisp as sugar, with a thick black velvet ribbon about the lace collar. Her lips were rich and smooth, and the surprising thing was that in her own expression there was something very personal; something rousing.

"How long have you been mustanging?" she asked him.

"A year. I was driven to it," he smiled. "I had a lot of need for money, but not much of it. So I sank all I had in gear and mustangers' wages, got myself a partner, and had a crack at it. If we cash out like we hope, we'll go into ranching."

Her smile deepened. "Why, you should settle near us! We're west of El Paso, on the border. A town called Amargosa—it's the seat of Doña María County. Do you know it?"

Up the tracks, the locomotive bleated. A volley of crashing reports ran down the line of cattle cars. "I've been through," Ross said. "Are you near town?"

"Fifteen miles out. Right on the border. It's called Pacheco Ranch, after the man who originally owned it."

No, ma'am, he almost corrected her. *After Pacheco Valley. The original owner was named Archuleta. My father bought from him.*

She raised the lines when he did not reply, as though she must drive on, and he said quickly, "Yes, I—I remember it was a nice town. Lots of chinaberry trees, and a bandstand. What about land prices?"

"Well, it's hard to say. But ranches change hands now and then."

And this girl with the dark-lashed pale eyes, whose skin was so smooth a man could not look at it without wanting to touch it—this girl lived in his home, and ate at his table, and perhaps slept in the bed that used to be his. Was that why they were looking at each other as though they had met before, and neither wanted to pass until the acquaintanceship had been made secure? All Ross was certain of was that she was looking at him in a very odd way. Not a come-on way, not brazen at all; but certainly with a message in her face.

"We'd like to find something we could manage," he told her. "But we might have to get it at a tax auction, something like that."

She regarded him with a steady curiosity; but soon she said: "I wish you'd think about it, anyway. Perhaps I could help you find something, if you should pass through."

This is impossible, Ross thought. *A girl I've never met before is asking me to buy a ranch near her, and I'll be damned if I think she's playing it fast and loose. I think she's just friendly—or else simple.*

"I'll sure come down there for a look," he said. "By the way— the name is Ross Chance."

"Chance?" she said, with an oddness in her eyes.

He spelled it. "Kind of an unusual name."

"Yes.... You don't have relatives there?"

Ross, for some reason, shook his head.

"A Colonel Bob Chance?"

Ross shook his head again.

"I just thought—Well, if you do decide to look around Doña

María County," the girl said, "why not write me a note ahead of time? I'm Laurel Shelton. Amargosa, General Delivery. I could make inquiries in advance."

On the heels of this startling offer, she made him a little nod, raised the lines and drove off.

After that it was like waking from a dream. As he sat his pony in the bleached sunlight, Ross wondered whether it had really happened. But it had: the buggy was in sight for one last instant before it disappeared behind the trees. A ruttish masculine strain in him said, *This one would be like shaking apples out of a tree*, but then again he was seeing the friendliness in the pale eyes, and the firm, beautiful features, self-possessed and intelligent.

Don't fool yourself, he decided. Anything out of line there would be a quirt across the nose. No, sir. Laurel Shelton had felt the same disturbing emotions he had, and knowing that the way things went they would probably never meet again if she stood too firmly on her feminine prerogatives, she had let the bars down for one moment.

With the intoxication of excitement still in him, Chance rode on to look for the girl's father.

Shelton stood at one side of a slatted chute up which cattle were being prodded into a car when Ross found him. His black Stetson was on the back of his head and he held a quirt in one hand, striking it slowly against his palm. Atop the car stood a tall, rawhide-thin man with a cigarette in his mouth and a tally board in one hand. Chance recognized George Gunlock, who had ramrodded the Chance ranch five years ago, when Ross lived there. Gunlock stared at him and then gestured and called a greeting. His nose was lean and high-bridged and his mouth was just a tuck in the long blue-stubbled chin. He had to glance down as two more steers lunged into the rocking car, made a note on the tally board and then called through the turbulence of the yards:

"Mr. Shelton—want you to meet a friend of mine—Ross Chance."

Lamar Shelton smiled tentatively as he looked at Ross. He was a larger man than Ross had realized before—taller and heavier than Ross himself, who stood six feet—and his features, though they had a rugged sort of handsomeness, were large and coarse. His brow was rutted by two deep lines, and sun wrinkles creased his eyes. He had wide, muscular-looking lips. There was a forcible quality about him, a feeling of energy merely in the way he transferred his quirt to his left hand and offered Ross his right.

"How are you, Chance?" he said.

"Good," Ross said. He looked closely at Shelton, but if the rancher were impressed by the name, as his daughter had been, he did not show it. "I've got some horses to sell. Someone told me you might be interested in buying them."

Shelton's eyes were busy with Chance's face. "How many?"

"A hundred and eighty. Most of them are canners, but there's a few good saddlers in the bunch, and a few more that wouldn't shake the ash off your cigar."

"Where are they?"

"Upriver a half-mile. I can take you there any time you say."

Shelton said the first thing that indicated an awareness that Ross's name was the same as that of the man he had bought a ranch from not long ago. "Any relatives around here? Your name's familiar."

"Not around here," Ross said.

"Or Doña María County?"

Again Ross denied it. He thought Shelton looked relieved. "How did you know me?" Shelton asked.

"Someone pointed you out when you left town a while ago. I spoke to your daughter just now and she said you were buying a few horses."

There was instantly a left-handed quality to the moment. Shelton kept his eyes thoughtfully on Chance as he raised his cigar and drew on it. But the good nature was out of them. Exhaling the smoke, he said, "I've got no daughter."

A puncher standing on the chute bars turned his head to look at Chance. His expression was unreadable, but there was wicked anticipation in his eyes. Puzzled, Ross said,

"A young lady in a green buggy—?"

"I judge it was my wife you were talking to," Shelton said. Chance's gaze wavered. He felt the hot embarrassment rushing to his face. Dumbfounded, he tried to recall what had made him assume the girl was Shelton's daughter, rather than his wife. But he knew it was simply that she could not be over twenty, while Lamar Shelton was more than twice that.

"I expect it was Mrs. Shelton," he said. "I don't know why I—"

Shelton interrupted: "Who told you I was buying horses?"

"Bartender at the Republican."

"I don't do business through the Republican," Shelton stated flatly, watching Chance with chips of malice in his eyes.

"I didn't judge you did," Ross said. "Well, if you aren't buying horses, we can forget it."

"I'm a cattle rancher and a beef contractor," Shelton said. "Nobody's eating horsemeat to speak of these days. If he does eat it, he doesn't speak of it."

Someone chuckled. Yet Ross could not be angry. Shelton was retaliating for an unforgivable hurt. Somewhere in Ross a fury was growing against Laurel Shelton, who had led him on. If she had not said she was Shelton's daughter, she had at least made offers no man's wife should make to any other man.

"All right, forget it," he said.

As he turned, Shelton said, "Where did you say these horses are?"

"Half-mile up the river."

"I'll be up in an hour to look at them."

"All right," Ross said, surprised. When he glanced back, Shelton said:

"'Chance...' You say you don't have relatives in Doña María County?"

"No," Ross said.

4

ROSS HAD BOUGHT a half-pint of whiskey for Blade while he was in the village. He uncorked it on the way back to camp and had a drink, his face grim with afterthoughts from the session with Shelton. A wind had come up during the morning. As he reached the camp on the graveled shore Ross felt its cold, raw sweep against his face. The Mexicans had curried the horses and arranged them according to Ross's orders—the culls in a large rope corral, a rope stretched between stakes serving as a hitching-rail for the saddlers. By itself on a picket line was the bay stallion Ross was saving as a stud. Ross tossed Blade the half-pint and the big, blond mustanger raised the bottle and said fervently, "Here's to brunettes!" and drank deeply, and after that he said, "*And* redheads!" and killed the bottle with a toast to the yella-headed little girl he was going to hunt tonight. Then he threw the bottle in the river.

Ross told him the news. They ate the stew Blade had prepared during the morning. The dark-lashed eyes of a girl with skin like sun-browned satin seemed to watch every motion Ross made. It seemed indecent that a little tart like that should have the face of an angel. It was not fair to the men she captured with her smile. It was not even fair to her: one day her husband or some love-sick rival would take a forty-five to Laurel Shelton and make a good girl out of her.

Shortly after noon, Lamar Shelton rode in with George Gunlock. Shelton inspected the horses. "That bay go with them?" he asked, nodding at the studhorse.

Ross shook his head. "I'm saving him for breeding. Don't walk too close to him. He's rough."

He started to explain about the saddlers, but Shelton asked abruptly: "Why did you tell me you weren't Colonel Bob Chance's son? Gunlock says you are."

19

"You weren't being very talkative," Ross countered. "Why should I open up?"

"On your way back, though?"

"Did I say I was?"

"Just guessing," Shelton said. Then he added: "It was too bad about your father."

"You mean his heart? Well, they sometimes live forty years after an attack, if they take it easy."

Shelton frowned. "No, you don't understand. I mean—"

When he hesitated, Ross prompted: "You mean what?"

"Didn't you know he was dead?"

Ross gazed blankly into Shelton's features. "Dead? Since when?"

"Last June. Hell, I'm sorry to be the one to carry the news. But he had his last attack early in the month."

Ross had a curious feeling of loneliness. A bridge had fallen over a stream, and he stood by himself on one bank, while a boy and an old man faded into mist on the far side. The boy was himself, fifteen years ago, the old man was his father, but they were both dead, now. He had never thought he cared at all for his father, not since he had finally learned the old man did not care for him. Perhaps it was knowing that a door had closed on part of his life which gave him this lost, aloof feeling.

"No, I hadn't heard," he said. "There was a letter for me at the hotel, but it was sent back. I guess that was it."

Shelton was drawing a cigar from his pocket. On second thought, he drew two and offered one to Ross, which Ross silently accepted. But when Shelton held out a light, he shook his head. He stood with the cigar in his mouth, numbly watching the brown currents of the river.

"I'm sorry," Shelton said gravely. Then he smiled suddenly: "You were kind of mysterious about being Chance's son."

"You were kind of mysterious about whether you were buying cattle or not."

Shelton did not comment, and after a moment he said, "Well..." and then turned and started up the line of rough-maned mountain ponies. Chance drifted back to the fire. Gunlock and Blade, sitting on the sand, were drinking coffee while the wind whipped grit against their chaps. In silence Ross poured a cup for himself. He put the cigar over his ear and frowned into the tin cup. He tried to grasp the meaning of this sweeping change which had just been made in his life, but it eluded him. He had this feeling of depression: that was all.

Gunlock was watching him. "I see Shelton told you about the colonel," he said. There was no sympathy, feigned or otherwise, in his voice. His long face was merely inquisitive as he studied Ross. His cheekbones were sharp, his mouth thin, and deep bays went into his hair at either side of a prominent widow's-peak. He had the same reckless expression about the eyes that he had had when Ross knew him—the inveterate gambler, the old month's-wages-on-one-throw ramrod he remembered well.

"What happened to the land?" Ross asked him.

"It went for taxes."

Ross glanced at Blade, who was beginning to look startled. "What land was this?" Blade asked.

"*The* land," Ross admitted. "My old man died. . . . Who got it?" he asked Gunlock.

Gunlock tilted his head toward Lamar Shelton. "Him. At auction."

"So he's got the whole works now," Ross said, with surprising bitterness.

"Well, he paid for it. Anybody could have bought it at auction."

"Yes, but why'd the colonel sell that first half? He couldn't have needed the money."

"If you wanted to keep tabs on things," said Gunlock, "you should have stuck around, and not gone running off." He began to smile. "You shouldn't have gone into that saloon, at seventeen, anyhow. Colonel Chance's son drunk and disorderly! It liked to shamed him to death."

Ross gazed up at him, annoyance in his eyes. But Blade regarded the foreman with interest, his face amused.

"Why, pshaw," he said, "Ross don't even take a drink. He hasn't let me have a bottle in camp for months."

Gunlock chuckled. "He took a drink this time—first time, wasn't it, Ross? He got fallin'-down drunk. One of the places he fell down was a straddlin' house. The old man liked to blew up! I heard him in the parlor the next day readin' the Bible to Ross for a solid hour."

Blade was grinning broadly. "Yeah? Then what?"

"Then Ross whupped the tar out of him. Man, you shoulda—"

"All right, drop it," Ross snapped.

Gunlock stopped speaking, still smiling. Both men gazed with broad amusement at him. But the ramrod did not continue. After a while Blade's smile faded. He began to frown.

"Where the hell does this leave us?" he asked Ross. "There's nothin' to put the money on, now, is there?"

"I don't know," Ross said. "I won't know for sure till I talk to the lawyer."

"Don't know what Henry Lyman can do now, Ross," Gunlock said mildly.

"Neither do I, but I'm going to find out. The first thing I'm going to ask is why my father sold that land in the first place. I was going to pay the taxes on the other half with what these horses brought."

Gunlock's eyes lighted. He glanced at the horses. He looked back at Ross. "Hey, wait a minute!" he exclaimed. "You mean this herd is free and clear?"

"Just the wranglers' salaries against it."

Gunlock's back straightened. "And you're looking for an investment..." But at that moment Lamar Shelton could be heard returning. Gunlock stood up. "Hang onto that money then, boys. I've got something to tell you pretty soon. The hottest thing in New Mexico!"

"It used to be Mexican lotteries all the time," Ross recalled.

"Yes, but this—" Gunlock broke off. "I'll tell you later."

"Here's one maybe you can tell me now," Ross said quickly. He had not meant to ask this. But suddenly, knowing he might never have another chance to find it out, he put the question that had bothered him since this morning. "Why in the hell," he asked, "does a girl like Mrs. Shelton marry a man like her husband?"

Gunlock looked down the beach at his employer. "He's only forty-odd. Plenty *macho*. I know *I* wouldn't want to tangle with him. And I allow he'll give a girl about as much lovin' as she requires."

"I didn't say he was old. But the girl can't be over twenty. And she doesn't seem like his type."

"Puzzles me, too," said Gunlock with a wink. "A year ago she was just the daughter of the marshal of Amargosa, Al Henderson—guess he was since your time. Nice fellow, beat Will Coles out in an election even though he was a newcomer to town. So Laurel was doing her own washing and setting her own rizbread. Then she married Shelton. Now she's got twenty gowns in her closet, according to one of the maids, and I hear she pays more for a teaspoon of perfume than Lamar does for a bottle of whiskey. I guess I never will figure it out," he concluded solemnly.

Because it was exactly what Ross had figured, he felt let down. He had hoped for some novel explanation. "So she married him for his money," he remarked drily.

"Why not? Never knew a better reason." Gunlock laughed.

Shelton had stopped to do some figuring in a notebook. Suddenly Gunlock hunched over his coffee cup and caught Ross's attention. "Get this," he said. "Shelton may scream like a banshee, but he'll pay twelve-fifty a head for these plugs. He's got a spot for every horse he can buy. Hold out for twelve-fifty."

Ross stared at him, trying to be sure he was not attempting a practical joke. But Gunlock was serious. Ross turned to gaze at Shelton; but just then he saw the rancher passing behind the bay studhorse on the line. He raised his arm quickly.

"Look out for that bay!" he shouted.

Shelton lunged away just as the horse kicked out at him. He turned angrily, his Colt half-drawn. "God-damned horse like that ought to be shot!"

"You can shoot him," Ross called back, "for two hundred dollars. I told you about him before."

With a settling shrug of his shoulders, Shelton came on.

The men by the fire stood up. Shelton asked Ross, "How much are you asking for them?"

"Twelve-fifty on the culls," Ross said. "Average of thirty for the saddlers. If you want the bunch, you can take it for three thousand."

Shelton smiled drily. "I'll give twenty-four hundred."

Then he began explaining, in a dry, take-it-or-leave-it way, how cull horses had slipped in price this fall, and how much it would cost to feed the herd while Chance and Ramsey hunted another buyer; but Ross interrupted him.

"I know what I can get in El Paso. I can knock off two hundred for freight and feed and come out even. But that's it."

Shelton dropped a cold, suspicious stare on his foreman. After a moment he said, "You don't dicker like a mustanger, Chance. You talk like you'd been reading my mail." Ross shrugged and, smiling faintly, drank his coffee.

"All right," Shelton said. "But believe me you hit me at the right time. I wouldn't give nine dollars for those brutes any year but this."

At that moment they heard a horse and buggy coming up the road from the village. Somehow, without looking, Ross knew that it was Shelton's wife. He felt his heart contract. They watched until the green livery buggy came into view at a turn masked by leafless cottonwoods.

"Didn't you tell Mrs. Shelton I said to stay at the hotel?" Shelton asked George Gunlock. His face was dark, hard as saddle leather.

"Yes, sir. I reckon she got tired of waitin'."

For one moment, Shelton gazed at Ross. Then he looked away, as the buggy ground up to the fire. He heard the labored breathing of the horse and the leathery squeal of the springs.

"I asked you to stay at the hotel," Shelton said to his wife.

"But I thought you might want to ride back," Laurel Shelton told him. "You've almost finished, haven't you?"

"Yes. . . . You know, I wouldn't have asked you to stay there if I hadn't had a reason," Shelton remarked.

"But the lobby was so cold and dirty, and all the papers I could find were ancient."

"And the men, too?"

The remark fell like a stone in a pool. As it became quiet, Ross was forced to look at the girl. He had meant not even to acknowledge her. Her face had colored. There were tears in her eyes—tears of shame, but also of anger, he recognized, and he thought she would have more courage than most women, if she could face this down. With a smile bright with maliciousness, she retorted:

"Why, Lamar, do you think I'd have to take a buggy to find a man, if I wanted one?"

"I reckon you could cause a stampede by dropping your handkerchief, if you wanted. I didn't mean to reflect on your charms." His irony was heavy-footed. Ross was aware that the girl could cut him to ribbons. But Shelton quickly turned back to the mustangers. "Chance, I'll give you a check for this. My foreman will identify you at the bank, if you want the cash."

He knelt by a rawhide *alforja* and began to make out the check with an indelible pencil. Ross looked again at Laurel. She was regarding him with appeal in her face. *Don't believe him*, she was trying to say. And Chance, who wanted to despise her, experienced a melting sensation as of tears trying to come to his eyes. In the sunlight her face was beautiful, with the clear cool beauty of moving water, quiet on the surface, but its quiet only proving its depths. She was not only beautiful, he decided, she was deep, full of spirit and the unpredictable. She was beautiful and unhappy and she belonged to a rich man who had bought her for cash. An emotion like despair shook him.

"By the way," Shelton said, "I'll be in El Paso two weeks from today. I'm going up to Santa Fe tomorrow. Now that you've got some cash, why don't you make it work for you? Buy all the horses you can find between now and then. I'll pay you the same price for anything you want to sell."

"I might do that," Ross said. He thanked the rancher for the check, folded it, and just before the buggy rolled away he looked once more at Laurel Shelton. Her lips were slightly parted and she was still gazing at him with that quality of appeal, as if she wanted to make something clear to him. But everything was perfectly clear: Laurel Shelton liked her husbands rich and her lovers young. That was what Ross Chance knew he should keep in mind in any future dealings with her.

5

ROSS TOLD THE Mexicans he would return with their pay before sundown. He put the bay stallion on a lead rope and the three of them rode to town. Blade had been quietly dreaming over the fortune in Ross's pocket, and now he sighed, "I've always had a hunch I could make a fool out of a roulette wheel, if I had enough capital. I've got a hunch now that I'm going to do it tonight."

"With what for money?" Ross smiled.

"Why don't we bank half of this, and put the rest into a game?" As Ross continued silently looking at him, the big blond rider said defensively, "No fooling! If I double or triple half of it, we'll be a lot farther ahead. Anyhow, what do we need cash for now? The ranch deal's blown up, ain't it?"

"I don't know for sure. Maybe we'll need all that money and more, before we're through."

They were passing near the railroad station, the wind of late afternoon ripping at their hatbrims. Ross saw the rising temper in Blade's eyes.

"Let's understand something," Blade said curtly. "I didn't marry you, last winter—I just went pardners with you. And I've had a bellyful of scratching. If that deal's blown up, we're splitting the money. Now."

"We're not splitting the money until we know the deal's off," Ross said. His steady assurance began to drive Blade to fury. Blade hitched his horse around toward Ross's, but at that instant George Gunlock spoke.

"Wait a minute, boys. Ross, did you ever think of money working for you, instead of you working for it?"

"That's the idea in saving it," Ross said.

"I'm not talking about ranching," Gunlock said impatiently.

26

"How'd you like to run that money up to a fortune, maybe, in six months' time?"

"I bought my last brass mine when I was ten, George," Ross smiled.

Ross still spoke banteringly, but he was aware of the desperate intensity in the ramrod's eyes. He remembered how Gunlock had always had a dream like this—a Mexican lottery or a mail-order mine—and he supposed this was the most recent.

"This is on the level," Gunlock insisted. "I could make all three of us a fortune in six months, if I had that money to work with."

"Sure enough?" Blade asked; but he was not joshing the man.

"Jesus, boys, if I'd once got my hands on that much money during this last year! Believe me, I wouldn't be ramrodding for a bull like Shelton. I'd be toting a gal like Mrs. Shelton on my arm, and walkin' in fifty-dollar boots. Only—God damn it," he said, with genuine tears in his eyes, "I can't tell you what it is till I get the money! You see, if I told you, there'd be nothing to keep you from walking right in and helping yourself."

"Gold mine?" Chance grinned. "Spanish Prisoner?"

Blade said sharply: "Shut up, Ross. Can't you give us a—a clue, or something?" he asked the foreman. "We'd be for something like that in a minute, if we knew it was straight. Even the top-kick, here."

The horses' hoofs scuffed, the cold dust swept ahead of them, as Gunlock balanced in decision. "Well—call it a land-title deal. Legal stuff. That's all I can say till I see the cash on the table between us."

"Legal stuff," Ross repeated. "Sometimes that legal stuff backlashes, doesn't it?"

Gunlock's lead-gray eyes were steady with secret meaning. "Believe me, Ross, *this* is backlashin' right now! It paid off for somebody once before, but he didn't nail it down. It paid off big."

"Shelton?" Ross asked; and he thought Gunlock looked astonished. And seeing that expression on the lean face seemed to light a small flame in him.

Gunlock scratched his unshaven chin. "Never mind who," he said. "Just savvy this, now: the minute I see that money, we're pardners. And you'll kiss me on both cheeks."

"God forbid."

"Okay!" Blade exclaimed. "We're in, George!"

"What the hell are you talking about?" Ross stared at him.

Blade's lips flared; his boyish eyes were vicious. "This is one game you ain't cutting me out of! I've got as much say about that money as you have. I think this fellow's on the square."

"I think it's a hare-brained deal like twenty others he's lost on," Ross snapped. "And we're keeping that money in one piece until I talk to the lawyer."

"You son-of-a-bitch!" Blade shouted suddenly. He reined his pony against Ross's, and swung hard at his head. Ross caught his arm and held it. He turned his horse away and dragged Blade out of the saddle. Blade landed sprawling, got up and began trying to haul Ross down, but Ross seized the coil of rope at his saddle horn and clubbed him over the head with it.

Gunlock shoved between them. "Jesus Christ, boys! I didn't want to break up the team."

Ross's anger burned out. Looking down at Blade, he felt sorry for him. His enthusiasms were as violent as a child's. He reached a hand down to the mustanger, but Blade stubbornly turned away.

They rode silently to the bank, where Ross, thinking a little more deeply into Blade's character, decided to take twenty or thirty dollars in cash and put the rest into a cashier's check which would be invalid without both their signatures.

Leaving the bank, Gunlock apologetically suggested they sleep on it. "I'll be around town till noon, when I take this herd back to Amargosa for Shelton."

He rode off. The street was full of cowpunchers and dogs, of wagons and autumn wind, and on the wind came despondency. "I'm sorry, boy," Ross told Blade. "But I've worked too hard for this."

"What are you going to do with it?"

"I don't know. But I want to talk to my father's lawyer before I do anything. I want to know why he sold all his good land to Shelton, when he'd refused a fortune for the land long ago. You don't reckon," he said, "that Gunlock could have been talking about Shelton just now, do you?"

Blade did not answer. "Where you staying?"

"Rio Grande House, if I can get a bed."

"I'll look you up in the morning."

Riding back to the horse camp, Ross paid off the wranglers. Then he saw to storing the harness and other gear at the railroad station, and rode into the village again. The day was dying in melancholy, wistful with long shadows, with woodsmoke like memories. He thought of a new grave in the family cemetery on Pacheco Ranch. He thought of the small chance of doing anything with the cash they had. And last he thought of Laurel Shelton.

It was a damned shame, he thought, to make a woman beautiful, and then give her the soul of a strumpet. It was typical of a wasteful Providence, however. Witness this bay stallion, which he was picketing behind the Rio Grande House after taking a room: the blood line of a fine horse, the heart and brain of a rattlesnake.

Ross left his saddle pony under the long shelter behind the hotel, with the other saddle animals of the guests. He went to his room and washed up, and looking into the triangular sliver of greenish mirror he saw a tall, sober-looking young man with very dark skin and brows and short, camp-cut dark hair. I don't look like I've got a grin in me, he decided, and so he smiled, and decided he looked even more sad. I don't want to get like the old man, he reflected. Money and cattle—all that counted—so that in the end those things had given him a stamp as plain as a notary's seal. He had a laugh like a cigar box full of nickels, a smile like a crack in a tombstone.

He tried to decide what it was he wanted, and all he could think of was the ranch, and the *álamos* along the stream; the big cool ranch house and the feel of solidness it had.... But it was gone now, and that feeling of loneliness came over him again. Brusquely, he lighted one of the Mexican cigars he had bought, tilted his Stetson at the town angle, and left the hotel.

He had gone a short distance in search of a café when he saw a familiar shape on the boardwalk before a saloon. It was the rancher, Tom Hackley. With his hands cupped, he was trying to light a cigar, but the wind snuffed the match and he swore to himself and dug for another. On an unaccountable impulse, Ross paused to hold his Stetson as a shield for him. Hackley could not see him because of the hat, but he murmured, "Thanks, friend," and puffed the cigar into life.

As Ross replaced his hat, Hackley recognized him, and his mouth froze into a sour line. The marks of his beating were deep and painful—an eye swollen half-shut, a split lip, a bruise on one cheekbone. Now that the horses were safely disposed of, Ross felt he could risk sympathy. He extended his hand.

"*Compadres*," he smiled.

"You go to hell," Hackley said.

"You tried a bluff and it didn't work," Ross reminded him. "I could forget it ever happened, over a drink. Buy you one, Hackley. Out of the profits."

Hackley exhaled the smoke with an angry puff. "You go back to the Rio Grande House and have a shot of chamber-lye, on me."

"How'd you know I was at the Rio Grande?" Ross asked curiously.

Hackley's face altered, lightening with some secret meaning. "Maybe I own it," he said, and passed on.

The damned fool, Ross thought. He was glad he had spoken to him. It made him less sorry for the beating. Moving on, he found a restaurant, but just as he was reaching for the knob the door opened and a young woman came out. It was Laurel Shelton. They stared at each other for a moment. Then she said in her slow, rather husky voice: "Mr. Chance, I—I wish—"

Ross tipped his hat. "A good evening to you, Mrs. Shelton." He went into the café and closed the door.

Afterwards it came to him that he was taking it hard, considering what had actually happened. He had spoken for two or three minutes with a girl whose eyes were gray with exciting depths, who had looked at him in a way that gave him gooseflesh. She had asked him to write her. Whatever it had meant, the plain fact was that all women were not chaste, any more than were all women virgins; and meeting a married lady who was available should not shatter a man for the rest of the week.

After dinner he had a drink on it. He had several. He was feeling reasonably cheerful when, at nine o'clock, he returned to his room. It was at the end of a long hall on the ground floor. The moment he opened the door, he saw the lamp burning on the small oak commode, and caught a fragrance of lavender. Then he saw a girl seated in a straight-backed chair by the shaded window, and his heart seemed to squeeze hard as a lemon, and then breathlessly expand. He moved inside and closed the door.

"Mrs. Shelton," he said, "if you could get into banks as well as you get into locked hotel rooms, you've missed your calling."

At Laurel Shelton's feet was a crocheting bag, while on her lap were laid out some bright afghan squares, which she had been stitching together. She seemed completely composed. She gave him a quiet smile.

"A bone hairpin would do for a key, on these hotel locks. But I happened to have my own key with me. I'm staying in the National Exchange. I just jiggled it a little, and it opened."

Chance was conscious of a savage desire to possess her. *She's fair prey...a woman like that....* He wanted to touch her, to hurt her. He wanted to idealize her. His mouth turned with bitter humor.

"You know the risk you're taking for us both, don't you? What am I supposed to do—make it worthwhile?"

The afghan squares dropped silently as she rose. She came toward him, her face strained, and stopped just short of him to strike him on the mouth. "No one has ever said such a thing to me before," she said. "No man but my husband. Just what do you think I am?"

She flung angrily away and stood at the commode, staring at herself in the mirror. She reached up to tuck a scrap of black hair into the *couronne* in which she wore it.

"I'll be damned," Chance pondered, "if I know what you are! I thought I knew when I opened the door and saw you here. It was what I'd decided you were before."

"What was that?"

"I figured you were the kind of woman who marries an old man for money and gets her loving from the ones she meets in railroad stations."

She shrugged. "I suppose any man would have thought that, after what I said to you, and what my husband said to me. But I can assure you you're wrong."

"Then I'm licked."

She turned slowly to gaze at him, and began to laugh softly. "You do seem a little surprised, Mr. Chance. Were you really so fooled? Did you think I would be so easy?"

Ross shrugged. "I kind of had that impression. And I was mad enough to want to try it, after the fool you let me make of myself with your husband. I told him I'd been talking to his daughter. You led me into that one, lady."

"I didn't mean to." Her lips held only a faint smile now. "I didn't say what I was to him. I just assumed you knew I was his wife."

The old Carcel lamp on the commode gurgled, and they both started; afterward they stared at each other, and Ross relaxed. "I don't know what we're nervous about, Mrs. Shelton. As you say, this is just an ordinary social call."

"I didn't say that. I said I didn't want to be made love to."

"Then what kind of a call is it?"

She did not reply at once, and standing close to her Ross breathed the faint, exciting fragrance she had brought—a breathless suggestion of lavender and sachet, odors a mustanger encountered so seldom that they were as rousing as the roundness of a bosom under a summer bodice. Either Laurel Shelton did not know much about men, or she had a slow way of getting to her lovemaking.

"Well, for one thing," the girl said at last, "I came here to try to change the impression you just admitted you had of me. That was one reason."

Ross grinned. "Impression changed."

"And the second reason—I wanted to know why you lied to me today."

"About what?"

"About being Colonel Chance's son. It's nothing to be ashamed of, certainly."

Ross's gaze stayed slowly and appreciatively on the pretty, faintly flushed features. He was thinking that her reasons for making nocturnal visits to mustangers' rooms might seem sound to her, but they rang like a lead quarter in his ears. Unless she had some deeper motive which she had not disclosed, the real reason seemed to be that she had wanted to see him again. And in this there was greater satisfaction than a sound excuse would have given him.

"No, it's nothing to be ashamed of," he told her. "Only it seemed like a good idea to play my cards close to my chest with strangers."

Her chin tilted. "So you let me play the fool by telling you about the country, when you knew it better than I did."

"Been a long time since I was there," Ross told her. "Things change. Maybe you know it better than I do, now."

She returned to the chair where she had been sitting when he came in. "May I sit down?" She smoothed her skirts under her and sat without waiting for his reply. "And now you're on your way home," she said.

"Maybe. If I do go back," Ross told her, "the first question I'll ask is why my father ever sold that first half of the ranch. I don't say I was cheated. I'd just like to know why he broke it up, when he didn't need the money."

"I don't know that myself. You know, I wasn't married to

Mr. Shelton when he bought the property. We've only been married six months. However, I've heard that your father sold because he couldn't operate the ranch by himself."

"Rot," snapped Ross. "He could have run it from a wheel chair."

"Well, that's only what I've heard."

"Did you hear what he did with the money from the sale? Because he couldn't pay taxes a year later. That's the part about it that—" He broke off and turned to the dresser, where his tobacco was.

Laurel Shelton sounded surprised. "You sound angry, Ross. You don't think he *gave* the land away?"

"Maybe he gave the money away. He must have done one or the other, or he wouldn't have been broke a year later." He struck a match and brought the flame to his cigar.

"I should think you'd have kept in closer touch with your father," Laurel said, "if you had meant to operate the ranch some day."

Ross puffed smoke at the battered lamp. "When I left home," he said, "I wasn't worrying much about keeping in touch with him."

"You do hear the strangest stories about why you left."

Ross turned. "Tell me one," he suggested.

"Well—for instance—that you became intoxicated in the Gadsden Purchase Bar, and it took ten men to keep you from destroying it."

"Wrong," Ross said. "It was six."

"Then you *did* get drunk—I mean intoxicated?" she asked.

"You mean drunk," Ross said, smiling. Somehow she made him see something humorous in a thing which had always seemed bitter to him. That night had always been part of the day which followed; and there had been nothing uproarious about the battle with his father. "What else do they say?" he asked her.

"That you had a four-alarm fight with your father before you left. Right in my own living room."

Ross drew slowly on the cigar, regarding her, seeing the seriousness behind her half-smile. He had the impression that she was sincerely interested in the life of the Chances. Women were like that: nothing absorbed them so much as why who wasn't speaking to whom.

"Well, I'll tell you," he said. "I did get drunk. It was my first time. And my father and I did have a tussle."

"Over that?"

"I expect that was just the last battle of a long campaign," he speculated. "He was more of a top sergeant than a father. There's nobody like a top sergeant to teach you what you ought to know. But ordinarily you aren't expected to love him. And it seemed like I didn't want to know anything he wanted to teach me."

"He taught you all about horses, they say. I've heard you could stay on a bronc longer than any man in Doña María County."

"Maybe," Ross agreed. "He had a game leg himself, and wasn't much of a rider. So I had to be good enough for both of us. When I was a kid, he'd put me on horses nobody but a bronc-stomper would fool with. That's how I learned to ride. I got a broken nose before I learned, and I lost count of the sprains."

"Didn't your mother stand between you?" Laurel asked. "I wouldn't let any husband of mine treat a boy so."

"My mother took off a few weeks after I was born. I guess the colonel tried to use a Spanish bit on her, like he did his riding horses."

His lips closed on the cigar. He looked down at the girl. Her eyes were on her needlework. She looked, thought Ross, intelligent and spirited and gentle. And he wanted to tell her about it all, but was afraid it would sound like whining. There was so much hurt there still, a boy's hurts, but he was a man and they no longer mattered to him. All the same, he thought, I'd like to tell somebody, just once, and forget it. The one thing on which he agreed with his father was that there was nothing worse than a whiner.

Laurel looked up. She was going to say something, but just then the sound of footfalls coming down the corridor reached them. Ross turned toward the door. He could hear the boots halt at the room before his, but there was a tentative sound about them—as though someone were looking at the number on the door. They came on again, and halted at Ross's door. Ross glanced at Laurel. Her eyes were full of alarm.

"Blade Ramsey," Ross said softly. "We had a falling-out. He's probably full of whiskey and remorse." He gathered her crocheting things and tucked them into the commode. "Stand back of the door," he said. "I'll take him to the bar."

For an instant her hand touched his arm. The gray eyes stayed sadly on his face, "I'll be gone when you come back. I do thank you, Ross. I'm sorry I acted so—so female. But I wanted to talk to you, because it seemed as if we had something in common."

Finally it came to Ross that she was telling the truth. Her only sin had been lack of judgment. Being female, as she said. He raised her hand, feeling a little foolish and yet wanting to do it, and kissed it. "If I settle in Amargosa," he said, "I'll probably see you once in a while. Only I wish I'd met you three years ago. Somebody made an awful mistake."

"Yes," she agreed. "I did...."

A man's knuckles rapped on the door. "Chance? I want to talk to you. Lamar Shelton."

Laurel's eyes were huge and dark. He could see the color bleach from her lips. Quickly he took her arm and led her to the corner behind the door. He returned to muss the covers on his cot; then he tossed on it a newspaper he had bought earlier. "Wait a minute," he said gruffly.

He pulled off his boots. After making the springs of the cot squeak, he walked to the door. Lamar Shelton stood in the shadowy hall, swarthy and smiling, wearing his Stetson on the side of his head. "Hello," he said. "Can I come in?"

Ross sighed. "For nine months a man sleeps on the ground. But the first time he comes face to face with a bed, somebody wants to chew the fat all night."

Shelton chuckled. "I didn't mean to upset anything," he said. "But as long as I've got you up, I'd like to ask you something."

"I'm listening."

Ross saw the rancher's eyes exploring the room. But after a moment Shelton shrugged his shoulders. "You're independent as hell, aren't you?"

"Are we buddies, or business acquaintances?"

Shelton's heavy features sobered. "Suit yourself," he said. "I can talk here, if I have to. In the first place, I know my foreman tipped you off to what I'd pay for those horses."

"If you knew it, then you didn't have to ask me."

"Right. What I wanted to ask is what the proposition was that he made you and your partner?"

"Who said he made us one?"

"I was in the livery stable when you and your partner had the ruckus in front of it. I heard a little. Just enough to make me interested. You see, I've known for some time that he was grinding his own axe."

"That's too bad," Ross said, "but I'm not going to lose any sleep over whether your ramrod is cheating you."

Shelton's muscular face hardened. "I can see that. It wouldn't have an odor of sour grapes, would it—because I'm running Rancho Pacheco instead of you?"

Ross kept his eyes on Shelton's, prying at them—attempting to see whether he really heard guilt in his voice, or imagined it. "Why should it?" he asked.

"Some men would be sore," Shelton retorted. "Figuring that because they grew up on the ranch, it ought to belong to them."

"I feel that way a little bit," Ross admitted.

"Well, you'd better get over it. The land belonged to your father. He needed cash; I had it."

"And yet the next year," Ross pointed out, "he was broke. How come?"

"When I gave you my check this afternoon, did I reserve the right to approve how you spent it?"

"No, but I'm talking about the proceeds of a ranch—not a year's work. How could he have spent that much? By the way," he asked, "how much was it?"

Shelton retorted: "That was between your father and me."

A feeling of exuberance, a fierce exhilaration, lifted in Ross. "The more I talk to you," he smiled, "the more I think I should come home and talk to Henry Lyman."

Shelton stepped back. "The hell with you," he said. "Maybe you need that sleep more than I thought. By God, you'll need it if you plan to come back to Amargosa and raise trouble with me. And I'll give you some more advice, too: Don't fool around with George Gunlock—not in anything. He's trying to get his nose skinned. I could handle two of you as easy as one."

"Try mine sometime," Ross snapped.

"Good night," Shelton snapped. But then, as he was about to turn, he said maliciously: "I hope you enjoy that bed, Chance. But be careful of the springs, you and your friend. I can smell her perfume clear out here!"

Putting both hands in his pockets, flipping back the tails of his frock coat, he walked back to the lobby.

6

AFTER ROSS HAD re-entered the room and set the latch, he sat on the cot and pulled his boots on once more. He glanced at Laurel. Still standing in the corner behind the door, she had begun to weep, her face turned away and one hand pressed against her eyes. Ross went toward her, smiling ruefully.

"He didn't know it was you. Nine women out of ten use the same scent you do, don't they? If he'd known it was you . . ."

She shook her head. She wiped her eyes on a handkerchief she tugged from a lace cuff, and went to sit on the cot. She appeared tired and disconsolate. "A woman wouldn't have to ask what was wrong," she said. "She'd know what it would do to her to be hiding behind a door from her husband, in another man's room."

Ross sat beside her. He wanted very much to put his arm about her. Instead, he took her hand. It was small-boned, firm and warm. "But you haven't done anything wrong," he said.

"It isn't what anybody did. It's—well, I'm married to him. And yet here I am trying to get sympathy from another man. Hiding behind doors. Marriage ought to be more than that, Ross."

"Sometimes it isn't," Ross commented.

"No," Laurel said quietly. "Especially when there was nothing there in the first place. Oh, the ladies of Amargosa could tell you all about it!" she admitted. "They know I've got four Mexican girls to help me with the house, and probably could tell me things I don't know about my own wardrobe. And I'll bet the banker's wife has let it out that I was overdrawn three times last month."

"People talk," Ross said.

"And the less they know, the more they talk! I could give them some things to gossip about, if they ever ran short! For instance, they know we have separate bank accounts and

37

separate lawyers—but do they know we have separate bed-
rooms?"

Ross was surprised and unaccountably pleased. He looked at
her. She glanced away, embarrassed now and quieting.

"Not that they don't invite me to join their sewing circles and
the like. Things they'd never have thought of doing before I
married Lamar Shelton. And of course the daughter of a man
who died in prison needs all the prestige she can get."

Ross frowned. "I thought your father was a marshal."

"Can't a marshal die in prison?"

"Yes, but he usually doesn't."

She frowningly looked at their hands, still linked on her lap.
"It was a Mexican prison. And he wasn't really guilty of
anything. I talked to him and he told me the charge was trumped
up. But he died before we could prove it."

She drew her hand away. She crossed to the commode and
gathered her crocheting. Then she walked to the door and
listened. She was a small, slender figure against the dark panel.
"I think it's all right now."

Ross reached for the lamp. "Take it easy, now," he said, and
extinguished the flame. He raised the window shade enough to
see out. The view was of the rear of the hotel—a woodpile, a
shed, the long roofed hitchrack where sleepy horses stood.

"I'll let you out the back way," he said. "If you're at the
National Exchange, you'd better cut south down the alley that
parallels the street, and then cut over to the main street. Will he
want to know where you've been?"

He found her in the darkness, inhaled the exciting fragrance
of her and heard the rustle of satin as she moved.

"No," she said. "We have separate rooms. And as I said—
separate beds."

Ross's throat tightened. He wanted to put his hands out to
clasp her waist. But immediately she was saying, "I don't know
why I told you that. Except that I—I'd like you to understand. I
married him to help someone. But my husband reneged on his
part of the bargain. So I reneged on mine."

Ross spoke through his teeth, his heart thudding against his
ribs. "Mrs. Shelton," he said, "I've been in the mountains for
nine months. You ought to know it isn't safe to tell me things like
that. You can blame yourself for what I'm going to do."

He pulled her against him. She gasped, but he crushed her
face to his and found her lips. He could hear her crocheting bag
softly strike the floor. A storm of desire rocked him. One hand

went up to tangle in her dark hair, and with his eyes closed he pressed her lips roughly.

"Ross!" she whispered. "Ross, Ross!" Then he held her tightly against him with his face turned toward the door, rocking slowly, agonizingly, there in the darkness.

"Will you tell me why the best things always belong to somebody else?" he whispered.

"They don't," she whispered. "It's just like you said—you've been in the mountains too long. And I've been lonesome too long to keep my head, too. So let me go."

Ross released her. He felt as though he had stood for a moment in the heart of a whirlwind. After a moment he unlocked the door and peered up the dim hall. She pressed close behind him. They left the room.

From the rear of the hotel, gazing along the vacant lot next to it, Ross could see the busy street, the wind-driven dust glinting in the light of the saloons, and the shops that were still open. The wagons of some ranch families were parked in the lot with canvas shelters beside them. Lamps glowed in two of them, but there was no one in sight. Nearer, he saw the shadow of his bay stallion on its picket rope. It was tugging at a mound of hay he had forked up for it earlier.

"All right," he told the girl. They walked quickly to the alley. Across it were the reeling picket fences of some homes, a couple of privies, and the gaunt skeletons of wagons. Ross escorted her to the corner of the big mercantile south of the hotel. Standing with her, neither of them speaking for a moment, he could hear the horses stir with restless whispers of harness.

"Will I see you again?" she asked.

"It would be better all around if you never did," he said. "But I'm leaving for Amargosa in a day or two. I don't know whether I'll stay or not."

"I hope so," she whispered. "Now I must hurry. Good-bye. I suppose you'd better not write that letter after all."

"No. I've an idea some folks would think it was asking for trouble."

He heard her gown rustling as she moved away into the darkness, holding her skirts up.

Ross turned back. A night had never seemed so empty. The wind was a toothed provocation, the stars glittered distantly and coyotes howled on a mesa above the river. The lights of the street looked foolishly gay. He passed along the horse shelter, stopping beside his pony to check it for the night. He spoke reassuringly and laid a hand on its rump. With startling force, the horse threw its head and struck him on the bridge of the nose. Stunned, he fell back. The horse tried to kick him and he stumbled away, but lost his footing and fell. It kicked once more and there was an explosion of pain in his head. There was a brief instant of agony, ending in a cold mist of faintness welling over him. With great effort he crawled away. The horse was still kicking angrily, lurching at the end of its short tie rope. Though it was dark, he recognized at last that it was not his saddle horse. It was the bay stallion. Someone had switched them.

From the alley, someone was calling. "*Ross! Ross!* Are you hurt?"

He recognized Laurel's voice, and turned to tell her he was all right, but the lamps in his brain seemed to puff out, and he fell forward into cold, drenching night.

7

BLADE AND SOME other men carried Ross into his hotel room. Ross learned this later. He was aware of Blade leaning over him, helping to undress him, and saying:

"God damn a horse like that!"

When Ross's head touched the pillow, the pain fountained up and he lost consciousness again.

A doctor came and poked a small knife at the hoof-cut on his head, and said, "If the horse had been shod, this man would be dead now. It missed a blood vessel by that much."

Ross lay in silent paralysis, gazing at these creatures who seemed to slide on a foggy background. One of them was a drunken-faced, foolish Blade Ramsey, who said, "The horse ain't been shod—but he's shore been shot, now, Doc. I seen to that. He's my pardner, this fella."

"Your partner should know better than to ride a horse like that," said the doctor.

"He was just a studhorse. Somebody must have switched on him."

This was the first time Ross thought of Tom Hackley. A moment later they pressed a cloth over him and he began to fight the sweetish suffocation that assailed him.

It was much later when he was able to sit up in bed. "It's been three days, mister," the stout, middle-aged nurse the doctor had left with him informed him.

His head was still a jellified sponge full of lights and aches. There was a thick bandage over his right ear extending to the back of his head. "Has my partner been here today?"

"That big yellow-haired fellow?" the nurse said. "No, not since the first day."

"That's funny," Ross said.

"Why, he left town. Didn't you know?"

"No, I didn't. When was that?"

41

"Monday—no, Tuesday, it was. The day you paid the doctor."

Ross tried to recall it. "What did I pay him with? I only had a few dollars, plus a check."

"It was the check. Your partner asked how much you would owe for everything, and you said it was all right to pay out of the check."

"But . . ." Ross had to slump to ease the pain in his head.

The woman told him, "Then you signed the check, and Mr. Ramsey signed it, and he came back and left money for the doctor. There's a little cash in the commode, here. . . ."

So he knew then that he had been robbed. Looking up at the fly-specked muslin ceiling, he realized Blade had seized the opportunity to decamp with all the money.

There was only two things of which he was sure: that Blade had gone with Gunlock, to invest in George Gunlock's wild-eyed scheme; and that one night, when Blade was having drinks with his little yellow-haired girl, an old partner would step into the room, and Blade would pay for every dollar he had stolen.

8

TEN DAYS AFTER the accident, when Ross was getting around without a headache every time his heels touched the walk, a letter came from Laurel Shelton. He took it to a café with him to read. For a while he seemed to have buck-fever. He let it rest beside his plate while he ate. At intervals he glanced at the copperplate inscription on the envelope. It came to him that she could have written no other hand but a small, neat one like this. He sniffed the envelope and recognized her scent.

"What the hell is she writing to me about?" he wondered.

But he feared to open it because he knew it might be the second chapter in something which already had gone much too far. Yet he knew that if she said, "Come to me," he would do it.

Finally he slid his table knife under the flap and read it.

"... *I can't tell you how much I have worried, though your partner told me the next morning that you were not seriously injured. By the way, he returned with George Gunlock and has taken a job trapping horses near us. He tells me you plan to join him later.*"

As he sipped his coffee, Ross's face quirked with grim humor. He turned the fold of the letter.

"*Mr. Shelton and I returned yesterday from Albuquerque. He will leave again in a week for El Paso to buy cattle at an auction. If you are able to travel by then, you might care to help him bring the cattle back. He will be leaving El Paso a week from Thursday.—I do hope you are fully recovered,*" she concluded.

That would be tomorrow, Ross realized, looking at a calendar on the wall. Shelton would be buying cattle in El Paso today. The letter had taken that long to reach him.

He walked to the ticket office of the Denver & Rio Grande and found there was a train leaving town at seven P.M., which would arrive in El Paso at midnight. He had little more than the price of the ticket, after paying his hotel bill. He bought the

43

ticket and returned to his room to rest until traintime. He was glad that he had not hurried anything. He was feeling stronger every hour, and he did not need instinct to know that he would require all his strength when he reached Amargosa.

He was able to sleep a few hours on the train, and finished the night on a bench in the station at El Paso.

As he washed in the men's room in the morning, he thought, *I'd like to talk to Henry Lyman before I see anybody*. Lyman was almost the only thing connected with Colonel Bob Chance for which Ross had any use, and that was because Lyman was a rough little East Texan lawyer who was his own man, even with a toughneck like the colonel. His legal and financial judgment was, Ross had long suspected, as much responsible for the growth of Rancho Pacheco as were Bob Chance's ways with cattle and land. He knew Henry would have something to say about the loss of the ranch, and he found himself pinning that hope up like a star to steer by.

This fall the yards at El Paso were more crowded than Ross had ever seen them. In the heavy, moist air of the October morning, the pens were patched with the reddish backs of Herefords, the off-breed coloring of longhorns, and a few of the new gray humpbacks called Brahmans. He was gazing through the bars at a pen full of these when a man said:

"They look like hell, don't they? But they beat the ticks and heat."

Ross stiffened, at once recognizing the voice as Lamar Shelton's. Evidently Shelton had not recognized Ross from the back, for when he turned the rancher stared in surprise. Then he grinned. There was an incisive quality in his smile—his teeth white in the strong, dark features, his eyes brown with a hard glitter. He was wearing a bleached blue work-shirt, a gray Stetson on the back of his head, and the black hairs of his forearms were exposed by his rolled sleeves.

Ross read more in his face than he could be sure of. He tried to keep his own feelings of guilt hidden, but he knew what Laurel had meant that night when she told him she hated to be hiding anything.

"I thought I was going to have a few more horses for you," he told Shelton. "But it turned out I already had one more horse than I could handle."

"Kicked the b'Jesus out of you, eh?" said Shelton, with obvious pleasure.

Ross glanced down the short line of cattle cars. "Is your foreman with you?" he asked.

"Yes. Do you want a job helping him? We're going out around sundown."

"Fine. I was on my way to Amargosa anyway."

"What for?" Shelton's words had a bite.

"I've got some business there," Ross told him, watching the narrow, shrewd eyes closely.

"Yes, I'd heard." An instant after he said this, Shelton did something so completely unexpected that Ross was caught offguard. He walked straight into the mustanger, jamming him against the chute bars, and drawing his Colt in the same instant pushed it into Ross's belly. Ross was sick with shock. He saw all Shelton's pretended affability vanish and a murderous anger surface in his face. He saw the flat lips stretch back from his teeth.

"I told you not to fool with Gunlock, didn't I? I told you he was going to get his nose skinned, and you'd better keep out of it. Now, by God, you'll know I meant it!"

Ross kept peering into that distorted face. He saw no dissimulation—if Shelton knew about Laurel's visit to his room, he did not seem to have it on his mind. He said, "Sure—he's some of my business. I'm coming back to cut the hide off him. The same for my partner."

"I told you!" Shelton repeated, as though he had not heard. "You were ready for the sugar—now, how do you like the pill?" When Ross's eyes flicked aside to where the men were working, Shelton drove the gunbarrel deeply into his stomach. "Do you think they'll hear it, Chance? With all the clatter that engine's making?"

"Are you crazy, Shelton?" Ross demanded.

Shelton kept crowding him as though he could push him through the barrier. "You got a wild idea, somewhere, that you'd been cheated of something, didn't you? And Gunlock just suited your notions. What kind of fool do you think I'd be, to pony up to you? By God, you want to chew on what you've bit off, do you—?"

He was out of control: Ross could see the unbridled rage in his eyes. He knew he was going to fire the gun, and knowing this Ross was able to do what he had to. When the hammer clicked, his hand snapped to grasp the Colt across the cylinder and trigger guard. He forced his thumb between breach and hammer. The blunt firing pin gouged his knuckle as it fell. Closing his grip on the weapon, Ross twisted Shelton around, thrusting out his leg to trip him. But Shelton was large and powerful. They were locked that way a moment, Shelton trying to rip the gun from him, Ross maneuvering to twist the rancher's arm behind him. About them were the sounds of restless cattle, the wooden clatter of chutes and the locomotive's iron chuffing. As they strained against each other, Ross felt pain rising in the recent wound in his scalp, and he knew that in another moment he would be in trouble.

Shelton suddenly panted: "All right—take it! There's a man coming."

Ross clung to the gun until Shelton released it. He eased the firing pin out of his gouged thumb. He saw the blood well darkly. A horseman was moving down the aisle between the pens. Shelton turned to gaze at the locomotive, putting his back to the oncoming rider. Ross also turned. As the horseman passed, he said breathlessly:

"I ought to turn you over to the marshal."

"I should have shot you when I had the chance."

"Cut it out," Ross said, "and tell me what you've been raving about."

"You should know," Shelton snapped. "My foreman sold you the idea in Las Truchas."

"Now, listen! You saw my partner swing on me that day? That was because I wouldn't buy the idea Gunlock was trying to sell. I don't know yet what it was. But I wasn't going to give a year's profits to find out."

Shelton studied him. "I'm listening. Tell a good one."

"It's true," Ross said. "But it's all the explaining I'm going to do. I've been two weeks getting the strength to go after those two—my partner and Gunlock. Ramsey took off with my money. I suppose he invested in your foreman's crazy scheme."

Shelton threw him a sidelong glance. "And you don't know what it is."

"No. I told you that."

"Gunlock said you were in it with him and Ramsey. He shook me down for five thousand dollars a week ago and said you were to get a share."

Ross stared at him. "You mean you paid him that much? What for?"

Shelton's lips hardened in a tight grin. "Going to play it

innocent all the way? They had me make out a check for your share. They took theirs in cash."

Ross studied him closely. He was convinced that Shelton was not going all the way with him. He did not believe Gunlock had said he was in the deal. When he was not crazy with anger, this man had a smooth and calculating mind, and Ross had the feeling it was working now. It came to him that if he opened up and told Shelton all he knew, it would be more to the rancher's advantage than to his own.

"Where's Gunlock?" he asked.

Shelton said the foreman would be away from the yards most of the day, buying supplies. "He'll be back around traintime."

"Then I'll be here when he comes back. We'll kick this around a little."

Shelton straightened from the fence. He glanced at the sky, which was shot with early-morning color, though heavy with clouds. "If you're going to Amargosa anyway, you may as well go with us. You can make a hand, can't you?"

Ross said, "Yeah," and kept trying to read Shelton's close-grained features as Shelton, putting out his hand for the Colt, said:

"Throw your gear in the crumby, then. We'll leave around six."

In his pocket, Ross Chance had three dollars and fifty cents, with part of which he bought smoking tobacco. He carried his valise and bedroll and saddle over to the caboose and established himself in one of the upper bunks forward, where he had light from the cupola. Off and on that day he lay there with his boots cocked up and his hands linked under his head, gazing up at a slot of tumbling winter clouds.

Toward sundown, the clouds massed deep and black over the gaunt hills about El Paso. Thunder crashed, and just before the cattle train pulled out, large, warm drops of rain began to fall. Ross Chance hurried from the railroad restaurant to the siding where the cattle train had been left after being made up. He had been wondering whether Gunlock had returned, but now, as he mounted the iron ladder, he heard Gunlock's voice in the caboose. He halted on the platform, a long, drenched shadow with a stub of cold cigar in his teeth. The door opened and the foreman threw a cigarette into the tracks. He said to someone, "Sure—you bet we'll talk about it!" and he was on the platform then, staring at the dark, dripping form of Ross Chance.

Ross had his hand on the wet grip of his gun. Gunlock slowly rested one hand on the brake wheel as they confronted each other. A lamp inside the railroad car threw a drowned light on his face, notching it with hollows. His pale eyes stubbornly, but in apprehension, stayed on Ross's face.

Though Ross had been looking forward to this meeting, he had not known what he would do when it came. He was only sure now of a somber joy.

"Go inside," he told Gunlock. "I've got something to say to you."

Gunlock's grin was a quick slit in the long face. "Same here, Ross," he said. "But it'll have to keep. They're about to roll this train."

Ross clenched his fists, breathing deeply. From the interior of the car, Lamar Shelton appeared in the door. "Let him go, Chance. We've got to get started."

Shelton came onto the platform as Gunlock dropped to the coarse wet gravel. "You said you'd make a hand," he reminded Ross. "Grab a slicker and get up on top. Watch the last three cars on this end. If a cow gets down, give me a lantern signal and we'll come back and help you."

Shelton followed after Gunlock. In his fishskin slicker, he was a large, flapping ghost with the rain pelting against him. Ross found a raincoat in a locker and pulled it on over his damp jacket. He lighted a lantern and climbed to the catwalk. The cattle were restless, bawling continually and lurching against each other. The cars stank of manure and wet hides. Lanterns bobbed here and there in the stockyards like lights in a sea. Ross saw sparks fountain from the diamond stack of the locomotive as the fire was stoked. Shortly after, the whistle blew a short, sharp signal and trainmen semaphored their lanterns up and down the line. Ross crouched on the catwalk to take the jolting start.

The train smoked northward along the Rio Grande in a broad valley guarded by the mountains on the east, the mesas on the west. Lamplighted windows glowed in the little Mexican villages they passed. His eyes yearning, Ross gazed at the little golden squares of light. A mustanger and line-camp cowboy lived without roofs and beds. He worked in tough country where the wild horses and outlaw cattle ran, dreaming of the ranch he would buy some day. Ross had known these men, had been one of them for years, and their dreams had been his. He had built his own cabin in those dreams. It had had a sound roof and walls, and windows which could be shut against sandstorm and blizzard. It had contained a stove, a bed, a table, a woman. The woman was entirely unlike the kind of women a man knew when he came to town for a week at a time. She was neat and attractive and had not lived so close to mechanical pianos that when she spoke her voice rang of untuned strings. She was thrifty and practical, but despite this she was always a loving woman whose arms were soft and white in the darkness.

She had been like Laurel, who belonged to Lamar Shelton. He thought of it with a stab. Perhaps he had lived too long among simple people like the border Mexicans, for whom marriage was something absolute: it was as sure as the seasons; as private as a love letter. He thought of the way a Mexican woman wrote her name when she was married. *Maria Gonzales de Perez:* Maria who belonged to Perez. Laurel, who belonged to Shelton.

A man was coming along the catwalk. Lamar Shelton sauntered with careless confidence down the lurching path of planks, stopped before Ross with rain dripping from his nose and said:

"Come on. Gunlock will be along. We'll have that talk."

"All right," Ross said. "I'm ready."

9

AFTER THE COLD RAIN, the air of the caboose seemed stale and overheated. Shelton threw some coal into the stove and clanged the lid on. He lifted a blue-enamel pot and poured coffee into an unwashed cup. Then he looked at Ross, as he tugged off his slicker. "How about it?" Ross nodded, and Shelton poured the second cup, but though George Gunlock was noisily descending the ladder from the drafty well of the cupola, he did not pour a third. He added five spoons of sugar and lounged into an alcoved bunk.

Taking his cup, Ross sat on an opposite bunk. Both he and Shelton observed every movement of the foreman as Gunlock removed his slicker and Stetson. Gunlock took a half-pint of whiskey from his hip pocket and had a drink.

"Colder'n a well-chain in December," he said.

"Heavy weather comin'," Ross said without expression.

"Hey! Coffee!" Gunlock said, noting their cups. He poured half a cup and filled it with whiskey. Then he sat at the far end of Ross's bunk. And there was silence. Lamar Shelton's mouth was set. He kept staring at his foreman. At last he said:

"I'll let you tell it. It's your party."

The ramrod gazed at Ross. He wiped his wet chin on the sleeve of his denim jumper. Then he rose to take a chamois clasp-purse from his pocket and open it. He extracted a folded check, which he handed to Ross.

"This'll tell it better than I can."

Ross examined it. It was for twelve hundred and fifty dollars, and it was signed, *Lamar Shelton*. Gunlock was saying exuberantly:

"I told you, damn it! But you wouldn't believe me. You ought to be glad you've got a partner like Blade who'll take a chance. And that he didn't get sore and just leave you out of it. You're a pardner in this, Ross. There's a fourth man I'll tell you about

50

some time. But this will give you back about all you had to start with—and you ain't begun to collect."

"There's one thing it doesn't give back," Ross said.

"What's that?"

"A whole head. . . . Who switched horses on me?"

"Tom Hackley," Gunlock returned at once. "That rancher you beat the hell out of. Blade figured it after the accident."

"I haven't been calling it an accident. Seemed to me it was the first part of a cute deal to get that money away from me. You don't know that fool like I do. He's got just enough caginess to steal bird's eggs out from under the bird—but not enough savvy to remember not to leave his calling card. The nurse told me about his rigging me on the cashier's check. I'll take one look at him in Amargosa, and know whether you and he did it, or if it was Hackley."

The train rocked around a turn. The hanging lamp swung. They were nearing the Union Ford crossing of the Rio Grande, Ross knew, from old familiarity with the train route. The train began to slow. Through a rain-slashed window, he discerned railroad shacks and ranks of ties, and finally a warehouse, before which they stopped. Voices sounded in the darkness; from up the line came the crisp fall of boots. Shelton rose.

"Hang on."

Opening the door, he stepped onto the platform. Coal smoke swirled into the caboose, the scent of wet cattle thickened. They could hear a man talking about a downed cow; then Shelton was saying:

"Take a prod and mash her in the bag. It's the only way to get them up. Let me know if you can't manage it." Returning, he left the door open, and standing with his back against the jamb he stared at Gunlock with dry contempt, his head lowered, his Stetson on one side. Ross remembered the cold thrust of his Colt against his belly that morning, and he thought, *I wouldn't push this one too far*.

"Now, get this straight, Ross," Gunlock was telling him. "We're pardners. We hang together, see?"

"Pardners in what?" asked Ross. "Blackmail?"

"In a land deal. The Chihuahua Land and Livestock Company. Headquarters—Villa Hermosa, Chihuahua."

"If you've tried to cut me in on any phony deal, I'll see you both in jail," Ross said flatly.

Gunlock bounced up. He strode to the ladder and hooked one elbow about the upright, smiling in an exultant manner.

"This is the legalest God-damn' deal this side of a judge's office. This is rent money—for some land Shelton's renting from us. You've got to have a little imagination to believe this, but it's all down in black and white. It seems that the title to part of the land your dad sold Shelton was sour as hell. He not only did not own it himself, but it didn't even belong to anyone in this country!"

Ross gazed at him in silence. "Who did own it, then?"

"A couple of ranchers in Mexico."

"You're crazy. Henry Lyman made the title search himself. He did it on every acre of land the old man ever bought."

"Sure. But he was assuming something. The south boundary of the ranch is the international line, ain't it? Okay. He was assuming that the international boundary was on the level. That's the joker. It ain't! Somebody moved the monuments thirty years ago. There's a ten-mile strip along there that's been shoved south. So the colonel was ranching partly in Mexican country. And Shelton's doing it now!"

A thunder of couplings reverberated down the cattle train. The caboose slid ahead, lagged, caught again and began to jerk forward. Some of Gunlock's coffee spilled. Ross continued gazing at him, thinking as he looked at the lanky features with their gloss of excitement, *He's crazy as a loon.* But Lamar Shelton was solemn, and the foreman began to laugh in his throat.

"Tell you who owns that land, Ross. *We do!* The Chihuahua Land and Livestock Company. That's why I needed the cash. To buy this strip of land from the Mexicans who owned the land adjoining Rancho Pacheco on the south. They sold it to us without knowing what was up. We own a ranch two miles wide and ten miles long, and it's the most valuable land in New Mexico. Ain't it, Mr. Shelton?"

"You son-of-a-bitch," Shelton said harshly. Gunlock laughed. He took a couple of strides down the car and smacked his fist against his palm, grinning at Shelton. Shelton now confronted Ross angrily. "Are you in this squeeze, or aren't you?"

"I'm in it for twenty-six hundred. Cash or hide. Are you going to tell me you paid five thousand dollars for a yarn like this?"

A sad anger burned in Shelton's eyes. "You know, there's just a hell of a lot of back rent and taxes pile up when they haven't been paid in thirty years. The interest on the unpaid rent alone would knock your eye out!"

"The way it works," Gunlock said, "Mr. Shelton will make installments on what he owes every quarter. It'd be hell if we had to turn it over to the Mexican authorities, you savvy, because they'd move right in. Take over the ranch house and sue Shelton right up to his eyeballs."

He finished the coffee. He threw the heavy china cup on a bunk. He looked drunk with importance and power. Grinning, he struck his fist against his palm. "Well, how's about? How's about, kid?"

"I think Shelton's right this time," Ross stated. "You're a son-of-a-bitch. In fact, I think I'll collect a little of that hide I've got coming, right now." He came to his feet.

Over Gunlock's face settled a swift fury. "Wait a minute, fella. I can ace you out of this and into trouble, you know."

"You can like hell."

"You ain't so clean," Gunlock's thin ironic lips said. "You stand there singin' hymns at me, and I'll wind your clock good."

Ross stood balancing to the lurching roll of the train. He studied Gunlock, in anger but in caution, finding sinister meaning in his manner. In the night, in the cold rain, the wet bleat of the train whistle came to them. Gunlock pushed his hat to the back of his head.

"That's the idea, Ross. Think about it a little before you shoot off your mouth."

Ross said, "You've got a mind like a pigsty, Gunlock. The only thing you're going to say about me is that I wasn't in this with you. Tell Shelton that. We'll talk about the money you and Ramsey stole from me when we get to a marshal's office."

Gunlock's face filled with sly contempt. "How you want it, boy. In the meantime, let's talk about chippy-chasers."

A brief ray of alarm flashed through Chance's mind. But it was gone, leaving his anger raw and exposed, and he took a step toward the foreman and said, "Damn you, sit down! Shut your mouth for one minute and listen to me."

"I don't listen to nobody, Ross," Gunlock interrupted. "People listen to me, now."

Ross stepped in and slapped him across the mouth. Gunlock fell back and his head bumped a cupboard. He swore, low and bitterly, but did not come back. His right hand went into his hip pocket and he pulled out a bright square of green wool. It was dirty and wrinkled with handling. His face became hard and triumphant. He tossed it to Ross.

"Sure—you talk, Ross! Tell us about the bedroom games you

play with ladies to take their minds off their crocheting."

Ross looked at the green crocheted square. He was shocked, knowing at once it was one of the afghan squares Laurel Shelton had had with her in his hotel room. But even more, he was saddened by the irrevocability of what Gunlock had done. He did not look at Shelton. He dropped the wool and walked into the foreman with a short, strong jab to the face. Gunlock grunted, his head banged the cupboard again, and he fell. But a moment after, he crawled toward the back of the caboose and lurched up.

A brakeman's bar lay on the end of a bunk; he seized this and rushed at Ross. Ross went in beneath the club. He jarred against Gunlock's gristled body and whipped his fist into the hard belly. The brakeman's bar struck an overhead as Gunlock swung it. It clattered from his hand and rolled away. Ross slugged the ramrod on the side of the head. Gunlock stumbled and crashed with a jolt into the trash of cigar butts and sandwich crusts in a corner.

Far ahead, Ross heard a change in the note of the wheels, a hollowness which denoted a bridge. He stared at the foreman as he stirred on the floor. He wished he had done something to shut his mouth earlier. He wished he had had the acuteness to know what Gunlock was threatening to say. He had done something now which must make it even harder for that unhappy, frightened girl.

Then he saw Gunlock getting up with one hand gripping the frame of the open door, his face mottled. His right hand was on the butt of his Colt, as he seemed trying to decide something. His voice was just audible over the racketing car.

"Damned chippy-chasing studhorse!" he said.

When Gunlock drew the gun, Ross lunged after him. Ross swung a roundhouse blow which collided with Gunlock's chin. The gun roared, dimming the lamp. The flame surged up with a ring of oily smoke. The bullet from Gunlock's gun had gone through a cupboard. Stricken, Gunlock reeled backward. All at once Ross rocked forward, shouting at Shelton:

"Grab the fool!"

But Shelton stood beside the door and watched his foreman stumble back through it. He did not raise a hand. He did not say anything nor change expression. Ross dived at Gunlock, but missed and collided with the edge of the jamb, becoming aware at the same moment of an empty roar in the car: the train was on the trestle above the Rio Grande. As he ran forward, Ross saw

Gunlock crash against the wet railing and poise for an instant as though he were casually sitting there. Beyond Gunlock, Ross caught a dark sheen of water and a gray skeleton of trestling.

With a glint of spurred boots, Gunlock was gone.

10

THE CAR RESOUNDED with the clatter of the trestle. Then it was quiet once more; the train had reached the west bank of the river and was heading into the mesas and desert mountains of the Mexican border. Ross and Shelton stared at each other. Ross stepped onto the platform. Barbs of rain darted through the green and red auras of the side-lamps. His hands locked on the railing, he stared down the tracks. But the trestle was drowned in night and mist.

As he stood there, he heard a man descending the ladder into the caboose. A trainman in overalls and sheepskin jacket came onto the floor and struck his hands together above the stove. "I hope you fellers ain't finished that coffee!" he said.

Shelton suddenly stirred. "A man just fell onto the tracks!" he said.

The trainman stood stiffly with the coffeepot raised. "Are you jokin'?"

Shelton joined Ross on the platform. "No—my God, I'm not joking!" he shouted. "We saw him fall."

"Where from?"

"*Where the hell would you think?*" Shelton shouted. "Off the catwalk, wouldn't you think? And we're getting farther from him every minute. Stop the train!"

The trainman scrambled up the ladder. The crawl-door banged after him. Ross had the coldly desperate feeling that all the blood was leaking out of his body. Shaken, he returned to the car and dropped blankly onto a bunk. He heard Lamar Shelton, following him, ram the door closed.

"Do you think he's dead?" Ross asked numbly.

"What do you think?"

Ross's fingers gripped his knees. "Maybe we ought to talk a little," Shelton said. "It might help me to know what to say when they ask what happened."

"You saw what happened," Ross retorted. "He pulled a gun on me."

"After you'd hit him?" Shelton reminded him.

"What would you have done?" Ross challenged. "He started it by calling me a chippy-chaser."

"I've been called worse things," Shelton told him, with a faint smile.

"And I'll bet you slapped somebody around."

"But I didn't kill anybody." Shelton's eyes were dark as old walnut, hard and steady under his heavy brows. The train suddenly jerked; it began to slow. "Those fools will dump every cow on this train on the floor," he said.

At a time like this, he can worry about cattle, Ross thought. He kept staring at the rancher, knowing he would speak sooner or later; eventually he would explain why he had lied to the trainman.

Shelton picked up the afghan square and frowned at it. "What was this supposed to be?"

Ross peered at him. Did Shelton fail to recognize it? "I don't savvy it. I never did know what he was getting at."

Shelton's eyes tilted somberly. "Didn't, eh?"

"He was accusing me of being a chaser, that's all I got out of it. I took all I could from him. He had a licking coming."

The woolen fragment dropped from Shelton's hand. "Don't lie to me, Chance," he said. "If you want any help from me, you'd better tell it straight."

"What do you want to know?" Ross protested.

"I want to know why he thought that would scare you."

Ross found a cigar in his pocket. He lighted it and stood at the door, watching the ties come into plainer view as the train stopped. He tried to push his brain, but it resisted him with a perverse weariness. Then an acceptable, if chancy, lie occurred to him. He breathed the smoke deeply before he said:

"It belongs to a girl Ramsey and I and Gunlock fooled around with in Las Truchas. Never mind her name. She was—her folks are pretty well known there. Blade and I met her when we came to town last summer."

He turned to scrutinize the rancher's face. Shelton's expression was cold. "Well . . . she came to us," Ross continued; "we didn't go to her. It was her lookout, wasn't it?"

Shelton began to smile. "How old was this girl?"

"Never mind. And she isn't in trouble, or anything—not as far as I know . . ."

Shelton pushed the afghan square with his square boot-toe. "And this was hers," he said, "and *you'd* be in trouble if Gunlock opened up on you, eh? Under age..."

"That's what Gunlock thought, at least. The girl had a bunch of these one night. She was crocheting them together for something."

"I'll tell you what I think," stated the rancher. The train had stopped and the drivers were thrusting it jerkily in reverse, now. Boots pounded along the catwalk toward the caboose. "I think you're a God-damn' liar. But I'll go along with you for a while. —Here they come," he said. "I'll handle it."

Every man except the fireman and engineer crowded into the caboose as the cattle train backed toward the river. There were four cowboys who were accompanying cars of cattle to one town or another. There were a switchman and some other trainmen and the man they had told of the accident, a brakeman named Campbell. They all crowded the platform, peering through the watery light thrown by bull's-eye lanterns.

"The damned fool," sighed Shelton. "I told him to lay off the liquor. But he kept hitting it. He went upstairs to check on that cow that was down at Union Ford. A minute later we saw him hit the tracks."

A man said, "We're coming to the bridge."

Slowly they pushed out onto the trestle. It was silent. Tension had Ross in a merciless grip. The brakeman, Campbell, said, "Funny. He told me he was going to catch some sleep when he went back."

They passed a red fire-barrel on its platform. Between the ties, the river was visible in dark slotted gleams. At last the water was gone. They were on gravel. The train halted and the men jumped out and some of them looked on the bank and two men started back along the ties at either side of the train. The brakeman ran back and set a flare. Ten minutes later they returned.

"Not a sign," said Campbell. "I expect he fell in the river. —Well, boy, this is going to sound rough. But we've got trains coming behind us, and if we don't want to get our behinds full of cowcatcher, we're agoing to have to move. Rain's no time to hunt corpses nohow."

All the men looked at Shelton. He said, "And good ramrods one in a hundred.... Campbell, will you send a wire ahead to Marshal Coles in Amargosa? They'll want to know about it."

11

DURING THE NIGHT they ran out of the weather. They had stopped for hours at some town where cars were uncoupled, rearranged, coal was taken on, and the interminable, mysterious functions of trains taken care of. In a clear, cold morning, they neared Amargosa. Ross stood on the platform to look the country over, feeling deeply an old thrill and satisfaction.

The sky was limitless, the thin blue of skim milk. Distantly he made out the Penasco Mountains on the border, behind miles of golden grass. They crossed the Rio Santiago and he saw the first of the little Mexican truck farms about Amargosa. Along the county road, weeds were smoking in bar-pits. Chilis lay drying, red and glistening, on every roof. Ross saw an oxcart lumbering into the village with a dripping load of vegetables. Far to the south, beyond the blur of trees and woodsmoke which was the town, he saw a familiar saddle in the mountains, and pictured at its foot a collection of adobe buildings among cottonwoods— Rancho Pacheco. He could not escape the feeling that it was his ... that for some reason it still belonged to the Chances. But it was no more his, he told himself, than it was that of any other mustanger who might drift into Amargosa.

Cold, sooty drafts of smoke swirled about the platform. He heard Lamar Shelton come from the car to set a carpetbag beside him as the train slowed. As Ross turned to go after his own gear, Shelton spoke.

"Not going to forget me, are you?" With his hands in his pockets and his coattails thrust back, Shelton smiled.

"I'll see you around," Ross said.

"Because I want to clean up this land-title fake," Shelton said.

Ross glanced at him. "Fake? I thought it must be on the level, before you'd pay on it."

"They didn't leave me much dickering room, you know." Shelton's face was guarded. Ross had begun to know his expressions.

"Do you reckon this was the first time he ever used this club of his?" Ross asked him.

"How do you mean?"

"I mean I never got it straight why my old man sold to you. He was making money. Even in bad years, the ranch always paid off. You don't suppose Gunlock had been putting the blocks to the colonel on this same deal, until he decided to sell and get out from under?"

"I wouldn't know about that." Shelton's voice was even. "I didn't know your father very well."

"You were a beef contractor or something before you bought the ranch, weren't you?"

"Who told you that?"

"Gunlock. He said you owned a little holding ranch near us where you kept herds until you were ready to sell them."

"Well, that's one thing he said that was true. Only a thousand acres. I bought most of my feed. . . . Here we are," he said drily. "For the time being, you'd better make peace with your partner. He's mustanging my range. Do you know the Paso Redondo area?"

"I grew up there," Ross told him.

"That's where he's got his camp. Move out there with him after you get squared away. Then come over and see me."

Without answer, Ross went into the caboose. He did not like taking orders from this big, self-confident man, but this was an order, and he was taking it. While he collected his belongings, he scrutinized for jokers every part of the story he and Shelton had tacitly agreed on. It seemed to him they were forgetting something. Yet the yarn was simple and serviceable. As the train stopped, he carried his luggage outside. Standing on the platform, he looked about.

Amargosa lay in a pocket of gaunt hills. The look of fall was crisp and golden on the country. The station was at the head of a secondary street running south to the plaza. Looking down the broad, uneven road lying between one-story adobes and rows of round-headed chinaberry trees, he could make out the east end of the plaza. There were puddles in the ruts of the road, a shining look to the leaves still on the trees. Some oxcarts were on the street, several horses, a few turnouts. Ross saw that a number of men and women were at the station—an unusual number, and he knew the word about Gunlock's death had been given out.

Shelton was walking up the tracks with his carpetbag. Ross followed him, carrying saddle, bedroll, and a cheap paper suitcase. He had to stop to rest, and while he stood there he saw a girl in a dove-gray gown step from the crowd toward Shelton.

"Lamar, is it true?" she asked.

"Sad to say," Shelton replied.

Breathing deeply, Ross gazed at the girl. It seemed impossible that he had seen her so little—that he had had a single letter from her. An irrational jealousy rose in him—that the man to whom she spoke first, the one who was now bending to kiss her with one arm about her waist, was Lamar Shelton. It seemed to Ross that a desire as strong as his should carry certain rights. But he was the extra one, and Shelton was the one she had been waiting for.

You fool, he thought savagely, *she's married! She writes her name Mrs.* But the recollection was empty. She was married, yes, but love did not require legalizing, like the begetting of children. Love was a phenomenon as independent as the weather.

As he walked to the station, he could hear the growing excitement of the crowd. Shelton and the trainman, Campbell, were recounting the story. The stationmaster hurried from his office with another man in a high-crowned derby who, Ross guessed, was an official of the line who had been dispatched from division headquarters. As he stepped up on the splintered planking, Ross did not acknowledge Laurel by even a glance. He was aware that she was staring at him; he also knew that Lamar Shelton might be observing them.

Setting his saddle and packages against the pebbly wall of the depot, Ross glanced around him. He had not been recognized yet. He supposed there was no reason why he should have been. He was simply a tall man in denim pants and horsehide jacket, who wore a work-stained Stetson and needed a shave. A transient; a horse-breaker; no one could guess or would try to. Ross heard a horse jogging up and saw a tall, stern-faced man pull it in at the edge of the platform. Lamar Shelton raised his voice.

"Marshal—over here!"

Ross watched the marshal dismount with ceremony, make some adjustment to his saddle, set his tall sombrero squarely, and walk through the crowd. He was a head taller than most of the men, and Ross could see his cement-colored face as he joined the rancher. It looked no more pleasant, Ross concluded, than it had when Marshal Will Coles was Lawyer Coles, scratching for a living.

"Now, what is all this?" Coles demanded of Shelton.

Shelton's expression was carefully compounded of respect to a man of authority, and amusement at a small man in a large pair of britches. Coles heard the story and then asked irritably:

"You the only witness, Lamar?"

Shelton's gaze immediately found Ross. "No. That man over there . . . Chance, will you come here?"

Ross had been lighting a thin Mexican cigar. He finished and dropped the wicklike wax match. He joined the men in the heart of the small crowd. "Hello, Marshal," he smiled.

Marshal Coles' weak, gray-green eyes regarded him with surprise. He was a man of sixty who wore a dirty collarband shirt without a collar, and unkempt sideburns which made Ross think always of goat's hair. As he stared at Ross, he put several piñon nuts into his mouth and his front teeth worked at the thin shells. He spat the shells and said:

"Well. Got all the hellin' out of your system and come back, did you?"

"Wait and see," Ross smiled.

"No—*you* wait and see!" snapped Coles. "We don't tolerate no rough stuff in this town, Chance. Not since the last marshal died. Just thought you'd want to know."

"What made you think that?"

"Things I've heard," Coles said mysteriously.

"Maybe you listen to the wrong people," Ross said. "I've been working, Will. And I never was much for helling. I suppose it seemed that way to you because my father took a saloon apart now and again."

"Well, just be sure it ain't a case of like father, like son," said the marshal.

Shelton came in tactfully. "Probably you want to hear Chance's story too, Marshal."

"Bet I do." Coles tilted his head back to inspect Ross through the steel-rimmed spectacles he wore. "Did you see it happen?"

"No, I was in the car with Shelton. Gunlock had been drinking. He'd just gone up when we saw him fall."

"Don't see how you could see him fall if you were inside."

"He fell off the back."

"What do you reckon he was doing on the back of the caboose?" Coles inquired. "No cattle back there, were there?"

He turned to stare at the caboose, and someone chuckled.

For a moment Ross was stopped by the marshal's random shot. "I doubt that he ever got set on the catwalk," he answered flatly. "He came out the crawl-door, I suppose, and lost his balance and fell across the cupola."

"Any kinda search made for him?" Coles asked.

"Not much. He fell in the river. There was a train close behind us, the brakeman said."

"You didn't actually see him slip?" Coles asked without looking at him.

Ross frowned at the marshal until he met his gaze. "What are you trying to do, Will—put answers in my mouth? I told you I was inside the car."

"Oh, yes," Coles smiled. His smile was thin and cold. "Well, you men come up to my office direc'ly and swear to this."

Now, with the crowd breaking up into groups, Ross glanced at Laurel Shelton. The first impression he had was of a very pretty, elegantly attired, and self-possessed young woman. It was hard to connect her with the frightened girl who had visited his hotel room that night. She wore a gray gown which just cleared her boot tops, and a small blue bonnet clung to her dark hair. Tiny diamonds sparkled in the lobes of her ears. She and her husband were standing alone, with Ross a short distance away. He saw the gay smile she gave Shelton as she said:

"Lamar, I've done the silliest thing!"

"No doubt," said Shelton.

"I've overdrawn my bank account again. There was this perfectly gorgeous material at Holabird's, and I knew if I didn't get it right then, someone else would. So—"

"So you gave a check, which happened to be no good because you'd already bought those earrings. Right?" Shelton asked in thin-smiling irony.

Laurel laughingly touched the stone in her right ear. "You do know me so well!"

Then she seemed suddenly to discover Ross, as he started to turn away. "Oh, Mr. Chance!"

"Yes?"

If you looked deep into those sparkling gray eyes, you could imagine you saw something graver than her smile. Ross was looking straight into them, and he was certain that he saw an appeal to him to understand her.

"Mr. Chance," she said, "we were so sorry to hear about your accident. Are you feeling all right, now?"

"Feeling fine," Ross said. "At least, as well as you could expect to feel after stopping a horse's hoof." He tipped his hat to her and walked through the crowd to his luggage. He carried it into the baggage room to store. He was there when the Shelton buggy, with the rancher driving, rolled out a few minutes later. Ross hoped Laurel would look at the window where he stood, but she was staring straight ahead and her chin was firm. He had been blunt enough in not staying to talk with her, and now he knew she had quite comprehended the gesture.

12

ROSS MET A few men he had known formerly in Amargosa. He spoke to them in the station. Yet all of them seemed awkward with him. Do they think I'm ashamed of needing a shave, he wondered. Or that my father went broke? Barkley, a feed merchant Ross's father used to deal with, invited him for a drink, but Ross told him he had a date with the marshal.

"He seems like a pretty important man, now," he added.

"He's all of that," Barkley smiled. "Old Coles went in on a platform opposed to sin, after Mrs. Shelton's father died. He locked the saloons on Sunday and chased all the girls out of Four-Bits Alley."

"Where are they now?"

"Pedregosà Street," Barkley chuckled. "Sin's a hard thing to put down. Don't let him talk you into signing the pledge."

Ross enjoyed strolling the dirt sidewalk from the station. He loved this bilingual town of dusty shade trees and adobe buildings. He liked the little plaza with its bandstand, pocked by Confederate bullet holes, and he remembered the Saturday-night exuberance of walking in it looking at the girls. He passed the stage depot, where lines came in from Mexico and from the silver mines a hundred miles north. As he neared the marshal's office, he heard the bell in the cathedral at the west end of the plaza begin to toll. A little Mexican girl in pigtails, with a black *mantilla* over her head, smiled as he passed her, and Ross reached down to pull a pigtail. She giggled and ran.

Next to the marshal's office was a vacant lot where assorted junk was collecting—old iron, hames with rusting bells, bottles. The marshal's office was a tawny mud-brick building shaded by a tree full of withered berries. Adjoining it was the jail, a long structure with a sheet-metal roof and four barred windows. Shelton had parked the buggy under the tree and entered the building. Laurel had dismounted to walk a few steps down the street. She was returning slowly, a parasol twirling over her shoulder, as Ross approached. Passing the jail, she came on toward him. Her features looked strained. She kept gazing past Ross. He realized what she must be thinking. That she had made all the overtures. She had visited his room, improperly, and she had written him. She had let him kiss her. But he had not even looked at her when he got off the train. She was ashamed and probably angry. Though it was chancy, with her husband in the office fifty feet away, Ross halted.

"Laurel—listen to me!" he said.

She kept moving. He put out a hand to stay her. His fingers touched the firmness under her sleeve. "Listen, Laurel— something's happened. I can't tell you now."

"You don't have to, Mr. Chance." Her voice was almost lighthearted; she was working at it. "Men have been telling women this same kind of story for years. I'm sorry I put you in such a position."

Ross stared after her helplessly—at the slender waist and shoulders and the mature roundness of her hips. At last he moved on, setting himself against his desire to explain to her. *It's got to end—it might as well end right now*, he told himself. But he paused before entering the jail to glance after her. As he stood there, he heard Lamar Shelton speaking low and heatedly in the marshal's office.

"I don't care a damn for that—this is the way it's going to be!"

"Like hell! You ain't going to tell me how to run my business," Marshal Coles retorted. He sounded breathless.

"I'm not, eh?" Someone moved in a chair. "Try me some time, Will. See if I mean what I told you when you took office."

After this there was a brittle silence. A tingling went through Ross. He felt that he had just heard something extremely important, and he stood there expectantly until he heard Coles grunt:

"I hate gambling, that's all. With money or—or anything." Something was deposited on a desk, with a thud, and Coles complained: "He should be here by now." Coles came toward the door. When he reached it, Ross Chance was standing about three strides from the corner of the building, striking a match for his cigar, which had gone out. Aware of his scrutiny, Ross made no sign until he finished lighting the cigar. Then he glanced up with a smile.

"Am I late? Had to store all that truck of mine."

Coles's sage-green eyes kept prying at his face. *Did he hear us?* his expression said. He looked to Ross like a husband interrupted at love-making with the maid. Presently Coles growled something and retreated into the building. Ross followed him into the office with its odors of cigar smoke, dust, and a faint trace of antiseptics. Seated in a rawhide chair with one boot crossed over his knee and his Stetson hung on his boot toe, Lamar Shelton was cleaning his nails with a pocketknife. He gave Ross a grin and a wink. *Stay with it, boy!* his expression said.

You liar, Ross thought. You bald-faced, copper-bottomed liar! You've got a deal of some kind cooking with Coles, but you sit there winking that you're still protecting me!

Behind his desk, Coles complained, "I swear I filled this inkwell last week. That cleaning woman would steal the blood out of your veins."

If you had any, Ross thought. He watched the officer search for the ink bottle among a wilderness of medicine bottles on a shelf. Even the stringy back of his neck looked guilty. "Damned if I don't clear this corruption of Henderson's out tomorrow!" Coles swore. Then he seemed to recall something, and told Shelton with irony: "Begging your pardon. I forgot he was your father-in-law."

"He was still a fool," chuckled Shelton. Rising, he glanced at the bottles on the shelf. "My God, he could cure anything under the sun, couldn't he?"

"Anything but dying in jail," said Coles. Finally he located the ink bottle and filled the crusted well on his desk. "Sit down, Chance," he said. "Pen and paper right here. Just write it the way you told me."

Ross gazed at him until he uneasily looked away. "Why don't you get Mr. Shelton to do the affidavit? He was Gunlock's employer. I'll second anything Shelton says."

"I'll get to him later," Coles snapped. "I'm talking to you, now."

Ross shrugged. "I can't write, Marshal. I was too busy hellin' around, as you say, to go to school."

Coles's eyes were weak but his voice was strong. "I told you we were running this town different, mister! When a man dies, we go to a little more trouble than buying him flowers. Now, set down there and give me your affidavit."

Pushing his hat back, Ross smiled at Shelton. "Were they all drunk the day Coles was elected? The man's crazy."

Shelton's face became sternly reminding. "Oh, I don't know. This is just matter of form."

Coles looked bloodless—like a scared old maid, thought Ross, and he could not help probing at the wound he had opened. "It's not that big a job, Will. It can't pay much more than you made handling divorces. Why get all heated up over it? In the first place," he mentioned, "it's none of your damned business about Gunlock, anyway."

"How do you figure that? Anything on this side of the Rio Grande is my jurisdiction—Doña María County."

"Sure—but Gunlock didn't die on this side of the Rio Grande. He died in the middle, if he died at all."

In Marshal Cole's office there was the soundless noise of something collapsing. Coles put his thin fingers to a sideburn and combed it. Shelton's foot stopped twirling his Stetson. In the jail behind the office, a drunken Mexican softly sang a ballad of unrequited love. Shelton's hat fell and he stooped to retrieve it.

"You know, Will, that's a point!" he remarked, straightening. "If Gunlock fell in the middle, it would be hard to say whether he's Texas's baby or New Mexico's."

"That could be," Coles said blankly. "That could be. Just save me that much grief if he's Texas's baby. We'll let it go for now, Chance. But if I want you, where will you be at?"

"Hard to say. I may do some mustanging out at Paso Redondo."

"Oh, yes. Your pardner's there, ain't he?" Coles commented.

"My pardner?" Ross frowned.

Coles seemed to hold his breath. His gaze flicked to Shelton. It was Shelton who replied:

"I was telling the marshal about buying the horses from you and Ramsey."

"Oh, yeah." Ross let his gaze linger on Shelton's face. As he was on the point of taking his leave, the marshal spoke.

"O' course you know about your father dying, Chance."

He did not meet Ross's gaze when Ross turned to him. "Yes, I know about it. About the land, too."

"It was too bad. But it's over and done, now."

"Is it?"

"Well, ain't it?" Coles challenged. "You just look in the recorder's office sometime, if you think it ain't. The Sheltons have bought and paid for it, and you might as well not come hankering after something like that."

"Oh, I'm not hankering," said Ross. "But I'll probably have a talk with Henry Lyman just to make myself fell better."

Coles's sage-colored eyes pinched. "Tell you what won't do you no good a-tall," he said quickly. "To drag Henry Lyman into it."

Ross perceived the urgency in the marshal's eyes, and probed it still further. "Why wouldn't it?"

Coles made an exclamation of disgust. "That dried-up little Blackstone! Just because he's had the devil's own luck winning cases, he figures he runs this county."

"The way I remember," Ross remarked, "he practically does. He's always handled all the legal business in Doña María County, except the divorces, and that was your specialty, of course."

Coles's stringy cheeks gathered smudges of color. "What's wrong with divorce cases?"

Ross began to chuckle. "I remember my father's joke about divorce lawyers. 'Most of 'em would sleep with a client's wife, to give the man grounds for divorce.'"

Coles spoke with vixen force. "Yes, your father had a lot of fine ideas, Chance, and look at the end he come to! With all his taste in lawyers, his own couldn't keep him from going under."

"That's what I wanted to ask Henry about," Ross said.

"Well, ask him! But don't think you're going to do yourself any good." Then, seeming to catch a stare from Shelton, the marshal growled, "Because he ain't a magician or nothing. He's just a lawyer, like myself, only he didn't have to scratch to put himself through law school, like I did. He's—Henry's had a lot of luck, that's all."

Ross gazed at him, this Abe Lincoln whose candlelight studies had brought him nothing but weak eyes. "That may be," Ross said. "All the same, I'll have a talk with him."

13

Ross WALKED TWO blocks south to the plaza, a rectangle of trees and withered shrubs reaching a long block off to his right. The small cathedral faced the square at the near end, where Ross stood. At the west end were the county courthouse and city hall. All the vital juices of Amargosa and Doña María County pumped in and out of this little plaza. You could get drunk in any of ten saloons facing the plaza, eat in one of the half-dozen restaurants, get a marriage license or divorce in the courthouse, and be married or buried in the church, whose round belfry frowned in whitewashed disapproval, across the dusty trees, at the venality of the courthouse.

Ross turned right and walked west along the plaza, in the galleried shade of the business houses. He had not seen Laurel when he left the jail. He had not looked for her. His mind was full of impressions he had gained in that brief talk with the marshal and Lamar Shelton. He felt as though a dozen keys were in his hand and a single lock was before him, but none would quite fit. He had heard Shelton's voice when his guard was down, and it was not the tough, genial voice he wore for show. It had sounded sharp and a little worried.

Ross was certain that he had told Coles what had really happened on the train. Yet he was convinced they did not dare, for some reason, to expose him, and so he had a little time to get his bearings. Time to talk with old Henry Lyman, his father's lawyer, and he experienced a warm eagerness as he neared the Gadsden Purchase Hotel, where Lyman had his office.

The hotel presented to the street a whitewashed adobe façade with deepset windows. An upstairs gallery supported by rough pillars formed the usual roof over the sidewalk, and along the railing of the porch was a sign: *Lyman & Chalmers, Attys. at Law*. Chalmers had been dead for twenty years, if he had ever existed. But in his two rooms of books and maps and cigar

70

smoke, Henry Lyman had strapped this county together with bands of parchment and revenue stamps.

Just west of the hotel saloon was a separate stairway to several upstairs offices. Ross ascended to the upper floor and entered an open door. He was in a small, dingy reception room where an old man with skin like dried flower-petals was copying papers on onionskin. You would have thought he was installed here with the furniture, many years ago, but Ross did not remember him, and so he introduced himself and said, "Is Henry busy?"

A voice in an inner office called, "Who is it, John?" and the old man was getting up to reply when Ross smiled and shook his head.

"I'll just see how good his memory is."

He went into the large, airy office with its whitewashed walls and dark cabinets. An elderly wisp of a man in a frock coat and pleated shirt sat at a desk. His back was to a door opening onto the railed gallery. The room was full of his cigar smoke. He had the bald head of an eagle and a thin, sharp nose. He looked to Ross as though he were eighty percent clothes and twenty percent laywer, a little dandy of a man with eyes like gimlets.

Suddenly he leaned back with a smile. "Is that you, Ross, under all that whisker-stubble?" he asked.

Ross touched his unshaven jaws. "It was me, the last time I looked," he said.

"Well, sit down, sit down!" Lyman got up and came around to look at him. "Colonel Bob Chance's boy all over," he declared.

"Well—not quite," Ross told him.

Lyman offered cigars. Ross took one from the box but eyed its rum-soaked, licorice-colored wrapper in suspicion. "Do I need a note from my mother to smoke this?"

Lyman smiled. "They're not for the faint-hearted.... Ross," he asked bluntly, "why didn't you keep in touch with me? I might have been able to save something for you."

Ross told him about the letter which had been returned from Las Truchas. "If I'd known he was dead, I'd have come back. But I thought I had plenty of time. I didn't know he was that sick."

Lyman's rich brown eyes seemed to pinch; Ross thought he was going to say something. But he set his lips and remained silent.

"Do you think I should have come back?" Ross queried. "The way things were between us?"

"All I know," the lawyer said primly, "is what I would have done. And I'd have come back, if I knew my father needed me."

"If he'd thrown you out?"

"He didn't throw you out," Lyman argued. "You got out. I never saw a man so lonesome as the colonel after you left."

Ross gazed at him. "That's a damned lie, Henry. You don't have to try to patch it up. It's too late for that. You couldn't even patch it up when we were both alive, often as you tried."

Henry Lyman snorted. "Not lonesome? For a week after you left, he came in every day to tell me what he'd do to you when you came back. Then he changed it to *if* you came back. Then he took to asking me if I thought he was wrong, and should he go looking for you. He sent Gunlock to El Paso to buy some calves he didn't need, hoping he'd run into you. After a while he got drunk and kept a nice edge for the next six months—just enough to keep him stumbling."

Ross looked away, but a sharpness stayed in his throat. He knew this little buzzard-nosed lawyer had never told even a white lie in his life, and he wanted very much not to believe this.

"If he'd wanted to see me," he said, "he could have written."

"Pride," postulated Lyman, "is the best and the worst trait a man can have. He had fifty percent too much. I don't know what the percentage is with you, but it's too damned high."

"If I'd come back," Ross declared, "we'd have been fighting again in a week. We were carbide and water. I don't know why. He didn't even know. But we couldn't hit it off."

"I know why," Lyman said.

Ross looked at him in surprise. Lyman said sadly, "Because he was the best man, but the worst father, I ever knew. He was ashamed of any weakness in himself, including being only five-feet-six, and he was ashamed of weakness in his family. He didn't know we're all weak, to begin with. The fact that you weren't born a bronc-stomper looked like cowardice, to him. So he put you on the worst outlaws he owned, until you could ride anything. The fact that you got drunk and went to a straddlin' house shamed him. Everybody in town knew it. He didn't mind your getting drunk so much as having to buy a woman. A young buck six feet tall and handsome ought to be able to get a girl by lifting his finger—a Chance, particularly. So he set out to teach you that."

"A blind bull," Ross said, "never taught anybody anything."

Lyman puffed on the cigar that was twice too large for him, and nodded in agreement. "All right, but you're older, now, and

I think you ought to know a little about your ancestry, before you go kicking over your tombstone. That's all I'm saying."

"I knew that particular ancestor pretty well," said Ross with a crooked smile.

"Did you know how many people he was supporting until the day he died?"

"A couple of saloonkeepers?" Ross guessed.

"Four broken-down cowpunchers who couldn't rope a tumbleweed, and an old Mexican woman here in town who had no claim on him except that she nursed you after your mother took off." His face grew sad as he drew on the cigar. "He was a damned fine man," he concluded. "I never had a better friend in my life."

Lyman rose, and Ross watched him go to a letterpress rack. He was a dandy with the mind of a philosopher, thought Ross, a man whose reticence might fool you forever, unless he chose to open up. He had opened up more today than Ross had ever known him to. He had divulged the fact, without saying so, that the death of Colonel Chance had left him desolate.

Lyman carried a volume of onionskin sheets to his desk. Handling the cigar with his teeth, he opened the book. "Maybe this seems like a lot of foolishness," he said. "I'm not trying to reconcile you to your father. Nobody ever got along with him except me, anyhow. But what I want to understand before I try to help you is whether you're his son, or just somebody with his name."

"I don't know that any more than you do," Ross retorted.

"Why'd you come back, then? To grub for nickels the creditors might have overlooked?" Lyman's eyes were harsh.

Ross looked into himself for an instant. There were so many emotions there that he could not give a straight answer. Laurel . . . Gunlock. . . . But behind all the other colors, swirling and mixing like a colored top, was the plain, understandable fact that for the last couple of years, coming home had seemed an end in itself.

"I came back because I've been thinking about the ranch," he said. "Because I always loved every acre of it, and if I'm not going to have it myself, at least I want to say a prayer over it before they bury it."

Lyman squinted. "What kind of a prayer?"

"I want to know why Dad sold it. He felt the same way about Rancho Pacheco, didn't he?"

Lyman smiled. "Hell, when he hit New Mexico he didn't have

half the price of Rancho Pacheco. We got here the same month, me for my health, him to get out of the mosquito country. I worked out a way for him to raise cash on everything, including his gold filings. He mortgaged his life to get that ranch. That's how much he loved it."

"Then why did he sell it?"

"I don't know."

"Didn't you handle the sale for him?"

Lyman swiveled his armchair to gaze out the window. A little band of goats was being driven across the square. Leaves were being burned and the incense of them dissolved through the streets and alleys and rose like memories to this room. Lyman watched these things and said:

"No, I didn't handle the sale. Will Coles did. Your father took all his business out of my hands the year before he died."

Ross took the cigar from his teeth. He said hotly: "And you stand up for him as the best friend you ever had! What was the matter—did you forget to dot an 'i' in one of his papers?"

"I refused to handle the sale, that's all. So he moved out. To that juiceless temperance deacon of a divorce lawyer!" He spun the chair. His eyes glinted with moisture. "Why the hell did he take Coles's advice over mine? Didn't I help build Pacheco to the third biggest ranch in Doña María County? Damn it, boy, I kept him out of jail when he horsewhipped the tax assessor for discriminating against him. I patched quarrels between him and the few friends he had. But when he got in trouble, he turned his back on me."

"What kind of trouble?"

"I just said I didn't know. He wouldn't share it with me. That's a nice kind of gratitude, ain't it?" He rose, threw the fresh cigar into the street, and stared hotly at Ross.

"I've got a little bit of an idea," Ross said, "why he may have sold. I think he was pressured into it. I think they gave him his choice: either sell half, or lose everything."

Lyman shook his head. "He didn't have any secrets. All his scandals have been public domain for years."

"Not this one. This involved his land title. Somebody found out the title of the ranch wa faulty."

"The hell with that. I prepared the abstract myself. He's only the second owner of the land since the bulk of this county came into the United States with the Gadsden Purchase."

"Sit down, Henry," Ross said. "Get out the brandy, if you've got any. You're going to need stimulants."

When Ross had finished, Henry broke the silence to say bitterly: "That Gunlock always was a cow-stealing son of a sheepherder. I told your father that. But he would keep him."

Ross shook his head. "My guess is that Shelton blackmailed Dad. Then Gunlock got hold of the same information somewhere and turned it back on him. Look at the possibilities! Back taxes—interest..."

Suddenly Lyman rapped: "This is a lot of hogwash. If your father swallowed a yarn like that, he deserved to lose the ranch. Hell! They checked that international line with calipers. There were surveyors from Mexico and the States both—and remember we were stealing land from them for the second time in two years, and Mexico wasn't hot for giving away acreage."

"But don't forget this: There's some pretty rugged country along the border. Suppose they set the monuments right in the beginning: would it be too hard to move them later—kind of bend the line say, to bring in Paso Redondo and some of the other choice land along there?"

Lyman's hands, lean as bird's feet, aligned articles on his desk. "I reckon not. There weren't many people around here then. The line could be turned south in the mountains and brought back again before it hit the plains. But—hell, it's fantastic!"

"Shelton believes it—enough to pay five thousand dollars to keep it quiet."

Lyman frowned. "You don't know who this fourth man is in the deal, eh?"

"Gunlock didn't tell me."

"As a man who's always despised Lamar Shelton," said the lawyer, "I'll bet he threw Gunlock off that train to get rid of him."

Ross gazed at him, holding his breath. "Take it easy, now, Henry," he said finally. "I happen to know Shelton *didn't* kill Gunlock."

Lyman's bright eyes were steady. "Are you sure of that?"

"I ought to be," Ross sighed. "I killed Gunlock myself."

The little lawyer's mouth opened; then he closed it and set his lips firmly together and spun his chair to look out the window. Finally he got up and took a gray stovepipe hat from a hatrack.

"Why don't we go down and have a brandy?" he said.

14

IN THE ADJOINING room, the old clerk was placing a damp cloth over a letter to be recorded in the letterpress. "Back in an hour, John," said Lyman. As they closed the door, the sound of someone coming up the stairs could be heard. The tread was light, and Ross was not surprised to see a young woman come onto the landing.

The surprise was that it was Laurel Shelton.

When she saw Ross, she hesitated with her hand on the newel post, a folded parasol over her shoulder. There in the dim hallway they gazed at each other. Laurel looked startled. Then she transferred her attention quickly to Lyman's face.

"I'm just too late, I see," she said. "I thought I'd run up for a moment while I was in town...."

Lyman introduced them. "Mr. Chance—Mrs. Shelton. You have something in common, you see—you're both clients of mine. As a matter of fact," he recalled suddenly, "Mr. Chance's father was the Colonel Chance who owned the land you bought last spring, at the tax sale!"

Even in the dusky light, color could be seen to rise to the girl's cheeks. Under Ross's astonished stare, she glanced down, but realizing she must react she looked at Lyman.

"Isn't that a coincidence!" she said. Then she ventured a timid glance at Ross.

"I would have thought," Ross said, "that your husband would be the owner of the property, ma'am."

Lyman explained: "*Mr.* Shelton owns Rancho Pachero—the half your father sold some time ago. *Mrs.* Shelton—she was Miss Henderson, then—bought the other half at the tax auction."

"I see," Ross said, still gazing at Laurel.

They descended the stairs together, the girl between them.

Ross took her arm. He held it with angry pressure; she caught her breath, but he did not relax the grip.

The lovelier they were, the more accomplished they were at lying. He had heard this, somewhere. He believed it now. Her husband misunderstood her. She needed help. But in her own name Mrs. Shelton owned half the land he had expected to have, some day. She had known that while they stood in his hotel room, in Las Truchas—but she had not seen fit to mention it.

At the hotel entrance they waited while a Mexican woman trudged by with a rack of red pottery on her back. Hats in hand, the men smiled at the girl, and Henry Lyman suggested that she shop a while, when he would be able to talk to her.

"No trouble regarding your ranch?"

"Oh, none at all! It wasn't in regard to the ranch. I—I'll explain it later." The blue silk shell of the parasol popped up. She put it over her shoulder and, turning, she walked away.

"She's upset about something," Henry Lyman frowned.

"She's always upset about something," Ross told him.

Lyman smiled. "What do you know about Mrs. Shelton?" Lyman exclaimed.

"Quite a bit. I met her in Las Truchas."

Lyman frowned. "When was this?"

"Last month."

"Didn't you know she was married?"

"Not at first. I found it out pretty soon."

Lyman seemed embarrassed. He gazed down the sidewalk. Then he said, "In view of everything, Ross, I think I'd—well, I'd watch my step, where Mrs. Shelton is concerned."

"I'm beginning to," Ross said, "right about now."

The Gadsden Purchase bar was a large, comfortable room where the best liquor was sold to customers from all parts of New Mexico and Chihuahua. There had been a time when a lonesome man could walk through a door in the rear and be transported across an alley to the comforting arms of any of twenty girls. Ross had gone through that door once himself, when he was seventeen and very drunk. And afterward he had been ashamed and could not recall having been particularly happy. It had been merely a fever he had had to recover from.

This being midmorning, there were only a few customers at the bar. Two barkeeps in tubular white aprons, and white shirts with the sleeves rolled to the elbows, were polishing glassware. Old Charlie Brown, who had been on hand that first and last

night Ross was here, recognized him as they passed down the
bar. "Well, Mr. Chance!" he said. "A long time, eh?" He was a
small man with shiny florid skin and a rabbitlike smile.

"A drunk like that lasts a while," Ross said.

Charlie laughed softly, but did not ask Ross where he had
been, nor what he planned to do. "A little touch before lunch,
eh?" he said.

"Just a touch. I won't try to create a shortage this time."

"Fine," the barkeep said. "Now, your partner—there's a man
to send us to the storeroom three times in an evening, eh?"

"Blade Ramsey?" Ross said. "We're not partners. We were at
one time. What's he done?"

Charlie Brown smiled a trifle ruefully. "It isn't the drinking so
much . . . But we have to be careful about the girls nowadays,
since Marshal Coles took office. Mr. Ramsey was in with a
young woman last week, and of course we had to ask him to
leave."

Charlie reflectively sawed a bar towel over the ruddy bronze
of a beer pump.

"What'd Blade do?" Ross asked. It was surprising how every
fiber of him seemed to sharpen at the knowledge that Blade had
been here . . . the hound scenting the fox.

"Oh, Mr. Ramsey was agreeable. They bought a quart of our
best and went along."

Henry Lyman spoke. "Some *aguardiente*, Charlie."

They trod fresh sawdust to a corner. At a table near the door
to the hotel lobby, his head pillowed on his arms, sat an old man
with a burned-out cigar in his fingers. A whiskey bottle, not
quite empty, rested near his hand. He was snoring slightly. He
wore a stained leather shirt with yellow suspenders crossed over
the back. There was something familiar about the massive gray
head, rough as a bull's.

"That's Pard Mallet, isn't it?" Ross asked the lawyer.

Lyman regarded the man disdainfully. "Yes—damned,
besotted old fool. Even your father got enough of him finally.
Fired him last year. I don't know why he ever tolerated him,
except that he inherited him from old Tomás Archuleta when he
bought the ranch."

Ross picked up the bottle. "'J.C. Cutter'. . . he's drinking
well, for a man out of a job." When he set the bottle down, he
saw the lawyer regarding Mallet in surprise.

"That's for damned sure," Henry Lyman grunted.

At a table remote from the bar they put down a shot each of

bright Mexican brandy. "I can stand it, now," Lyman sighed. "What about Gunlock?"

Ross told him about the fight. "He came after you with a gun," Lyman recapitulated, "and you protected yourself. And he fell."

"That's about it."

"Then why in hell did you tell Coles a phony story like that?" Lyman demanded in a tense, angry voice.

Ross said it had been Shelton's idea. "It seemed like a good one, to me. Old Coles would have me in the pokey right now, if I'd told the truth."

"And I'd have had you out by nightfall. For good. But this way.... If Shelton ever opens up, you're cooked, boy! What I don't see is why he's kept silent this long."

"Because he knew that if he turned on me, I'd tell all I knew about the ranch. And he'd be cleaned out."

Slowly Lyman thumped the table with his fist. "Don't you see what you let him do? If he hadn't maneuvered you into this corner, you'd have had *him* in a corner! Now, you don't dare go after him."

"That won't keep Blade from blackmailing him. And it was his idea and Gunlock's to begin with."

Lyman shook his bony head. "You wait! As soon as everybody's got his breath after this investigation of Coles's, Shelton will come to you and say, 'If you don't keep your partner off my back, I'll turn Coles loose on you.'"

Ross reflected. "Yes. That's about the way it'll go. Then what do I do?"

"God knows. Did you sign a statement?"

Ross shook his head. Suddenly he said, "Damn that girl, Henry! Do you suppose she's been playing me into her husband's hands all the time?"

"I wouldn't know," Henry said primly. "But if you want to tell me how you happen to know her, I may be able to tell you a few things of interest about her that *I* happen to know."

Ross explained about the meetings with Laurel in Las Truchas. "But she wasn't offering me anything. I thought... hell, I don't know what I thought! I figured she was a nice kid, though, and was—mixed up somewhere."

"She's good and mixed up," Henry Lyman said sadly. "Now, keep quiet about what I'm saying. You knew her father died in jail?"

"In Mexico. She told me that much."

"Did she tell you who the complaining witness was—the man who had him jailed?"

"No."

"Lamar Shelton," Lyman said.

Ross's head came up. "How do you know that?"

"Mrs. Shelton—she was Laurel Henderson, then—came to me last spring, after her father had been gone for two weeks on the trail of some stolen horses. She'd heard from a trader that he was in jail in Villa Hermosa, Chihuahua. She wanted me to go down and try to get him out. I tried, but I couldn't. He was being held on an open charge. You know those people—money's all that talks, and even that didn't talk this time. So I knew somebody else was paying more to keep him *in* jail than I offered! Finally I found out that the complaining witness was Lamar Shelton. Marshal Henderson didn't even know about it himself. All he knew was that he found these stolen horses—they belonged to Shelton, you see—near the border, in a stone corral. When he tried to drive them out, some Rurales jumped him. He woke up in jail."

Ross turned it over in his mind, seeing some basic order to it, some dark undercolor staining it all. "Did they hang him?"

"No. He was in jail about a month. Of course everyone in town knew it by then. They began gossiping about whether or not he'd been running a border-jumping trade. Marshal Henderson had been popular enough, but some of the old biddies like Will Coles's wife hadn't liked the way he kept the floosies bottled up across the alley. Stamp 'em out! That was the war cry whenever Annie Coles's sewing club met. Sure! Stamp out lechery and we'd all ascend. Better to know where they were than have them turning every hotel in town into a straddlin' house."

Lyman squinted at the fuming tip of his cigar.

"They made it pure hell for Laurel. A woman can hurt another worse by the way she says, 'Will you have lemon or sugar?' than a man can by stripping the hide off another. I liked the way that girl stood up. She give it right back to Annie Coles on the street one day. I heard part of it. Man!"

The inevitable question that came to Ross's head every time he thought of Laurel came out. "I don't see what good marrying Shelton did. A little prestige to throw at them, maybe."

"A hell of a lot of prestige. Shelton's substantial. But I don't know..." Lyman shook his small, bony head. "It was out of character for a girl like that. I remember the day she told me she was marrying Shelton. God! I didn't know what to tell her! I hadn't wanted to upset any applecarts until I was ready, so I'd kept quiet about Shelton. How was I going to prove it, anyway? But I told her then."

Ross's eyes came up, hard and black. "What'd she say?"

"For about two minutes she didn't say anything. Then she said she didn't believe it. She said she was going to marry him anyway. But that was beside the point. The main thing was, this tax land of your father's that was going to be auctioned off, she wanted me to get it for her."

"A marshal's daughter doesn't have that kind of money."

"She gave me a blank check signed by Lamar Shelton. It was a wedding present. I got the land for her, after I couldn't contact you. She didn't come around any more, but I knew Shelton went to Villa Hermosa a couple of times to try to get the marshal out. So *he* said. He never did, though. Henderson died a month after Laurel was married. Typhoid, down in Mexico."

Two men came into the saloon. The doors whipped behind them. At his dark table, Pard Mallet stirred and overturned his whiskey bottle. In bleary remorse, he watched the liquor drip from the table into the sawdust. He looked at Ross but did not seem to recognize him.

Ross glanced down. With the base of his glass, he made wet marks on the wood. "At least we know what kind of a woman Mrs. Shelton is," he said.

"What kind is that?"

"The kind who'd marry her father's murderer for money."

Lyman smiled wryly. "Oh, now, I wouldn't—"

Ross got up, finished his drink, and set the glass down. "I would." He sauntered back to Pard Mallet's table.

15

PARD HAD RELIGHTED the stale cigar with which he had gone to sleep the evening before. As Ross approached, he was letting the match burn out in his short, scarred fingers. Ross looked into the swollen drinker's-features and tried to recall the affection he had had for him long ago, when Pard, who had worked as blacksmith and handyman on his father's ranch, had befriended him. But it had dissipated like a dream—they were both forgotten, the boy and the blacksmith. Yet he could not go out without speaking to him, and he stopped by the table.

"What are you doing, Pard—boarding here?"

Pard's muddy gaze came up. He dropped the match on the table. Then he rose unsteadily with a guilty grin and took Ross's hand in both of his own. "Ross, boy! Never did look for you to come back. How are you, boy?"

Ross said he was fine. "Back on a visit?" Pard asked him. Ross told him it was hard to say, but as he watched him brush his tough gray hair with his hand, he realized Pard was having difficulty to maintain the appearance of surprise. A thin line of suspicion ran across his mind. Pard kept grinning, and now crushed the burned matchstick on the table top with his forefinger and applied the charcoal to his eyebrows—a ridiculous touch of vanity in an otherwise completely careless man.

"What do you figure to do, boy?" Pard Mallet asked.

"Little mustanging, maybe," Ross said.

Pard said solemnly: "Say, wa'n't that hell about George Gunlock? Wa'n't that a hell of a way?"

"You got to go sometime," Ross said.

"Yes, but . . . say!—you was with him and Shelton, wa'n't you?"

"I saw him fall."

82

"Well, God damn." Pard's ponderous body wallowed around in the chair. "That was the way it was, hey? Off the top of the caboose?"

Ross nodded. He waited, watching Pard drily, but Pard veered away from it. Presently he said: "Too bad about your old man, Ross."

"You got to go sometime," Ross repeated.

"Drug by a horse," Pard declared. He shook his head.

"Was that the way it was? I thought it was his heart."

Pard looked shocked. "He had a seizure, I guess. Then he was drug. Oh, God, you should've seen him."

"Where did you see him?"

"At Paul Fleming's—the undertaker's. After he was laid out." Pard wagged his head again.

"Surprised you were interested," Ross remarked. "I thought you and he had a falling-out."

Pard made a mincing shrug. "Oh, well—you know how the colonel was. I guess you know better than anybody. But he was all right underneath it."

Ross rose, and punched the blacksmith on the shoulder. "Take 'er easy."

"You the same."

In afterthought, Ross lingered at the table. "Pard, you worked on the ranch before Dad bought it, didn't you?"

"I worked on that ranch from the day it come into the States on the Gadsden Purchase," Pard declared proudly. "For old Tomás Archuleta, you know. He's still around town. Older'n God."

"But you're not working for Shelton now?"

Pard appeared surprised. His little bloodshot eyes opened. "No, no! I'm just—doin' a little pickup work. Helping out Bob Frazee in the hot-mill. Sweat out the old whiskey and buy the new." He laughed. But as Ross started to leave, he shook his head. "Poor old Gunlock. Just fell off the car, hey?"

"Yep," Ross said sadly.

"Him and Shelton . . . were they gettin' along all right up to then?"

Ross squinted at him. "I didn't notice. Why?"

"They haven't been hitting it off. I was just thinking—Shelton would feel real bad, if he'd been layin' the gad to George just before he died."

"I can imagine."

Ross walked out with Henry Lyman. The air was heating, a

final day of summer before the frosts. Mexican women and girls were carrying water from the stone well in the plaza, the brown ollas balanced gracefully on their shoulders. Across the square, a string of freight wagons rumbled in on the Chihuahua road.

"I may not know much," Ross said suddenly, "but I know one thing, now. Pard Mallet's the fourth partner in this deal."

Lyman glanced quickly at him.

"He did everything but ask me, flat out, if Shelton murdered Gunlock. Old Pard's sweating, Henry! He figures if Shelton's started protecting himself by killing off the opposition, he'll get to him sooner or later."

"May be," said the lawyer. "Pard knows that ranch better than any of us. Maybe he stumbled across the fact that the monuments don't line up . . . assuming this whole thing isn't a fraud."

From his pocket, Ross extracted the check of Shelton's, which Gunlock had given him before his death. "Will you advance me fifty on this, Henry? I'd like to keep it a while as a souvenir."

"Yes, and you'd better let me lock that souvenir up." The lawyer took some gold coins from his pocket and dropped them on Ross's palm. He appropriated the check. "There's one thing you could do, while I start digging. Go over and talk to Thomás Archuleta. It'd look better than me going. He'd suspicion something sure."

Ross walked to the barbershop and spent seventy-five cents on a haircut, shave, and bath. He liked the fiery chill of the bay rum on his face, and let the barber put some tonic on his hair. Leaving the barbershop, he started west toward Acequia Street, where Archuleta lived.

A horseman was riding north along the plaza when Ross turned south toward the *acequia madre*, the main canal which brought water for drinking and irrigation to the village. Ross recognized Shelton's strong, energetic figure on a buckskin horse, his gray Stetson shading his face. He stopped in the feathery shade of a desert cedar to wait for him. Shelton handled the horse smoothly around to the walk. In his heavy, dark face, his eyes were sharp.

"Coles was suspicious as hell," he said tersely. "I've got him tamed a little, but don't cross him like that any more."

"Then keep the damned old maid away from me," Ross said.

"Maybe you'd better stay out of town for a couple of days. Are you going out to Paso Redondo?"

Ross squinted. "I might as well. That partner of mine will be getting worried about me."

"I've got a wagonload of groceries parked by Griggs's Mercantile." Shelton glanced back the way he had come; the mercantile was on the southwest corner of the plaza. "The horses are behind the store. Why not drive it out to the ranch for me? Tell Rafael Ruela I said you were to have your pick of the riding horses in the corral."

"What's this going to cost me?" Ross grinned.

"Nothing. It's just a loan. Better take out some food for yourself, too. Ramsey won't have anything but whiskey there. Charge it to me at the store."

Ross's feeling was that he was seeing surface-deep into a well that went down to blackness. Shelton kept his gaze steadily on him while he considered. "Okay," Ross said.

"What'd you work out with old Lyman?" Shelton asked.

Ross saw his cocksure smile: *Don't try to go around behind my back!* it said. He gave Shelton the same smile. "Not much. He was holding a pocket watch and two rusty razors of my dad's that you missed when you took over the ranch. He thought I'd like to have them."

Shelton exasperatedly shook his head. "Still think I rigged him, don't you?"

"I'm just guessing," said Ross, "but I think maybe you put the same squeeze on him that Gunlock was putting on you."

For several seconds, his face growing somber, the rancher stared down at him. "All right," he said, "if you want to think so. But one thing I never tried to steal was another man's wife." He swung the horse back into the street.

With the shock of realizing that Shelton had understood from the first what Gunlock was implying on the train, Ross watched him ride away. After a moment, his face set, he walked on.

Ross left the central area, walking a block west on a potholed street and turning south again toward the canal. Tomás Archuleta lived at the end of this street. Children, pigs, and dogs played contentedly before the small adobe homes he passed. This town, Ross thought, was as careless of itself as an old man spilling food on his vest. A town of bells and blackbirds, rubbish and potholes, where ninety percent of the women on the street were Mexican or Indian, and about the same percentage pregnant. Yet it had the warmth and ease of a hot bath on a cold night.

For several minutes after he had left Shelton, Ross's mind had been numb. Ever since Gunlock threw down that green square of wool in the caboose, he had waited tensely for Lamar Shelton to make the connection. Now he realized that Shelton had known from the start what Gunlock meant. Shelton must have guessed at a lot more than had actually happened.

With cold force, Ross recalled that Shelton had not been alone with the girl since the death of Gunlock. They'll be driving out there tonight, he reflected. She'll be in danger from now on. He stopped at the edge of the street, staring southward across the tattered line of cottonwoods bordering the canal, over the golden grassland sweeping on to the blueness of the Penasco Mountains of northern Chihuahua. He felt that somehow he must prevent the girl's going to the ranch with Shelton. After a moment, his boots falling slowly in the hardening day-old mud, he walked on.

He knew now that the affair with Laurel had gone too far for him to turn back. Whether Lamar Shelton was watching them or not, he must let her know that Gunlock had given her away.

16

THE *acequia madre* was a murky little stream flowing between green ruffs of cattails and reeds on raised banks. A few hundred yards beyond were the slaughterhouse, a brickyard, and a cemetery where bright paper flowers hung on crosses among yellow weeds.

On the north side of the canal, unseen behind a high adobe wall, was the house of Tomás Archuleta. Frost-killed roses climbed over the cracked plaster facing of the wall and the coping of broken glass which topped it. There was a weathered gate and a bellpull, which when Ross tugged at it brought a Mexican boy to admit him. He was escorted across the drab yard into the *sala* of the house.

"*Ahorita bien!*" the boy said, hurrying to bring Don Thomás.

Ross pushed a cat from a chair and sat down. Cats, dogs, and their odors were everywhere. A parrot in a large cage shouted words from a Spanish toast. The furniture of the room had been magnificent in gold and green; the piano was a huge, flat one of a type Ross had never seen outside of a theater. But everything in the room was dusty and tattered and the cloth ceiling was stained with leaks.

Don Thomás entered. That phrase of Pard Mallet's sounded in Ross's mind: *Older than God!* He came forward, offering Ross a waxen hand, a specter in a gray bathrobe.

As Ross shook the old man's hand, he could feel the bones of it, like matchsticks. Archuleta tottered to a great, dark armoire, blew the dust out of two glasses, and poured wine. He spilled half of Ross's on the way to his chair. Then he retreated to a sofa.

Ross told the Mexican something of why he had come back. "I thought I might ranch again. But now I find everything is gone."

"Your father..." Don Tomás touched his heart. "I was

87

saddened by your father's death, and to see him split the ranch as he did."

From across the room, the dark eyes with their hedges of tangled gray hairs flashed to Ross an instant, and fell. Archuleta finished his wine. He rose and moved aimlessly to the piano. "Did I tell you," he asked, "that this piano once belonged to Maximiliano?"

"No," Ross said.

The Mexican punched an untuned chord on the instrument. "*Pobre Maximiliano*," he murmured. "Shot by a mob." Then he moved to a huge leather-bound Bible on a reading stand. "And this Bible . . ." he said. "You would not believe it is three hundred years old."

Ross's eyes followed him about as he exhibited his possessions. At last he said, "Why would he have sold, Don Tomás, if everything was all right? He wanted the ranch badly enough to pay you a fortune for it."

Archuleta stopped in the act of stroking a tortoise-shell cat on the sofa. "It was strange," he agreed.

"Was there anything wrong with the title?"

"There could not have been. I was the first owner of the ranch after this land was annexed to the United States. I owned it when it was still a part of Mexico. My name is the first one in the abstract of title."

"You were here when they surveyed the international line, then?"

"*Si!* I knew the chief surveyor well. I gave a banquet for Colonel Emory one night in the very ranch house where you were born. He was a fine man—*muy buen' hombre*."

Ross tried another sip of the stale wine. It left a dry vinegar taste on his tongue. "I ran into Pard Mallet this morning," he said.

Archuleta sat down beside the cat. "*Verdad?*"

"He was telling me about the old days, when he worked for you."

Archuleta smiled. "He was *muy bravo*, then—much of a man. He killed six Apaches one day, when they raided my ranch. And then he made the hair from their scalps into a bridle for his horse!" He laughed softly.

"Where did you come across him?" Ross asked.

Again there was a hesitation. "He was with Colonel Emory," said Don Tomás. "A meat-getter for the party. When they reached Nogales, he tired of it and came back. He always loved this country. I hired him as an *herrero*, and—for his bravery."

Ross finished the wine and rose. "No telling how long I'll be around. But I thought I'd say hello, while I'm in town."

The Mexican did not speak until they reached the gate. In the sunlight he resembled some ancient garment long preserved in a dark commode, yellowed now and utterly fragile. He pulled at the frowzy imperial he wore.

"*Buena suerte*," he said. "I am sorry you did not see your father before he died. To this day, I have a novena said for his soul."

Looking into the bleached blue eyes, the Castilian face, Ross thought of some long-preserved Don Quixote—but a Don Quixote who wore his remorse like ashes. Don Tomás knew much more than he had said about Rancho Pacheco: Ross took this conviction with him.

Off the plaza was a small Mexican restaurant where Ross had liked to eat when he lived here. It was still there, a bare room with tiny tables painted orange, and a brick stove in back. He had not been sitting long at the odd-legged table, alone in the empty café, when someone else entered. He had placed himself where he could see the door; he had not been quite sure why he did this. It was Laurel Shelton who entered. Without a glance at him, she took the next table. Against the window he could see the girlish silhouette of her face, her nose small and even, her brow, rising to the curled dark hair, clean and high. When she rested her hand on the table, he noticed how fine-pored her skin was. Ross finished his food and carried his coffee to her table.

"I'd like to talk to you, Mrs. Shelton," he said, formally but with good nature.

Her smile was quick but strained. "All right—if you won't call me 'Mrs. Shelton.'"

Ross sat down. "Did you follow me here?"

"Of course. I watched you from the plaza."

"Why?"

"Because I wanted to know what happened on the train. There's something wrong, isn't there?"

Ross nodded. "But it isn't what happened on the train, Laurel. I think it's what happened in Las Truchas."

She slowly lowered her fork, staring at him. "I don't understand."

"Gunlock was watching us. He made a report to Shelton last night, before he died. He produced one of those woolen things you'd been crocheting. I think he came to my room with Blade after I was hurt, and found it there."

A swift anguish twisted the girl's face. "Oh, no!"

Ross said in a low, tense voice: "So if I were you, I wouldn't go out to the ranch again. I don't know much about your husband, but if I thought my wife had been crocheting in another man's room—I'd kill one or both of them."

"Did Lamar say anything to you?"

"About an hour ago he let me know that he knew what had been going on. I don't know what he plans to do about it, though."

Her fingers were meshed tightly and she continued gazing at him. "I think I know," she said finally. "Something just about like you said you'd do. To one or both of us. Only, knowing him, I can't understand why he didn't kill you last night, as soon as he heard about it."

Ross frowned. "He's a practical man. With Gunlock and me both dead, he'd have a lot of explaining to do. Another thing, he's in a bind right now. Killing me would only make it worse for him."

"What kind of bind, Ross?"

"Financial, call it. But the main thing is, what about you?"

Her eyes wavered. "I've taken care of myself so far. I think I can continue to."

Smiling, Ross patted her hand. "Don't be silly! You haven't been in a mess like this before.—Know what I'd do?"

The dark head shook.

"Get out of town. Move to—well, anywhere. But don't leave a forwarding address."

She pouted, in an attempt to lighten the mood. "You aren't very gallant, Mr. Chance."

Ross turned her hand over. The tender warmth of her palm against his was obscurely exciting. He looked into her eyes, and they were as gray as smoke, as sad as a winter sky.

"Could you stand it if I did say something gallant?" he asked her.

"Could any woman?" She smiled faintly and her eyes watched his lips.

"Well, I've been thinking. That it was almost worth being kicked by a horse, to have met you."

She laughed. "I never heard anything so gallant, Ross."

"Because you were the first woman I'd ever met who could get me really mad. I could have killed you for letting me tell your husband I'd just met his daughter . . . instead of his wife. I'd have liked to give you a hiding for talking to strange men the way you did me. There wasn't a thing about you I liked except your looks."

She was still smiling, but he saw her lower lip tremble. "You did like my looks, though?"

"At first. But I got tired of seeing your face every time I closed my eyes. I decided what I should have done was to force myself on you in the hotel. Then I'd have been able to say to myself, 'She was just another cowtown floosy,' and I could have forgotten you."

"And since you didn't, Ross, what *do* you think?"

"I think that the worst thing that ever happened to me was leaving Amargosa just about the time your family moved here. Because if I'd seen you first, believe me you wouldn't be Mrs. Shelton now. If it was money you'd wanted, I'd have robbed a bank. If it was excitement, I could have made it exciting, too. Because, damn it, Laurel, I love you."

Something very surprising happened. Her eyes filled with tears, and her lip quivered so that she put her finger against it and turned her head away.

"Not—not so gallant as that, Ross," she pleaded. "There's a limit."

"Hey!" he said gently. "I didn't mean for you to break down. This is just a four-bit mustanger, you know, who happens to have fallen for somebody else's wife. It doesn't have to spoil your sleep, too."

"It wouldn't," Laurel said, "if I didn't love you, too."

He sipped his coffee. Laurel took a handkerchief from her handbag and blew her nose. She dabbed at her eyes and then looked at him with the moisture still on her lashes.

"Always the female," she said. "Crying because my husband almost caught me in your room. Crying because you love me. And if we could turn the clock back and find each other first, I suppose I'd cry about that."

"I could cry about that, myself," said Ross. He looked at the pretty and wistful helplessness of her. "Laurel, baby," he said, "this is as good a time as any to get it straightened out. We've got to put a lid on this right now. A good, strong one that we won't keep raising to take a peek under. I'm in no position right now to help you get clear of him. I'm in enough trouble myself. So stop being female for about twenty-four hours and get yourself on a train. Stay out of town until you know it's safe to come back."

Her finger traced a corded vein on the back of his hand. "If I can be female for just a moment longer," she said, "I might suggest that we go away together."

Ross put his hand over hers and gripped it. "Now, cut it out! I'm a little crazy myself; it wouldn't take much persuading to send me roaring off to Mexico with you for one grand tour before somebody caught up with us—your husband, a marshal, or God-knows-who! But here is how it is with Chance as of this morning: I haven't got a hundred dollars. I've got other troubles, too. And if I ever go away with you, it will be on a honeymoon. You'd be a bad habit to get, if a man didn't know he could keep it up."

"I—I meant on a honeymoon. I'm going to get an annulment, Ross. That's why I was at Henry's office today."

He gazed out the door into the muddy street. "Is that all you know about your husband?" he asked her. "Do you really think he'd give you up because some judge banged a gavel in his face? No, ma'am. He may have taken you for worse—but he also took you forever."

"Then what can I do?"

There was something like fear, and appeal, in her face. She was asking for help—for an answer she could not find herself. But at his back were a dead man floating down the Rio Grande, a vindictive marshal, an angry husband, a thieving partner....

"Honey," Ross said softly, "I can't even make my own decisions. The only advice I'll give you is what I already did: get out of town. Then wait. We can correspond through Henry."

She began to nod. "I'm going to take your advice, Ross. When I went to see Henry, I didn't know Gunlock had given us away. I expected trouble with Lamar, but now—I'm afraid to think what he'll do."

Ross finished his coffee. He fished two twenty-cent pieces and a dime from his pocket for their meals. "Put yourself in Henry's hands," he said. "He'll supply you with money and anything else you need, and if an annulment can be got, he'll get it."

He ran his hand up her arm to the elbow, feeling the fineness of her flesh and hungering to embrace her, and looking into her clear, beautiful eyes, he said:

"We'll have to call this good-bye for a while. But some day we'll have the most wonderful hello anybody ever had."

"No, it's not good-bye. Lamar told me you were driving a wagon to the ranch tonight for him. I'll meet you at the Acequia Street bridge at sundown and tell you good-bye then."

Ross smiled wryly. "When crazier girls come along, they'll probably be your daughters! No, sir—"

"This is less crazy than you think," she protested. "There are some papers at the ranch that I must have. I'll have a list of them for you tonight, and you can take it to Rafael Ruela, at the ranch. He's reliable; he'll bring them in. You must, Ross."

Leaving the café before Laurel did, Ross walked across town to the railroad station, where he procured his suitcase, saddle, and carbine from the baggage room. He returned to the plaza and found Shelton's wagon where he had been told to look for it, behind Griggs's Mercantile. He stowed his saddle atop the tarpaulined load of supplies the rancher was sending to Pacheco.

In the dwindling sunlight, Ross inspected critically the shirt, trousers, and jumper he was wearing, those veterans of a year's mustanging, and he decided to get out of them. In the store, he purchased new denims with their strong soapy smell. Feeling somehow restored, he bought a few supplies and carried them outside. He stood by the wagon to draw his carbine from the boot and examine the lightly oiled mechanism. It had picked up dust in the baggage room. With his bandana, he cleaned the action and loaded it. He drew the paper plug he had inserted in the muzzle before leaving Las Truchas. Then he threw it to his shoulder and squinted down the browned barrel. Finally he placed the gun under the seat of the wagon.

Dusk brought the smoke of charcoal fires to Amargosa. From the streets and alleys of the village, Mexican women and girls returned to the stone well in the plaza with their ollas; merchants in shiny rigs drove home and the first flush of gaiety came to the saloons. Men on their way home, cowboys in from the range, a few trainmen had set the beer pumps and bar-bottles in action.

Standing with his shoulder against the corner of Griggs's Mercantile, Ross watched the evening pageant without being part of it. He was looking for Shelton or Marshal Coles. Suddenly he saw a man on a buckskin horse rein in before the Gadsden Purchase Hotel. He straightened from the wall. At this distance, through the dust and smoke and with the light failing, he could not be certain, yet he was almost sure the man entering the saloon was Lamar Shelton. The doors closed behind him and at once opened as a pair of cowboys sauntered out. They selected their ponies at the hitch-rail and rode off.

Ross quickly walked to the rear of the store and untied the reins from the whipstock. He had left the horses in the collars. Clucking the team up, he drove out the back of the yard onto Acequia Street, turned right and headed toward the bridge, where the Chihuahua freight road crossed the canal. This was only a block west, opposite Tomás Archuleta's walled home. As he drove, he peered ahead in the smoky dusk. He discerned no one by the little stone bridge, but as he neared it a girl slipped from the shadows of a motte of cottonwoods. She ran up as Ross pulled in the team at the edge of the bridge. Laurel had the high collar of a dark cape pulled up, the cord snug about her neck. She carried a small traveling bag, which she handed up to Ross. He took it and stowed it under the seat.

"What do I do with this? Is this the list?"

Laurel was raising her skirts to place her boot against the spoke of a wheel. "Help me up!"

Ross leaned forward. "Wait a minute! You don't mean *you're* going!"

"Not all the way. Just to the old place on the part of the ranch I own—the Tecolote Canyon camp."

Without word, Ross clucked up the horses. The girl was forced to step back, but she cried out, "*Ross!* You can't leave me—"

"Can't I?" Ross said. The hoofs of the horses struck the cobbles of the bridge. The wagon lunged onto the small stone arch. Holding her skirts up, Laurel ran beside the wagon.

"Listen to me, Ross! He won't know how I got there. But believe me I can't stay in town!"

Ross pulled in the team. "What do you mean?"

"I mean that he discovered I'd been at Henry's office today. He questioned me until I told him what I planned to do. He was furious."

"Well, what did you expect? Why did you tell him?"

"I—I had the wild idea that I might be able to convince him we'd never get along together and we might as well separate. But instead of that, he threw up to me what Gunlock had said."

"What did you tell him?"

"I lied, of course. I told him I'd missed one of the afghan squares on the train, and I supposed Gunlock had picked it up."

"Did he believe you?"

She shrugged. "He took me to a hotel and got me a room. He said I was to stay there. But I was afraid to. I don't know what he plans to do. As soon as he left, I left too." She raised her arms to him again. "Ross, help me up, quickly! We can't be seen here."

In desperation, Ross pulled her up and started the wagon again. "Why didn't you to to another hotel?"

"Because I was afraid he'd find me. I decided to go to

Tecolote myself for those papers, and I'll ride back tomorrow and get the noon train."

Ross gazed across the reedy canal into the dark plain. "All I know is that if he finds us together again, any doubts he may have had about my intentions toward his wife will be gone. But I guess we're in it together anyway, now that Gunlock's spilled it."

17

ROSS COULD NOT RELAX until the final color scaled from the sky and darkness closed about them. Then there was a great sense of release. He found comfort in being again on the range where he had grown up. He felt as though he had come after many years to a place to which he belonged. He knew every turn in the road. He remembered the fragrances released by last night's rain, the blackstrap odor of sage and the smell of the wind itself, which had taken the clean breath of the mountain passes it had rushed through. Beside the deep-rutted wagon road was the rattle of dry screwbean pods in a thicket. Far off, coyotes howled.

If I knew he stole this from me, Ross thought, I'd kill him to get it back. It seemed to him that a man had some hold on the land he had grown up on, just as it had on him, and to come between him and that land was criminal.

"You loved this place, didn't you?" Laurel said.

"I didn't know how much until I got away from it."

"What did you think when Henry told you that I own half of it?"

Ross thoughtfully adjusted his feet. "When I found out how you got it, I didn't think much of you."

"Is that what you still think?"

He could see her looking at him. "I haven't learned any different."

"Then why did you say you loved me?"

"When did love start having anything to do with common sense?" She was close to him, soft and desirable, and Ross found her hand and held it. "I suppose I'm waiting to hear that I guessed wrong about you. But if I don't hear it, I'll forget it."

She sat straight on the seat and gazed ahead of the wagon. "You'll hear it now, Ross, if you want. Why I married Lamar, and how I happen to own Tecolote ranch, and everything."

"I've been waiting to hear why you married him ever since I met you."

Laurel was silent for a while, and the wagon wheels ground crisply through the hardening mud of the road. At last she spoke.

"I married him to get my father out of prison. If that sounds foolish, it was. But Lamar convinced me he could get Dad out of Mexico if I'd marry him. Any girl who wasn't completely gullible would have known better. But it killed me to think of him dying there...."

It was a long way from convincing. But Ross's silence held as they worked up a long pitch toward a pass in the desert hills.

"Dad was the craziest person who ever wore a badge, I guess," Laurel went on. "But he was wonderful. He always wanted to be a doctor—did you see the medicine shelves in his old office? I used to think he arrested drunks just to experiment with his hangover cure. If you mentioned you had a cold, he'd send you away with a porous plaster on your chest and medicines he made out of desert herbs running out of your ears. When he wasn't poisoning people with his medicines, he was working up deals of one kind or another. He'd buy a ton of chilis in Chihuahua and get them as far as the border before they found they were full of worms and he couldn't bring them across. But I worshiped him."

She looked away and the little laugh that had come to her voice was gone. "But someone didn't love him. Will Coles hated him because he was so free and easy, and because he and Coles ran for the marshal's job, and Dad, a comparative stranger to Amargosa, beat him out."

The breeze, stiffening, whipped her cape across Ross's arm as they came to a pass in the low hills, and the touch of the fabric was somehow personal. The wagon for a moment was lumbering through a shallow cleft in the foothills. They had left the flat country behind them. From this pass they would descend into a long basin called Pacheco Valley, with the main ranch headquarters at the eastern end of it. Laurel's ranch, with its headquarters at the old Tecolote Canyon line camp, was a short distance to the west of the pass.

As they started down, Laurel told him, "We turn off at the foot of the grade to my headquarters. Your father split the land north and south when he sold to Lamar. The line more or less follows this road, you know."

"I know," Ross said. "Paso Redondo and all the best water is in the first section. And of course the headquarters building. It's pretty much of a puzzle why my father would sell the best land and keep the worst, isn't it? But I'll tell you what puzzles me most of all: Why you married Shelton after you knew he was the one who'd had your father jailed."

"I didn't know it when I first planned to marry him," she said. "Lamar had been attentive for a long time. I think he really does love me. He began mentioning all the ways people can be got out of jail in Mexico, but they all seemed to involve a lot of money. Then he took to saying, 'After we're married, I'll move heaven and earth to get him out.' Well, it wasn't hard to understand that. So we began to plan."

"I gather you did some planning of your own."

"Naturally," she said. "A man who'll use misfortune as a lever to win a girl can't be trusted very far. So I told Lamar I'd like to have something in my own name, and since he planned to buy your father's land at the tax auction, why couldn't it be mine? Just nominally, of course. He'd really own and operate it. Then when I asked Henry Lyman to arrange it for me, he told me the truth . . . that Lamar had had Dad jailed, and was keeping him there, though he knew he was ill."

"Then for God's sake," Ross asked angrily, "will you tell me why you went ahead and married him?"

Laurel's voice took a brittle edge as she faced him. "What I wanted was to get my father out of jail! He was dying there. Don't you understand that? I didn't care how I got him out . . . just so I did it. What good would it have done to run around telling everyone that for some private reason Lamar had had him jailed? Even Henry Lyman knew the end of that: Lamar would say he'd been trying to spare me the shame—that Dad had been running off stock, and the Rurales caught him at it. Everyone in town knew he hardly made enough on his salary to get by on."

Suddenly Ross glanced back up the road climbing to the pass they had just left. The high splinter of moon gave a frosty light. He had heard a scrape of sound behind them. Yet the white road was without shadows, and after a moment he decided he might have heard the creak of a distant windmill.

Relaxing, he said: "That makes sense, Laurel. More sense than most women would have had—and more nerve."

"Not nerve," she smiled. "Just a strong lock on my door, and a way of letting him know I meant to be left alone."

Ross squinted. "Why do you suppose he went after your father in the first place?"

"Because Dad was investigating your father's selling the ranch."

Ross faced her quickly. "Henry didn't tell me that."

"I don't think he knew it. You see, the colonel and Dad had got to be good friends. When the colonel sold the ranch, Dad had sense enough not to ask him why: that would only have antagonized him. But he began investigating everything connected with it—the land maps, the boundaries, and everything. And just as he was beginning to think he might have found something, the colonel died."

He kept watching her face, the subtly changing expressions of it, but said nothing. With one hand, Laurel held the cape close about her throat.

"So then," she went on, "Dad was more suspicious than ever. He questioned Pard Mallet, who found the colonel's body . . ."

Ross grunted. "Pard told me that the first time he saw Dad after he died was in the undertaking parlor."

She shook her head. "He lied to you, then. He's so full of liquor most of the time he doesn't know what he's saying anyway. At any rate, he couldn't tell Dad much. And just then this gang of Mexicans began raiding the border herds, and Dad had to go after them. He went into Mexico a few miles after a herd of Lamar's horses. He didn't come back."

A few miles ahead, the cold slice of moon was well above the serrations of the Penasco Mountains. They were on the floor of the valley, with low hills before them, coveys of trees in watered places. Once more Ross's attention was drawn behind them, and this time he saw a shadow cross the road just below the pass, and vanish into the brush. He said nothing. He reached down to ease his carbine slightly from the boot.

"Except for your father dying," he said, "I'm glad Shelton reneged on his promise."

"Except for the same reason," said Laurel, "I'm glad, too. In my way, Ross, I'm rather old-fashioned myself. If Lamar had claimed me, I'd never have looked at you in Las Truchas."

She smiled at him, and Ross put his arm about her and pulled her against him. She was soft and fragrant, bringing a catch to his throat. But now he was certain that they were being followed, that Shelton had meant to ambush him tonight when he sent him out with the wagon. A man in a wagon was a sitting duck.

Laurel turned her face up to him. "At this point," she said, "I was almost certain I'd be kissed."

Ross put his boot on the lines and turned her to him. His hand found the light boning about her waist. He kissed her, clutching her suddenly tight, and the feel of her lips on his mouth was warm and sweet. He was caught up in the pain and joy of this moment. Then her fingers touched his wrist, and she whispered:

"No, Ross—!"

Quickly Ross turned away, catching up the lines again. He let the horses break into a run across the rough, watered basin toward a dark cloud of trees, and finally he told her:

"We're being followed, Laurel."

"Followed!" She looked back.

"I saw them a minute ago. I think they're after me, not you. Shelton planned this when he asked me to drive the wagon out. Do you have a gun?"

She reached for her crocheting bag under the seat and withdrew a small nickeled pistol. "But I'm not going to leave you," she said.

He patted her knee. Her eyes were large and frightened. "Yes, you are. About a half-mile ahead you can get off in those trees. Then cut down the gully to Tecolote camp."

"No, Ross!"

"And take off for Amargosa as soon as you can find a saddle horse. Now, don't argue!" he said. "There's a rider about two hundred yards to our right. About the same distance on the left, there are a couple more. I'm going to let the horses run for it now," he told her.

But at that moment there was a barb of yellow light where the man on their right was. A few seconds later a bullet struck with startling force high above them on a hillside at their left. After this shot came a cascade of reports as the gunshot echoed down the shallow *rincón* through which they were passing. Laurel began to tremble, and he heard her trying to say something, but could not understand it in the clatter of the wagon.

"Now, understand this!" Ross said tensely. "I'll let you off by those trees. I'll make enough noise going up that next grade for you to get away without being noticed...."

A few feet behind them, a bullet struck a stanchion with an explosion of oak and lead. Ross instinctively ducked, clutching the girl against him. They heard the departing wail of the ball as the horses crazily sought to break. Fighting the team back to the road, Ross began talking to the girl.

"I've got to put you off, Laurel. We can't make it in the wagon. The line camp's only a mile west of here. Get a horse there and head back to town."

Laurel still tried to protest, but Ross said angrily: "Do as I say! You'll only get us both shot if you stay with me."

Right and left, Ross could hear horses running. Another bullet ricocheted off the road before them, and the thunder of that shot mixed its echoes with those of the gun on their right. But again he heard the impact of a bullet high up on the slope at their left, and he had the curious thought:

Is he firing at us, or them?

The wagon was in the trees now, drawn not by a team, but by two terrified horses running free, and Ross released the girl and rising to a crouch set his weight against the taut lines. Resisting, they threw their heads angrily. With his foot on the brake, the iron tire smoking under the shoe, he fought the horses down. When the wagon stopped, Ross quickly swung Laurel down, yet she continued to hold on to his arms.

"I can't leave you, Ross!" she sobbed.

"And how do you think it is for me?" Ross asked her. "This is the first time I've loved any woman, and it has to be like this— leaving her alone in the dark with bullets flying! But sweet, it's the only way—the only way we'll ever see each other again. So run!"

It seemed to Ross that the horses were within a hundred yards, now, bearing savagely in on the road. The guns lashed furiously at the road but the trees prevented accurate fire. Laurel seemed suddenly to become calm. Her features were small and firm as she released his arms. She caught her cape closed with the hand that held the gun, and stepped into the buckbrush beside the road. In an instant she was out of sight.

18

As THE WAGON started on up the slope, more slowly because the rocky grade was steepening, Ross collected everything he would need for a break. He had bought a gunny sack of food supplies for the Paso Redondo camp, and reaching back, he was able to grab out a package of jerked beef. He tucked this into his jacket front. He found the box of forty-four caliber shells he had purchased and dumped them in his pockets. The wagon crested onto a long ridge. He ran his gaze from the dark eastern pocket of Pacheco Valley down the length of it to the group of hills divided by Tecolote Canyon. Straight ahead of him, somewhere at the base of the mountains, was the Paso Redondo line camp where Blade Ramsey was shacked up.

Starting down the slope, Ross was surprised to discern a horseman several hundred feet to his right, among the piñons of the hillside. Unless it were a fourth rider, the man had swung around the scope of trees in which he had left Laurel, and had reached this spot in time to intercept the wagon. Ross did this random figuring while he raised the carbine he had placed across his lap. He took a snap shot across the slope. The shock and lift of the gun, the concussive report, was a stimulant. He heard the bullet strike stone and carom across the hills and canyons of the valley. The man shouted something. He worked the loading lever and fired again, and the horses, unbroken to rifle fire, were running out of control.

In a minute, Ross realized, *this thing's going over.* He began picking the chances along the road ahead. There was a sandy branch of Turkey Creek at the base of the hill. There was dense brush here, and if the wagon should capsize at this point he had a gambler's chance of coming up without broken bones. The horses would be unable to slow for the ford; he was certain of this now, feeling the iron resistance of the reins, but there was an old stagedriver's trick he had used before when a team got away from him, and he meant to try it.

That fellow will have to be dropped, Ross thought coolly, seeing the horseman angling toward the ford, now. He was coming close enough that he had form: a big, lumbering man who carried his saddle gun shoulder high as his horse lunged down the hillside. Ross raised the gun again, hating to waste the shot, but wanting to hold the gunman back until he finished the business at the ford. The shot was close; he could see a spark where the slug struck stone. And now when the horseman shouted, he could understand him, and even the voice was familiar.

"Christ sake, boy—*I'm with you!*"

It was Pard Mallet's voice. Though Ross did not understand why the old Pacheco hand should be out here, he called back to him.

"I'm going to spill it down here, Pard! You can swing around to pick me up."

And he was slanting down that last rough hundred yards to the shallow ribbon of dark water and getting set for the jump in case he failed to pull it. The road flattened. The horses' manes streamed. They were hammering wildly toward the low cut-banks. Ross took the pliant ribbons and put each horse into an opposite lead. There was an instant when they were throwing over, one trying to draw the tongue this way, the other drawing that, and then the off horse lost footing and was down on its side with a crash of harness. Dragged half under the wagon, it screamed in terror and pain. The other horse stumbled, reached, and tripping once more, went down. The wagon slewed toward the bluff cut of the roadside. Ross seized his gun and prepared to leap from the off side. But again the wheels cut into the road and the screaming of the horses was terrifying, the dust a choking fog, and at last there was the presence of water close by. The wagon went up on two wheels, balanced an instant, and fell upside down in the water. Ross leaped and landed in the brush. As he lay there, he could hear the creek bubbling around the downed horses.

Somewhere, old Pard Mallet called tensely: "What's left, guy? Ross—you all right?"

Ross staggered onto the wet gravel. He stood a moment staring up the hillside. Far above, he glimpsed two riders in silhouette. He took time to flip a shot at them and they wheeled away. Then he looked down at the injured horses and knew,

They'll never be worth a damn, even if they aren't hurt. He put a bullet into the head of each, and reloaded his gun before he walked up to Pard Mallet, sitting his pony before a clump of brush at the stream's edge.

Pard—this big, whiskey-soaked man with the hearty voice and the guilty grin—reached a hand down to help him up. He kicked his foot from the stirrup and Ross toed into it and swung up behind. From the crest of the ridge, two guns rammed bolts of flame toward them. The horse tried to buck and Pard cursed it and yanked the reins as he spurred, putting the horse into a futile pinwheel. A bullet threw a silver plume from the water. The horse stopped pinwheeling and commenced to pitch.

"This son-of-a-bitch," Pard panted, "has got some manners to learn . . . !" He clubbed it over the head with the barrel of his gun. It staggered. When it recovered, Pard had things in hand. The horse moved out. With Ross's arms around the slack body of the old ranch hand, it cut at a slant across the sagebrush of the hillside, working southwest. They rode hard, the horse grunting at every stride, but the men on the ridge did not fire again. From high ground, Ross peered long in the direction of Tecolote Canyon, but darkness held the story of whether Laurel had got away.

After a mile, Ross dismounted and walked beside the exhausted horse. "How about this?" he demanded.

"That was Mister Shelton," Pard said. "And I reckon an old buddy of his, Marshal Coles. I see Shelton leaving town about dark, just after you left."

"How'd you know when I left?"

"Oh, I don't have much to do," Pard joked. "I just set around in front of the Gadsden Bar, spitting on my shirt and watchin' what goes on. I seen you leave Griggs's place."

"That's right, I was taking a load of things out to the ranch for him. I was to get the loan of a horse for it." Then he said, "Thanks, Pard. What'd you do it for?"

Pard's face was pouched but stern. "With me," he said, "a man's either my pardner, or he's a bad Injun. I've got no damned use for Shelton. Kill a man for what he had in his pockets. That's why I asked you this morning, what about Gunlock falling off that train."

"I gather I'm your pardner, eh?"

Pard gazed down at him. Under that slackness of his was a

hard spine of toughness. He looked Ross over and said drily, "You could be, Ross. If you ain't like your old man."

"Some say I am, some say I'm not," Ross joshed, watching the blacksmith and waiting.

"What about Gunlock?" Pard persisted. "Who killed him—you or Shelton? I wa'n't born yesterday, Ross. I know it was one of you."

"No," Ross said, "you were born just about in time to scout for Colonel Emory's surveying party, weren't you?"

After a long stare, Pard began to chuckle. "Yes, sir!" he said. "By the way, how do you like it down here in Mexico?"

"You mean we're in Mexico right now?"

"According to the way me and old Archuleta figured it, about nine-tenths of Pacheco Valley is in Mexico. That's all the best of Rancho Pacheco, boy. Just about takes in all the water you can drink in this area without getting a bellyache."

Ross stopped walking, and while he breathed deeply from the climb, he sought a cigar and matches in his pockets. He got it going, dropped the match and trod it out in the sweet dry grass, and asked Pard coolly:

"Who put the screws on my father, Pard—you or Archuleta?"

Mallet shifted in the saddle, expectorating thoughtfully into the grass. It was not obvious that his hand was on the butt of his gun, but in the darkness Ross saw how his palm caressed the Colt.

"Now, ain't that a hell of a thing to ask a man, Ross," Pard complained. "A man that's just saved your life, and you even taken a couple of shots at, and you ast him a question like that! Why, God darn you, Ross!"

"Sorry, Pard," Ross smiled. "I kind of lost my manners when your partner set that horse to kick me in the head."

"*My* partner?" Pard repeated. Then gradually his big, guilty grin came, and with a chuckle he said, "Why don't we hike on? We'll have all day to talk at the horse camp. That pardner of ours has got a little old yella-headed gal using the extra bunk now, but we can put her out quick enough. We got a lot hotter business than gals."

"There's nothing hotter than gals," Ross said sadly. "Probably that's what started this whole thing. Shelton or somebody wanted money to whirl the gals with, so the colonel had to go.... Was that it?"

"I wouldn't know, Ross," Pard Mallet said seriously. "I shore would not know." He put the tired horse into motion up the hillside.

"I'll bet I know before noon tomorrow," Ross said quietly. With the rifle over his shoulder, he followed.

19

PASO REDONDO WAS a pleasant spot at the mouth of a narrow canyon whose low, rimrocked walls cut into the flank of a steep mountain a mile south. Turkey Creek had been diked here to form a pond about a hundred yards across. It was sunup when they came in sight of it. Ross felt a tug of emotion. He remembered swimming in this pond, fishing in the willows, riding bucking horses in the pole corral across the creek where the camp was. This had been Ross Chance's favorite hideout. Whenever the colonel needed him, this was where he sent a man to look. A rush of forgotten dreams came to him, so impossible, so lost, that the tears came to his eyes. He felt genuinely sorry for that black-haired boy who had yearned to be the biggest something-or-other in New Mexico—he hardly remembered what. He wished he could have told him some of the things he knew now.

The sun was on the pink sandstone peaks and blue pines of the Penascos, but down here in the shadows it was still chilly. Fish jumped temptingly in the pond. A mule deer was watering at the mouth of the canyon and there were the waking sounds of a camp where many horses were kept. A spice of piñon smoke was in the air; the pencil of smoke ascented vertically from the rock-and-mud chimney of the adobe shack on the far side of the pond. It appeared that Blade Ramsey and his woman were already up.

"*Vámonos*," growled Pard, tilting his head left, toward the shorter way around the pond.

With Pard riding the fagged horse, Rose trudging wearily behind, they reached the south side of the creek and approached the cabin. The sun threw a few arrows of light through the passes. The corral was full of horses. A quarter of beef hung in a cheese-cloth cooler from the branch of a cottonwood shading the cabin. Under the tree there was a concrete water tank with a washstand fixed to the tree trunk and a mirror nailed to it. Someone was at the washstand. As they entered the yard, Ross had the scabbard of his rifle under his right arm and his finger through the trigger guard. The person at the washstand came forward unhurriedly. It was Blade's girl, and looking at her, Ross decided his old partner's taste in girls equaled his taste in whiskey.

She had the languorous grace that one connected somehow with bare feet. She moved her hips in a special way which seemed perfectly natural to her. The sun fired a shaft of light over a far ridge and as she walked into it her hair shone like pale bronze, and Ross noticed that she was brushing it. She stopped before the cabin and regarded them, standing with her feet a little apart.

"Hello, Francie," Pard said, in a gruff, weary voice. "Where's your man?"

"He's yonder, looking at a trap he set last night. Some puma's been scaring off all the mustangs."

She smiled and gazed at Ross. Her eyes, brown and glistening, were as personal as a chemise. She kept looking at him in that teasing way while Pard growled:

"How'd you ever get that lazy soak up before noon?"

"Oh, we've been up for hours," smiled Francie, stretching like a cat. Then she commenced slowly brushing her hair again, drawing the bristles slowly along the underside of the thick strand she held out, as though she enjoyed the sensation of it.

Pard, softening, grinned at Ross. "Makes you think of your mother, don't she?"

"Who's this?" Francie asked.

"I'm a friend of Blade's," Ross said. "Ross Chance. Didn't he tell you about me?"

"He may have. I don't remember. But any friend of Blade's is a friend of mine."

Pard led his pony off to a shed and began unsaddling. Ross sat down on a bench by the stoop of the cabin, put his back against the straw-tufted mud bricks, and closed his eyes. He felt as though if he sat here two minutes he would fall asleep.

"Do you mean to say," Francie exclaimed, "that you walked all the way from Las Truchas?" She sat beside him on the bench. He opened his eyes and glanced at her. Her brows were quite dark beneath her blonde hair. He did not think she could be over seventeen. She looked like some very sweet child who was playing with men the way she had played once with dolls, without realizing that men were less easily controlled.

"Las Truchas, eh?" Ross smiled. "So you do remember me?"

Francie smiled. "I guess I do." She put her hand up to feel the spiny black whiskers of his jaw. "You haven't shaved in a week. I'll bet you'd be good-looking if you shaved."

"I had a shave in the best barbershop in Amargosa yesterday morning," Ross said. "But it's like a meal in the best restaurant in town: you still get hungry again."

"I should think so," she giggled.

Ross leaned his head back again. Sooner or later this girl had to be told that she was through here. She had to go home, or back to the parlor house where she had been working, or wherever Blade had picked her up. "How long have you been here, Francie?" he asked.

"About two weeks."

"Where are your folks?"

"Dead," she said cheerfully. "I live with my grandparents, in El Paso. I got sick of being read to from the Book of Revelations. So I took off for a while."

Ross chuckled. "I left home over being read to from the Bible myself."

Francie clapped her hands together. "Oh, that's funny! Did you have as much fun as I'm having?"

Ross reflected. "I don't know how much you're having, but I haven't had a lot. I've worked like a mule. And I finally wound up getting kicked by a horse. See the scar?"

She gazed at the crescent of pink flesh in the roached black hair. "My! Do you think that will happen to me?" There was a suggestion of humor in her voice.

"No," Ross conjectured. "But what happens to you might hurt a lot worse in the long run. . . . If your folks live in El Paso," he demanded, "what are you doing over here?"

"Enjoying myself," Francie smiled. "I'm grown up—you don't have to start warning me about things."

Ross gave up. "When will Blade be back?"

She glanced up the rimrocked hillside rising to a mesa behind the cabin. "He should be back now. He didn't eat any breakfast. I've got to tend to it, too."

Rising quickly, she touched Ross's knee. "Come on in and help me."

"I will for a cup of coffee," Ross said agreeably.

He went into the cabin with her. There were a couple of cots, but only one was made up. Beneath it lay a familiar pair of black boots—Blade's, so he must have purchased new ones with part of his dividend from the Chihuahua Land and Livestock Company. The cabin held many little tokens of come-easy wealth: a new Colt hanging in a holster on the wall, a welter of liquor bottles with good labels, two hams hanging from the ceiling in a corner, new clothing lying on chairs.

On the Mexican tile stove, a large skillet of potatoes and side pork were frying. Coffee bubbled in a black pot. Ross found a cup and poured for both of them, with another for Pard Mallet, while the girl turned the potatoes. She looked sweet, standing there—perfectly innocent. There was a call from the mesa, and Francie stepped quickly to an unglazed window and waved. Ross stood behind her. He could see the rider on a bay horse at the top of the rim. He could hear Blade Ramsey call:

"Hey—draw one! I can smell it up here."

Francie laughed and turned from the window. Ross took a deep breath and passed his hand over his hair. He felt the scar from the horse's hoof; the place was still sensitive. At this moment he did not yet know what he was going to do about Blade. But as he started out, the girl called:

"Ross!" He looked back. Her face was soft and full of appeal. "Don't hurt him, will you? He—he just—doesn't think, sometimes. He's been feeling terrible about it."

"So have I," Ross said.

Pard Mallet was still busy with the horse. A man who had probably not bathed in years, he was scrupulously sluicing the sweat from the back of his pony with a wadded rag dipped in the horse trough. Ross watched him clean the soaped places where the cheekstraps of the bridle had rubbed. As Blade reached level ground at the foot of the mesa, riding on with a high-shouldered look, Ross walked to the concrete tank under the cottonwood. Francie came from the cabin and stood timidly near the door. With his Colt loose in the holster, Ross stood half-hidden by the tree. He observed the mustanger ride into the yard, and swing out of the saddle. He wore new wine-colored boots and a black Stetson not a week old. He looked relaxed and healthy, Ross thought, as though there was nothing at all to disturb his mind. Blade walked to Francie, put his arms around her and swung her about. Then he kissed her and held her back to gaze at her. Just like a young husband coming in from the range, thought Ross. He started across the yard.

"Blade, there's—there's a man to see you!" Francie faltered, staring at Ross.

Blade turned quickly. Ross halted. He saw the softness slough away from Ramsey's face. He was surprised by the changes in him. Blade had been drinking steadily ever since he hit Amargosa—he had the puffiness under the eyes to show that—but he had been thinking differently, too. There was a truculent cut to his mouth, and a sharpness of impatience about him. Ross observed the way he pressed his palm against his chaps, just below his gun, and it seemed to Ross that his hand trembled slightly. Then, unexpectedly, Blade put his hands on his hips and grinned.

"Ross, you shore look like the wrath o' God! Where you from?"

Without answering, Ross crossed the yard to him. Then he unbuckled his gunbelt and let it drop. He still said nothing, gazing at the mustanger through a long moment. At last he spoke.

"You can grin at me like that after what you did to me! You haven't got the brain of an ape, Blade."

"Aw, hell, Ross," Blade grinned. "I stole a march on you, but look where you are now! A check for most of what I took from you in your pocket already. And plenty more on the way."

"A check I wouldn't dare cash," Ross said.

"Why not? Mine's cashed and spent."

"Then you could go to jail for blackmail," Ross said.

"Blackmail, hell!" Blade protested. He gazed across the yard. "Pard—didn't you tell him what the deal is?"

Ross spat on the ground between them. "All you're concerned with right now is answering for Las Truchas. The doctor said if that cut had been a little deeper, I'd have died. You switched horses on me and then got me to sign that check while I was half-dead. By God, I wouldn't give four bits for a dozen men like you."

Blade's face hardened. "Because I was smarter than you? If I hadn't signed up with George, you'd be right back where you were—a bronc-stomper with a thousand bucks in his jeans."

"Okay, and what about the horse trick?"

"I didn't switch them on you," Blade snapped. "It was that fellow Hackley."

"How do you know it was Hackley?"

"I saw him when I was going to the hotel that night."

Ross's grin was swift. "You saw him, eh?"

Blade's gaze faltered. "Why should I have warned you? You weren't doing me any favors."

Ross pulled up his belt, his eyes on Blade. "You can call this a favor, though. This is a lesson you've been needing a long time."

His fist came up from his hip. It smacked into Blade Ramsey's jaw and drove him back into Francie's arms. The girl cried out and tried to hold Blade as he lunged back, but he struck her with the back of his hand and went in with a smashing swing at Ross's head. Ross ducked under it and stabbed straight at Blade's nose. He saw the blood spurt as the mustanger stumbled aside. Blade shook his head and pivoted, but he was not so fast in coming back. A little cautiously, he jabbed at Ross's face and then tried a wild right which cut the air.

Blade was off-balance now, and Ross knew he was going to hit him with everything he had. He threw his fist hard and straight against the mustanger's face, and Blade grunted. Hurt, he wallowed back. Ross saw the marks he had put on the man, and felt a wicked joy. The long, hard road from Las Truchas had laid mercy in its grave. He hooked one in under Blade's guard and saw his head jar. Blade fell back against the wall of the cabin. Doggedly he came forward again. Ross took one step to meet him. His grin was a white splinter. He slammed Blade on the cheekbone with the full force of his back and shoulder, and Blade fell forward silently and without fuss, falling on his face but turning almost at once onto his back. He pulled one leg up under him, and then lay still.

Now that the craziness was out of him, Ross felt suddenly relaxed. He could feel a feverish spot on his cheek where Blade had hit him. He had the thought that at least one injustice in this world had been atoned for. But when he looked from Blade to Francie, he saw that she was crying. Her small fists were clenched.

"I hate you for this," she choked. "If I were a man, I'd beat you. I don't ever want to see you again." She marched to the reservoir for a bucket of water with which to restore Ramsey.

Pard helped Ross carry Blade into the cabin. The boy came to in a few minutes, too dazed to speak. Pard patted his head as he turned away.

"Even Stephen, Blade," he said. "I reckon you had it coming. Now, let's have no more of this or I'll cut the throats of both of you."

20

ROSS ATE SOME breakfast. After this he went outside and looked over the horses in the trap—the long fenced pasture which funneled into the main corral. He saw nothing worth more than cull price, and supposed Blade, to keep up an appearance of industry against possible official inspection, was merely running in a few broncs from time to time. On impulse, he mounted Blade's horse and rode up to the mesa. From here, in the fresh light, he gazed across Pacheco Valley. It looked like a tawny, wrinkled hide slung between blue hills. He could not quite discern the Tecolote Canyon camp, where he had left Laurel. He wondered whether she had made it back to town yet; he would not consider that Shelton might have intercepted her.

The dry, tangy air of the border highlands blew gently. Ross took it deeply into his lungs. For some reason he thought of his father. It seemed to Ross that life found a man's weak spots and went to work on them. The colonel had loved this border ranch more than anything; he had put it between himself and his own family. But in the end he had lost it. It was different with Ross: he loved it too, but he loved a woman more. So it was the woman he could not have. You could get bitter chewing thoughts like this, he decided. He put the pony down the steep trail to the horse camp again.

He wanted to go into this session with Pard and Blade with a sure and confident manner, but he was tormented by pressures. Nothing was right. He was brain- and bone-tired. He felt that Shelton could be jarred loose from Rancho Pacheco, but he dared not take him to court. He was in love with a girl who loved him, but she was Shelton's, too. And all these things seemed poised on a shaky foundation of rotting minutes—minutes that other men were using to scheme, while he himself was blocked. Blocked in every direction, and he struck his thigh heavily with his fist and swore.

Francie was sitting on the stoop as he rode into the yard, but she rose and flounced into the cabin. Ross grinned. *Just wait*, he thought. *One of these days he'll take off on you, too—and you expecting, like as not. Then you'll know why I took a little skin off his nose.*

He stepped into the narrow portal. Standing there, he looked the room over. Blade sat at the table with his curly blond head in his hands. Pard was standing at the window, gazing out. Francie was fussing with riz-bread under a dishtowel, at the sink. Ross went inside. They all glanced at him. He put his fists on his hips.

"Well, let's get to it," Ross said. "Did Pard tell you about Gunlock, Blade?"

Blade's left eye was swollen blue. His mouth was cut. "So you killed him," he said.

Ross started. "Who said I killed him? We don't even know that he's dead. All I know is that he fell off the caboose into the Rio Grande."

Pard turned from the window. He wiped his nose. "You know what I been figuring, Ross? Shelton's nobody's fool. He wouldn't come larrupin' into the hills trying to murder a man unless he was covered on it. He and Coles are thicker'n thieves anyhow. I figure they teamed up on it last night. I'd give horse-collars to nuggets that there's a warrant out for your arrest right now—that Shelton swore it out for the murder of Gunlock, and he and the marshal came out to kill you last night. Resisting arrest—ain't that what they call it when a marshal murders a man?"

Blade listened to the blacksmith. He stared hotly at Ross. "By Jesus, that's it!" Rising, he kicked his chair back. "I'll bet Shelton killed Gunlock himself and left him up there to roll off. So he's cut us down to three. Then he jugs you for murder, and that leaves two."

Pard grinned fatly at Ross. "Kid's got a head on him. How do you figure it?"

Ross felt as though he were walking a narrow path in the dark. "About like that," he said. "But I don't know how we're going to prove it. Personally, I don't give a damn. What I'm interested in is getting out of this deal of yours with a whole hide. Then I'm going after the ranch."

"*And* the woman?" Pard asked.

"What woman?" Ross had not thought, up to now, that Pard had seen Laurel that night.

"Shelton's woman," Pard said. "I seen her. Good thing I

wasn't Shelton, hey? My pappy always told me that that strange stuff wa'n't worth goin' after, Ross. Man always winds up with the woman or her husband fillin' his tail with lead."

At the sink, Francie turned on Ross a look of astonished delight. Blade was staring at him, too, with a tilted grin. "So that's what Gunlock was laughing about the night we came to your hotel room!" Blade chuckled. "He picked something off the floor and said, 'This'll come in handy,' but I never did get what it was.—How is she under the sheets, kid?" he asked.

"Blade!" Francie exclaimed, smiling and blushing. "I'm getting out of here, if you men are going to talk like that...." Hurriedly she picked up a wooden water bucket and marched out. As they laughed, Ross's chin jutted.

"It was all clean," he said. "The only reason she was there ... well, it's none of your damned business why she was there."

They continued laughing while he took a chair across from Blade. "Laugh your damned heads off," he said. "And then stop and think about this: You turned the gun on all of us when you put the screws on Shelton. I don't know what the price is to have a man killed on the border now, but it didn't use to be very high."

"No, Shelton ain't going to do that," Pard said. "He knows we've got it fixed where if we die, he loses the ranch."

"Whose idea was this Chihuahua Land and Livestock Company?" Ross demanded.

"Gunlock's," Blade said. "He tried to tell us about it up there in Las Truchas, but you wouldn't listen."

"Was ruining my father his idea, too?"

Pard Mallet's big, liquor-pocked face toughened with old rancor. "No," he said. "That was mine. *I* wrecked the old bastard."

Ross stared at him. "Why?"

"Never mind why."

"You know you're going to tell that story to a judge, don't you? Because I'm going to have that land back."

Pard's eyes were cold amber. "Kind of like it this way, Ross. This way we're all makin' money, includin' you. Put you back on the ranch, and the rest of us are out in the alley."

"Yes, and what's going to be left after you get through bleeding Shelton? He'll mortgage to keep you from exposing him. But in the end he'll go under, and the land with him."

Pard slowly shook his head. Under his bloated exterior could be detected a tough and ruthless core. "That's what we're going to wait and see. Now, I'm going to tell you how she lies, Ross, just so you won't be asking foolish questions. Though you ought to know why I went after your old man."

"No, I don't. I know he kept you on the payroll long after you weren't worth powder to blow you to hell."

"I'll tell you why," Pard declared in sudden heat, his eyes full of old anger. "Because I was with him for twenty years—and then he canned me. He gave me one of his damned temperance lectures, and I told him to go to hell. That was when he canned me. I said, 'Colonel, you're supporting a Mexican hag in Amargosa because she wet-nursed your boy when he was a baby, and you've got at least three cripples on the payroll right now.' Then I said, 'I shore would recommend keeping me on, Colonel.'"

Blade Ramsey was following it with the simple enjoyment of a man who liked a good story. "What'd he say?"

"Said I was canned," Pard repeated. "So I went over to Shelton on his little saddle-blanket holdin' ranch. I laid it to him straight: I could put Rancho Pacheco in his hands if he wanted it. He said why didn't I grab it myself, and I told him I was kind of legally involved in it and didn't want to stick my neck out. So Shelton paid me what I wanted and that was it...."

Ross stared out the door, despising Pard for the coarse enjoyment he took in reciting his crime. He thought, If I'd stayed, I could have helped. I could have sweated him down somehow.

Pard was going on, telling it with relish. "But the main thing I wanted was to see the colonel sweat. All Shelton wanted was that ranch. He just had this little holdin' ranch of his and he was forty-odd and not getting rich very fast. He took me to Coles—this was before he was marshal—and had me tell him the story. About them surveying for the new international line after the Gadsden Purchase. I was a meat-getter for Colonel Emory's surveying party. Seems like the line cut right through some of the ranches, and the rancheros had hell deciding whether they were Mexican or American. Tomás Archuleta didn't get hit quite so bad, but you can see he didn't have it like a man would want it. Twenty percent of his land was below the new border, and that was the best of it—Pacheco Valley and his home place and all. He couldn't ranch on both sides without a lot of rigmarole, so he played it another way."

Pard spat on the floor. He rubbed the spittle into the limed earth with his boot.

"He invited Colonel Emory and the surveyors to the house and wined them proper. Fed them barbecued buffalo and antelope and all the wine they could drink. They didn't have to look far to find a girl, if they felt liké it. But it didn't take. Emory was official as all hell. The wind blew wrong there, so old Tomás came to me and laid the proposition out cold: If I could get those monuments moved south, he'd give me five hundred gold dollars and a job for the rest of my life. I studied on it a while. Then it hit me."

He walked to the door and gazed east at the long cowhorn curve of the mountains as they swung north. "Who was going to notice if I moved some of them monuments in the hills? You don't get a straight look at the line like you do on the desert. So I done that. Brought it down two miles, straightened it out, then cut it back north ten miles west. Jesus," he recalled, "I done five hundred dollars worth of pick-and-shovel work moving them stone-and-iron outfits!"

At the table, Ross struck a match. It made a harsh sound, and Pard glanced around. Ross lighted a cigar.

"Evidently Archuleta scared out before long," he remarked. "He sold to Dad a few years later."

Pard didn't comment. "Well, that was the story I told Shelton. He had it surveyed and seen I was right. He put Coles on it and Coles drawn it up—splittin' the ranch in two. Shelton wasn't going to take it all away from him, because where would the advantage be to the colonel not to just let the Mexicans take Pacheco Valley for back taxes and rent payments?"

Blowing smoke at him, Ross drawled: "You're a pretty foxy business man, aren't you? Get money out of Shelton to help him wreck the colonel—and then money out of him not to wreck Shelton himself! But you don't seem to worry much about blackmail."

"I would," said Pard, "if I was mixed up in any of it. That was what it was when Shelton took the ranch away from your father. I didn't want any of that. But I got a better idea and hit Gunlock with it: If we could raise a little money, we could buy this no-man's-land strip and charge rent on it! It took a little doing, but thanks to you and Blade, we finally raised it."

"Yes, and you've had your cut out of it now," Ross told him. "You've had your high living and your brags. But now you're all through. You're going to turn the rest over to me."

Pard slowly turned. His face thickened with emotion. His hand went out to grasp a rifle from its place by the door, and he walked across the cabin. The muscles tightened down Ross's back. He was poised as he watched him come on. Pard did not raise the gun. He said in a low, vicious tone:

"Don't raise your voice to me, you four-bit horse-trapper! I thought you were a cut above your old man. Hell! You think you're going to nose us out when you hadn't the sense to git in the game in the first place? By Jesus," he said, "I'd blow your belly open!"

Ross was not unaware of Blade. He saw that Blade still had his hands on the table—neutral until he saw how the wind blew. Ross came carefully to his feet.

"I'm telling you, now, Pard. You and everybody else will keep your hands off Pacheco Ranch. And your dirty mouths off Laurel Shelton's name."

Pard had an unhealthy look. "How are you going to do all this, mustanger?"

"The same way you're doing it—with the old knife at the back. Take one more nickel out of Shelton, and I'll turn you over to a U. S. marshal. You'll spend the rest of your life in Leavenworth for tampering with those monuments."

"Taking mighty good care of Shelton, Ross, considering all he done to your old man," Pard said scornfully.

"I'll take care of him in time. You, too. You're in it as much as he is."

"Oh, no. Not quite. I helped kill the horse, but I didn't bury the body."

"What's that mean?"

Pard shook his head. "Figure it out."

Ross suddenly closed the distance between them. He kicked the rifle away and seized Pard by the shirt-front. "What happened to the colonel, Pard? Is that what you're driving at?"

Pard's mouth achieved irony. "Come to me with your hat in your hand sometime, Ross, and ask me that."

Ross's palm struck the brown cheek, fat and stubbled as a flitch of bacon. He was conscious only of what he saw in the murky depths of the blacksmith's eyes.

"Come on! What happened to my father, Pard? You'll never walk out of this cabin till you tell me...."

Francie suddenly came in from the yard. Ross's glance flicked to her. The girl's face looked strained. "Blade—" she said. "Blade, there's a man coming! I think it's Mr. Shelton."

Blade bounced to a glassless window in the deep mud wall. "By God," he said, "it *is* Shelton! What's he want here?"

Ross dropped his hand and let Pard move back. For a moment they regarded each other with the dregs of anger in their eyes. Then Pard said, low and bitterly:

"Save a man's life and he turns on you like this! You bet you're on your own next time, Chance...."

21

ROSS WATCHED Blade tensely observing Shelton's approach. He could hear the brisk clatter of a horse through the stream a few hundred feet to the east of the cabin. Blade's hand rested on his gun. "Pard," he said, "you'd better talk to him. I'll cover you from here."

Ross laughed drily. "Thought you had him figured out. What's worrying you?"

"Nobody ever figured that one out," Pard growled. "He'll take some shoving, but we don't know how much."

"That's the danger in this business," said Ross. "You don't know how much shoving anybody will take, till you find out. I've got an idea Shelton found out my father wouldn't take quite as much as he thought."

Pard did not reply, did not so much as glance at Ross, but Ross had a hunting-dog feeling—a tingling of his whole being. Walking to the door behind Pard, he watched Shelton come on. He was a massive figure in the saddle, a canvas roll behind his cantle. The high winter sun flashed on the silver conchos of the harness but left his face in the shadow of his Stetson. He had a carbine in the crook of his arm. A short whip was coiled about the horn of his saddle. He halted by the old spring wagon in the yard and looked the cabin over. After a moment, Pard moved out. Ross heard the oily click of Blade's Colt going on full cock.

Shelton moved the pony ahead, turning it broadside to stare down at Pard Mallet. "Where is she?" he snapped. "Is she hiding out here with you tramps?"

"Now, that's a hell of a way to talk," Pard scolded.

"I know a lot worse ways," said Shelton. "Where is she?"

"Missus Shelton?" Pard asked. "I jest wouldn't know." Then he turned his head. "Ross, did you see Mrs. Shelton when you drove out last night?"

120

Ross stepped from the cabin. He moved a pace to the right and leaned against the wall. He studied Lamar Shelton's face, this man who was so full of deception you could never know when to believe him. Just when you thought he was protecting you from the law, you heard him making a deal with the marshal. His first reaction on hearing him say Laurel was missing was shock. It still lay in him, but he kept his eyes on the rancher's hard-fleshed features as he said: "I wouldn't have had time to notice if she had been on the road."

Shelton was balanced carefully on the saddle, keeping the yard and cabin in his field of attention. Ross had the thought that he had probably heard Blade cock the gun—that if all three of them now threw down on him, he would make a good showing before they got him. He looked like an intelligent, strong, and utterly ruthless adversary. He gave Ross a stern glance.

"You made a fine job of hauling supplies for me, Chance. I found the horses shot and the supplies dumped in Clear Fork this morning. What the hell happened?"

"Make a guess," Ross retorted.

Shelton's eyes slanted to Pard, then came back. "I could guess," he said. "When a man's got as many irons in the fire as you have, he's apt to get hold of the hot end of one once in a while. My guess is you were elected for extinction last night. Some people are saying that's what happened to George Gunlock."

"But we know better, don't we?" Ross said.

Shelton's faint smile told nothing. "And we'd better not forget it," he said. "Well, you got away, so there's no harm done. I can write off the supplies, but not my wife. Where is she?"

"I couldn't keep track of your supplies, Shelton, let alone your wife."

Shelton's mouth stiffened and the horse moved restlessly under him. "She was supposed to stay in town last night, but she wasn't at the hotel when I came in around midnight."

Pard chuckled. He flicked out the blade of a spring knife and began cleaning his nails. "My sight ain't what it used to be, Ross, but I coulda swore a lady got out of the wagon just before it turned over last night. Seems to me, Shelton," he observed, "other fellas are getting more fun out of your marriage than you are."

Staring at Pard, Ross straightened from the wall, but after an instant he looked at Shelton. Alarmed, Ross turned a few inches so that if he had to, he could draw his Colt. Deep in Shelton's eyes was the rage of a bloody street fighter struggling up to the jeers of a crowd. Across the yard with its latticed shade they stared at each other, this man who thought he had been cuckolded, and the man with the guilty, yet still innocent, love. Gradually the heat in Shelton's eyes banked. Ross saw an acceptance of violence in them, a conviction that it would come sooner or later, but in his own way.

Shelton took his gaze from Ross's face. He swung his pony and peered along the crumbled base of the mesa, his brown face working.

"She's got no more sense than... With the brush full of cow-thieving outlaws, she takes off alone! Well, if she comes by here," Shelton directed Pard, "tell her I'm expecting her at the ranch."

Shelton's heavy body tilted forward as he started to spur the horse. But Pard called to him quickly.

"You know, I'm glad you stopped by this morning," he said. "Because that five thousand was nice, but money don't last forever. You know what I mean?"

Shelton turned the pony and bore quickly down on him. Looming above him, he said in a hard voice:

"I told you the five thousand would be the first and the last money you got out of me. If this is another demand for it, I'll put you all where you won't need money."

Pard faced him with thick-featured confidence. "That wasn't even a good start. Gals like Francie come pretty high; they need a lot of fancy fixin's. And old Pard's got to where he can't drink the rotgut he used to. Cuts me up like soldering acid. I don't know about Ross," he said, "but if Blade and me don't get another five thousand against the back rent and interest you owe us, we're apt to—well, I don't know what we would do."

"You gave me your words you'd keep your mouths shut," Shelton reminded. "If you open up now, it'll be the last time you do. That's God's truth, Mallet."

"No, it ain't," Pard replied. "It's a lot of talk. But I'll tell you what a man might do, in a case like this. Suppose he decided he didn't care too much about part of his ranch—like your wife's Tecolote Canyon place—and he deeded it over to the fellows who were badgering him. Then, do you see, they'd be under the gun, too, because their title could be wrecked as quick as his! Now, wouldn't that be a way out?"

"No," Shelton said bluntly. "I paid twenty-four thousand

dollars for this ranch. I gave the Tecolote Canyon piece to Mrs. Shelton as a wedding present. But that don't mean I'd give it to you."

Pard grinned at Ross. "Man, he never had twenty-four cents left to pay for Pacheco, after he got done paying me! It was given to him free and clear by the colonel."

Staring at Ross, Shelton said: "That's a damned lie. I told you how he happened to sell. He couldn't handle a place that big any more. I don't know what Mallet's been feeding you, but that's the truth."

"What's the truth about what happened to the twenty-four thousand?" Ross demanded. "He couldn't pay taxes a year later."

After a moment Shelton spoke. "Walk over to the pond with me, I'll tell you the truth about something else, if you're so hot for it."

As he started for the hoof-pocked shore of the pond, Pard called after him. "I'm not joshing about that deal, Shelton! You've got three days to make up your mind."

Shelton reached the water before Ross and let his horse drink, dismounting to gaze stolidly at the slow currents of the pond. Ross came up. Instinctively, he knew what Shelton was going to say, and he did not know how to answer. There was only one weak spot in his armor, now, and the rancher had found it. Standing near him, Ross gazed at a *guajalote* wriggling in the mossy shallows.

"What about it, Chance?" Shelton asked suddenly. "Did you bring her out here last night?"

"I'll give you straight answers when I begin getting some from you," Ross told him.

Shelton turned on him with a quick movement of his body. His eyes were narrow with anger. He had his left fist balled, and he shook it slightly. "Do you think I don't know what's been going on behind my back? Do you think I've been afraid to tackle you?" His voice broke and he wiped his lips.

Ross had a queer, confused impulse: Though he despised Shelton, it seemed very important that the rancher believe there had been nothing furtive in his relations with Laurel. He told him flatly: "Nothing's been going on behind your back. I brought her out here last night, yes. But she sat on her side of the wagon, and I sat on mine."

Shelton, breathing deeply, tried to master himself. "Why did she come out here?"

"Because she's not the kind you can ramrod around. You can't set her down and say, 'Now stay there.' Because she'll walk out on you. That's what she's been doing. Showing you she can't be handled with a Spanish bit."

Shelton shook his head. "She's never tasted a Spanish bit yet. But by heaven she's going to, when I find her!"

"If you touch that girl..." Ross began breathlessly; but Shelton interrupted. There was a hard varnish of excitement in his face.

"Do you know what they do to adultresses in Mexico? They cut off their hair, strip them to the pelt and drive them down the main street.... That's a kind of fun they don't go after twice."

"What are you trying to do?" Ross asked. "Keep her, or drive her away?"

"I'm going to teach her that my wife isn't going to shame me before a whole county. She isn't a filly that every stud in the herd is going to cover if he feels like it, and she'd better learn it. She's had her fun acting like a duchess, spending more on clothes and trifles in a month than most women would spend in two years. But she's going to come to heel pretty damned quick."

"She'll never come to heel," Ross said doggedly.

"Won't she?" Shelton grinned. But it was a desperate, meaningless gesture. "If she can't tell me how Gunlock came by that crocheting of hers in your hotel room, I'll do what I said. I hope you're in town to see it. Because I'll have something for you when I'm through with her."

"Would you take Gunlock's word over hers?"

"In the matter of her sleeping with other men—yes."

Ross could feel himself breaking. It was like a cold snake whipping in him, driving him to something violent. He clenched both fists and heard a knuckle crack. "Listen to me!" he said. "Laurel did come to my room. She wanted to tell me something about my father that she thought I'd want to know."

"No fooling!" Shelton scoffed.

"She said the colonel'd been a close friend of her father's. And before he died he told Marshal Henderson he'd been wrong in the battle we had. He hoped I'd come home some day. That was all she had to say."

Shelton's eyes roved his face, looking dry and brutal. "Was this before she took her clothes off," he asked, "or after?"

It broke, then, like a flood of hot blood in his head. Ross hit him, clean and hard. Shelton reeled into the clayey mud beside the pond, groped for balance, but fell. His left arm splashed in

the mossy water. Looking down at him, Ross had never hated
anyone so fiercely. He wanted to trample him. He wanted to
gouge his face with his spurs. He hated the strong, coarse
features and the thick blood running slowly from his nose.
Shelton's face, clearing of shock, suddenly distorted. He rolled
from the water and came to his feet. He was a huge and wild-
looking figure with blood dripping from his nose onto his shirt-
front. He came at Ross in a rush.

Ross braced to meet him as the rancher lunged forward. But
Shelton was a jump ahead of him. As Ross cocked to strike him,
Shelton pulled his Colt. Shock poured through Ross. He saw the
gunbarrel tipping up, but it did not emit the flash he expected—
that was not Shelton's intention. He kept coming in, the gun
rising, and then with a swift savage motion he chopped at Ross's
head. Ross ducked and threw up an arm. He plunged into the
rancher and tried to bear him back into the pond, but Shelton set
his strength and weight against him and his arm fell again.

The gun struck Ross over the left ear and that was all he
knew.

22

WHEN ROSS RECOVERED, he was lying near the pond with his right arm outflung in the mud. He opened his eyes and without stirring looked around. Shelton was gone; the horse was gone. The cabin looked silent.

His head was being torn apart by the ache in it. He tried to sit up but sagged back and lay in a rocking black sea of stars, sick and dizzy. He felt terribly vulnerable, knowing the men in the cabin were stronger than he, now—that they might kill him if he stirred. They were talking in there, trying to decide what to do about a partner who would not cooperate.

He sat up at last. Fatigue and sickness turned dizzily in his head.

He tried to think back to the last sleep he had had. That night in the caboose? No, Gunlock had died that night. In the station at El Paso, then, a few hours on a hard bench with a newspaper spread over him...how many nights ago? Forty-eight hours...seventy-two hours...Those sick, frightened hours flapped up at him like buzzards rising from a carcass. Those packed hours of treachery and violence and scheming, and love.

Ross groped for a cigar in his pocket and found one, broken. He tore off the shredded end and took the rest in his teeth, but after striking a match he sat numbly without lighting it, thinking of Laurel. *Where was she?* My God, hadn't she made it back to town? No, he recalled—Shelton left Amargosa before she'd have been back. She was all right. Unless Shelton found her before he did. He knew he should be on a horse right now, going to her, but he did not seem to be able to move. Something stung his fingers and he snapped his hand; it was the unused match, which had burned down to his thumb.

He rose to go to the cabin, aware that he was not functioning right somehow. As he walked up the slope he saw Francie at the tank, filling the water bucket, and he tried to remember why she

126

had never finished that job, which she had started hours ago. Shelton had come; that was it. Francie glanced over her shoulder as he neared her, pouting. She looked like a child; it seemed a pity that she should be in any way involved in this. As he came abreast of her, she turned with the wooden bucket dripping-full. Ross put his hand out for it.

Then the ground tilted, and he had to lean forward to keep his balance. He stumbled, caught himself, and stood looking foolishly at her. Francie gazed at him with a reproving but worried expression.

"You should lie down, Ross."

Ross frowned at the rise in the ground which had fooled him. "Lie down? I think I'll just wait and fall down."

Francie walked to him and splashed a handful of water from the bucket into his face. The coldness stung. His head cleared a little. "Here—sit on the chopping block," she said.

He sat on the block and gripped his knees with his hands, his head tipped down and his eyes closed. The blonde girl lowered the bucket, appearing concerned. Her anger with him was gone; she put her fingers under his chin and turned his face up.

"What's the matter, honey?" she asked. "Did he hurt you so bad?"

"No," Ross smiled. "I'm just getting old." Then he heard himself plaintively asking, "How am I going to lick it, Francie?"

"Lick what?"

His hand stirred. "All of it. They're blocking me. All I want—"

Francie knelt by him. "You're sick, Ross. We'll get you to bed."

Bed! It was a beautiful word, the name of something forbidden. He wanted to go back to what he had been saying, but the thought had danced away. Vaguely he was aware that the doctor had said something about taking it easy for a while; lots of rest, plenty of sleep, don't overdo...

"Ross, you'd better go as soon as you can," Francie was saying. She held his chin between her fingers to make him look at her. The clear brown eyes seemed concerned. "You shouldn't have whipped Blade. And Pard's mad at you, too. They were counting on you being as pleased as they are."

"Pleased about holding myself up? This is my land they're kicking around."

Her fingers touched her hair, while she frowned. "I—I don't

understand what it all means. But I think you ought to go back to town pretty soon."

"I'm going to," Ross said. "Right away. I've got to sleep first, or I'll fall off a horse onto my head like my old man did."

Francie glanced toward the cabin. "Listen! Can you saddle a horse?"

"I expect so."

"Then ride up the creek a ways. I'll tell them you said you were going to get on high ground and see where Shelton went. Then you can stop somewhere and get a little sleep. When you wake up, you'd better keep going."

Glancing toward the cabin, Ross saw Blade come into the doorway to throw a cigarette butt into the yard. As he observed Ross and the girl, Blade halted to watch them. Ross got to his feet.

"That's pretty good advice," he smiled. "I'll take a drink of that water, and then I've got some advice for you." He raised the bucket and drank from it, feeling the restorative coldness clear to his fingertips. Wiping his stubbled mouth, he said, "Make him marry you, Francie. Else get out."

Francie smiled. "He's not the marrying sort, is he?"

"No. That would be your good luck, though. He's got no more control than a rodeo bronc. But you're going to be hurt if you stay with him. Either from the law or from him."

"Oh, I don't know," she said.

"This is a hard-luck outfit," Ross insisted. "They're trying to shove two men who won't take much shoving. It's going to end in shooting, Francie. I can't see any other end to it. Someone's going to be killed. Being innocent won't keep you from getting hit by a stray bullet."

"Shoving—Mr. Shelton, you mean?" the girl frowned. "Who else are they shoving?"

"Me," Ross said. "And I've just about come to the shooting point."

Walking to the little stone corral where a few saddle horses were kept, he had the distinct impression that there were bedsprings under the ground. Also he knew that a violent pressure was growing in his head, trying to find a seam through which to escape. Ross lifted a bridle from a peg in the wall of a shed and slipped through the gate of the corral. He cornered a horse and shoved the bit into his teeth. Leading him, he took him from the corral and threw a ragged Mexican tree onto his back.

Then there was a bad moment of wondering whether he could hoist himself into the saddle. He gripped the huge Mexican horn with both hands and drew himself up. After he was in the saddle, he pressed his fingers against his eyes and waited for the dizziness to pass. He let the pony move out. He rode past the water tank and paused before the cabin, wanting to make a convincing show of it. If he knew his partners, they were men who would go after a sick enemy the way roosters attacked a wounded member of the flock.

"Francie!" he called. "Will you bring me my carbine? I don't want to get in a long-range shoot-out with that fellow with no more than a Colt."

The girl brought him the rifle and he secured it under the saddle fender. Then she handed him a half-pint of whiskey, with a wan smile. He found a smile for her. "Bring you a quart of Mexican perfume sometime, sweetheart," he said.

"Good luck," she said.

"You, too," Ross smiled stiffly. "The best thing I could wish you would be to get out of here and go home. There's worse things to be read to from than the Book of Revelations."

"I don't know what," Francie said archly.

"The criminal code, for instance," Ross said.

Between the creek and the rough wall of the canyon ran a narrow shelf cluttered with willow and boulder. Along this trail Ross let the horse pick its own way. It climbed rapidly, after fifteen or twenty minutes topping out on the mesa onto the well-rutted freight road. Ahead, through a sparse forest of gray-green piñons, the mountains soared blue and rugged. Somewhere—perhaps he had already passed it—was the false international line. Ross kept the horse moving rapidly, holding the horn with one hand.

He came finally to a hill from which he could see the brown cowhorn of the valley. The sun and wind, pressing the grass on the hills, created a pattern of gold and tan, with stipplings of late green in watered creases. He could not find Lamar Shelton. He had probably departed in the direction of the home place a few miles east, but the trail, hugging the foothills, was hidden. Turkey Creek wandered in its stubbled greenery to the Paso Redondo camp, and broadened into the pond, and far beyond the cottonwoods ran up against a prow of pink sandstone and split into two streams. A mile and a half along Clear Fork, the right-hand tributary, lay Laurel's Tecolote Canyon headquarters. But this place, also, was hidden. Ross told himself, sensibly, that of course she had made it back to town. But saying this did not settle his anxieties.

He was about to head on when he heard a distant fall of metal on stone. He turned quickly back. The trail he had taken was plain for some distance. He put his gaze on it and waited for movement. His head began to pulse crazily and he could not draw a deep breath. He was shaken by sudden uncertainty, and had all the physical symptoms of having run uphill beyond his endurance. He cursed this weakness, but could not drive it off. While he waited, he drew the saddle gun and pulled down the lever. There was a roughness to the action which caused him to frown and glance into the breech. He gazed at the ruined mechanism without comprehending for a moment what had happened. The interior of the breech was crusted with some black substance. He dug at it with his fingernail and sniffed the scrapings which came away.

Powder, he recognized: gunpowder had been poured into the gun and ignited. He tipped the gun up and inserted his finger into the muzzle. Powder had been burned here, too, so that even if a shell could be forced into the ruined breech and made to fire, the slug would jam and cause the carbine to blow up.

He sat dully, again hearing the sound of a hoof. *I wonder when they did it.* While he was talking to Shelton, he supposed. He wondered if Francie were in on it, and whether it was through motives of delicacy that they had tolled him away from the cabin for the execution or to remove the danger of Francie's talking about it. He carefully thrust the gun into the scabbard again. A smile opened the grim line of his mouth.

By God, boys, he thought, you've got to tree this cat before you can skin him!

Waiting for a look at the men, he twisted the cork from the half-pint of whiskey Francie had brought him. He knew exactly what was in this bottle as he raised it to his lips; for a man as depleted as he, a half-hour's rebirth of strength and confidence. After that, the walls would come tumbling down.

Far below in the oak brush, a horse moved past a point of trees. For an instant it was patterned against a tawny hillside. Ross scrutinized the rider, a big man who wore a new black Stetson and carried his carbine carelessly in his free hand. As Ross studied him, the rider drew the horse in and tilted his face upward to search the steep plateau which crumpled into the hills. At once he saw Ross and turned to speak to a second rider who came into view, a man who looked too big to be riding a horse on a mountain trail. . . . Ross could see in his mind the cold-blooded eagerness in Blade Ramsey's battered features.

The distance was too great even for a rifle shot, and Blade suddenly struck his pony on the rump with the stock of his carbine and the horse lunged on up the trail. A moment after, Pard Mallet cut from the trail to the west, breaking wide across the mesa on a line which would cut off Ross's escape in that direction. Thus they held the strings of the sack in their hands.

Ross rode on. He had drunk half the whiskey, and its warm, spreading confidence was in his belly. It did not change the impression that there was a single, large blood vessel in his skull which leaped painfully every time the motion of the horse rocked him.

As he rode, he tried to see a way out—a quick escape. He was on a plain, much-used road, the main horse-trail to the Mexican ranches across the mountains and to the town of Villa Hermosa. A quarter-mile to the left, the mesa sloughed off into the rugged canyon of Turkey Creek. He knew from old experience that there was no quick crossing of that canyon. Blade and Pard Mallet realized this, also, and were basing their strategy on the assumption that Ross would try to outrun them to the west.

Ross halted in a half-height thicket of ironwood. He reached up to wipe his forehead with the back of his hand. Though the air was brisk, he was perspiring. He gazed straight ahead. The mesa, with its deepening forest of gray sage and piñon, was already breaking up, becoming the apron of the mountains, but only a half-mile ahead was the first dark palisade of the Penascos. Ross recalled the trail: a cliffside, switchbacking ascent to the first saddle, an hour's ride above. So Blade and Pard knew he would not try that. And they knew he would not risk making the canyon crossing on the east. They were perfectly confident, as the dust Pard was raising on his tangent to the west showed, that he would try to outrun them on that flank and double back to the valley.

As he sat there, Ross heard a sharp crackling in the brush. He started, and it was a moment later that the clean, thundering report of the rifle shot came to him. He looked back, surprised that he had left himself exposed. On a ridge a few hundred yards back, Blade Ramsey had halted to try a long one. It seemed, to Ross, more of a sad thing than a frightening one, that a man with whom he had labored for a year should now have annulled all the companionship of that time. It spoke of the vast and sinister power of easy money.

While they were broke and working hard, Blade had been a good-natured man who desired little more than three squares a day and a pint when he could get it. But Gunlock had sliced away all that soft exterior of his. What he had exposed was raw and ugly. It was the core of a weak man, greedy, reckless, and ruthlessly selfish. It had taken the reins of Blade's mind and kicked off the brake. Blade was in downhill flight, headed for the surest of disasters.

Ross touched the horse with his heels and it moved deeper into the brush. Blade did not fire again. A sudden, sharp loneliness descended over Ross. He thought of Laurel, hiding somewhere within a few miles of him; belonging with him. Yet perhaps they were now as far apart as life and death. The thought was intolerable that Shelton might find her before she reached safety. But even in town, how long would she be safe from him? Perhaps Henry Lyman himself could not help her. She was legally Shelton's, and who could stand between them? And when this came to him, Ross knew he must return to Amargosa; and presently he knew exactly how he would do it.

From the next high ground, he sighted northwest and found Pard Mallet's dust moving along on the same line. Again he heard the passage of a bullet in the brush, nearer him this time, and once more the high, powerful explosion of the shot. Down there, Blade lowered the gun from his shoulder and spurred his horse on up the trail. Ross rode over the crest of the ridge and plunged into a motte of piñons resembling a forest of tired Christmas trees. He rose straight through it until the depth of the trees between him and the ridge he had just crossed was enough to hide the animal. Then he dismounted. He took another drink of the whiskey and threw the bottle aside. He started at a run back to the ridge. But his head began to roar with a vast and thunderous pain, so that he halted with a groan and pressed his palms against his temples. At last the pain slackened. He walked on and heard a horse coming to the top of the ridge. He drew his Colt and rocked the hammer back. With the gun on full cock, he walked into a low thicket of buckbrush and sank down to leave just his head exposed. The brush was like a gray lace of thorns. A man could throw a stone to the spot where the trail crossed the ridge. Perhaps, Ross thought, if he could stop the shaking of his hands, he could do even better with a bullet.

23

THE WIND WAS from the north, a cold draft carrying the dust of Ramsey's approach. Drifting fast, it crossed the stony pass and swept into the thicket where Ross waited. There was a coldness in his body. He regarded the heavy Frontier Colt in his hand as though he had never seen it before. It looked ugly and ponderous. The bluing was worn from the high points on the cylinder, and the cedar grips were dark with handling. They talked about carrying a gun for snakes in this country, but you could kill a diamond-back better with a forked stick and a rock than you could with a gun. When the chips were down, you knew why you had been carrying it all your adult life: something about the country made man think of killing before he thought of reasoning. And when the man coming toward you carried a gun, the pattern was set for you, as well.

The horse scuffed briskly up to the crest, but just short of it Blade Ramsey halted. Ross's heart compressed. *If he loops around behind the thicket and sees the horse, I'm licked....* Holding his breath, he waited. Suddenly the pass, the gray trees, swam giddily before him. You son-of-a-bitch, he thought, hurry up! He forced a long breath into his lungs and held it, sucking all the strength out of it. He let it go, and just then the pony moved into the gap.

The first thing Ross was aware of was Blade's rifle, held in both hands with the reins trailing from his left, the muzzle covering the trail. Then he noticed Blade's face. It made everything easier.

He had seen this kind of obscene eagerness in the face of men coming up to a treed lion. Blade had a small grin on his mouth; a man who grinned by himself, Ross thought, must be crazy. And his front teeth were set together and his lips were tight, and there was a wild hunger in his eyes. He looked as bright, sharp, and dangerous as a dagger.

But as he reached the crest and failed to see the quarry at the base of the palisade, he frowned. He turned his head toward the canyon and scrutinized the trees, then swung his gaze the other way and tried to find a trace of the lost fox there.

"Throw it down, Blade," Ross called.

Blade saw him at once and the gun in his hands moved fast. Ross knew then that he should have fired first and talked later— he was too slow and sick to keep up with Blade. An avalanche of sound rolled upon Ross, a roar in which he seemed to be caught up and hurled backward. The bullet stirred the brush beside him. The flash of the powder was like a glimpse into an evil flower. Blade's pony reared. The mustanger was jerking the loading lever down and keeping his eyes on Ross.

Ross pointed the Colt as he would have pointed his finger. The gun leaped, raising his forearm. The breeze drew the smoke away and he saw Blade drop his rifle and clutch the pommel with both hands. Ross brought the forty-four down slowly and the mustanger was hung on the sights for an instant. But there was no point in firing, now. The black Stetson fell and Blade twisted in the saddle with his face turned away from Ross. The horse brought its forehoofs to the ground and pitched forward, stopping post-legged to throw Blade to the ground. Then it shied and began running sidewise, but Ross broke through the brush and caught the trailing reins. Holding the pony, his feet braced wide, he stared at Blade.

The boy was moving a little, but his eyes were glazed with shock. Ross could hear him breathing. He sounded like a troubled sleeper snoring. Quickly, Ross picked up Blade's rifle and mounted the horse. Then in afterthought he dismounted and retrieved the black Stetson. It was so new the sweatband was hardly stained. It was almost Ross's size. Wearing Blade's Stetson and riding his horse, he went a short distance up the trail.

Presently Pard Mallet came in view a short half-mile west. He came at a lunge to the top of a rise and stared toward Ross, evidently alarmed by the shooting. Ross waved his rifle at him. Under Pard's gaze, he put the carbine to his shoulder and fired up at the base of the palisade. Then he shook the gun again and spurred on along the trail. The trees hid him in a few moments. He pulled rein and heard Pard following his false lead toward the mountain.

He returned to where Blade lay beside the trail. He was still, now. Ross knelt by him, pressing his ear close to his lips. The boy was dead. Ross gazed off across the valley. Under the sun it was quiet and beautiful. Just a piece of real estate, he reflected. Nothing wrong with that land at all—grass, trees, rocks, a peacefulness that went deeper than a man could ever dig. It was men who spoiled land; who spoiled everything that was worth having. Land, women, horses, and liquor. We spoil everything we get our hands on, he thought. We ruin ourselves in the process of doing it, and finally we lie asleep on a hillside, and none of the things we've fought over are our own. Except peace, and we had that in the beginning.

He went through Blade's pockets. But there was nothing except a chamois pouch which contained one three-cent piece, some Mexican coins, a gold eagle, and two brass tokens stamped: *Good for One Beer. The Gadsden Purchase.* Ross closed the boy's eyes and placed a couple of copper coins over them. He considered keeping the gold piece, but it seemed that in a way it would be profane to take it, though it had been borrowed against his own land. He dropped the money in the dirt beside Blade and rode away.

There was plenty of time, now. He took a trail down the canyon to the valley, rode east a mile to a mulberry cloud of leafless trees where there was a spring, and slid from the saddle. Two cows that were licking a yellow block of salt gazed stupidly at him. He meant to lie down, but it was more like collapsing. His arms failed to support him as he let himself go prone, and he came hard against the dry, dead leaves beside a tree. *I'm dying*, he thought. *I'm dead. It's a lot better this way. Blade and I've found the answer.*

But as soon as he was asleep a black-haired girl with gray eyes came to torment him with her weeping.

A sunset like spilled wine was in the sky when he awoke. He had rolled over onto his back. The dry branches were black, like threads in the burgundy of the sky. His body refused to move. Nearby, cattle stirred, and he heard the horse shake itself with a loud popping of harness. If Pard or Shelton should walk up now, and point a gun at him, he knew he could not stir.

He lay there until the sky was a rusty green. At length he sat up. He sat with his knees drawn up and his head resting on his forearm. The peace of the evening entered him. He moved his head and it did not pound. He shook it gently and it remained normal. He stood up. He was ravenously hungry.

He gazed around him, now, and recognized the place where

he was as Roblero Spring. The runoff of a small but faithful spring had been dammed with earth to form a tank, bound now by thick growths of willow and reed. He had worked cattle here many times. Soon, as darkness came on, animals that came to drink, and animals that came to kill, would file down from the hills behind the spring. Directly north, hardly more than an hour's ride, was the Tecolote Canyon place. Ross felt a rising compulsion to visit it. If Laurel, for any reason, had changed her mind about going back to town, it was possible she might have left him some indication of what she planned to do.

His desire was to leave at once, but he stayed on while night formed against the mountains to the west and flowed out over Pacheco Valley. He found a cigar in his pocket and lighted it. He smoked slowly and thoughtfully, and when it was finished he threw down the butt, trod it out, and walked to the horse. Before mounting, he examined Blade's saddle gun. It was a brand-new Winchester .38-40—undoubtedly one of his acquisitions with the blackmail money from Shelton. It was a thirteen-shot carbine and there were nine shells left in the magazine. After those shots were exhausted, he would be back on his Colt.

In the dry chill of the early night, he started for the line camp.

They called it Tecolote Canyon, but it was more of a shallow scoop of a valley, a long twisting valley down which Clear Fork ran between low, rimrock mesas on either side. The hillsides shelving down to the stream were almost bare of growth, but at the bottom were oaks, hackberries, and a few poplars. On the west side of the stream—just before it looped east to the ford where Ross had turned the wagon over last night—the colonel had chosen a little cleft of ground a hundred yards back from the creek to build a line shack. Traveling cautiously, Ross came in view of it in about an hour.

It had the look of a completely desolate place, an ancient camp long abandoned. There was hardly any use prospecting it for the girl: she would not have stayed here longer than to get a horse. The place looked too silent and sinister to be investigated without apprehension.

Ross dismounted and walked to the edge of the yard. The colonel had evidently added a couple of rooms to the original shack. An ell had been formed by the addition. Branding irons were hanging from the branch of a tree in the middle of a corral. The sheds were lean-to affairs. There were a couple of mounds of hay, black with weather.

Ross had a pain in his heart, thinking of the colonel living here. You would look at this yard and expect a shiftless one-mule cropper to shamble out to meet you. But instead of that, the cabin had housed the proudest cattleman ever to come out of Texas. This was a poor stage for Colonel Chance's sort of doings. It was no backdrop for his countywide barbecues. It would scarcely do to entertain the territorial governor in. And his famous remark, made on receipt of an inquiry from a Denver cattle buyer as to whether he could supply one thousand prime steers, would have sounded ludicrous.

"Write back and ask that gentleman," he had ordered his foreman, "what color steers he has in mind."

Ross scrutinized the oiled-rawhide panes of the windows. He tried to decide from which window he would watch if he were a gunman, and decided the one on the right, which was not quite closed. He kept his gaze on it while he approached the porch. Reaching the cabin, he stared at the dark crack between frame and sill, but he could see nothing.

The cabin was empty—that began to seem obvious. He stepped onto the porch and covered the door with the rifle while he tried the knob. The white porcelain was ice-cold. Though it turned easily, the door did not give. It was bolted. Ross moved back. He looked at the window again; he turned his ear to the door. He heard his horse yank a tuft of grass from the ground. He could hear the creak of his belt as he breathed. He turned the knob and prepared to hit the door with his shoulder, but now it gave in easily.

The door had been unbolted.

He was becoming familiar with terror—the various sorts of terror a man discovered when he went outside the law. He knew what it was like to have a marshal look at you and ask, *How did this man die?* and how it felt to confront the husband of the woman you loved and lie to him about your relations with her; and he would never again have to wonder what it was like when a bullet went over your head. But the worst fear he had known was standing on the other side of a door from a man who was waiting to kill you.

After the explosion of blood from his heart to his brain, there was a sick coldness, a desire to run. The hairs on the back of his neck bristled. He wet his hips. Then it came to him that it might be Laurel in the cabin. No, he thought. She'd have recognized me. This was Shelton, or one of his men; or Pard Mallet. Or Coles.

God, is there anybody I don't have to be afraid of? he asked himself.

With a motion of his whole body, he hurled the door inward,

dodged inside and crouched on one knee with the gun directed into the cabin. Frightened and angry, he shouted:

"Come out, you bastard!"

A girl cried: "Don't—don't shoot!"

Ross dropped the gun and stumbled forward. "Laurel!" he said. "Oh, my God!"

Something clattered on the floor. She came into the portal and stood there with her hair hanging forward over her shoulders in braids, and tears on her cheeks, sobbing.

"Ross—oh, Ross!"

Ross crushed her in his arms. He thrust his fingers into her hair. They were so close that they were like one person. Nothing would ever separate them again. Not Lamar Shelton, not Marshal Coles and his rope, no one.

He whispered in her ear, "Never, never, never!" and though she did not reply he felt her press against him closer still.

24

Ross LED the girl into the cabin and closed the door. The darkness was like a warm blanket wrapped about the two of them. He held her while her hand reached up to touch his cheek, and an emotion sweet and powerful choked him. He had the thought that both of them had lost their old identities; they had found a new one, of which each was part. He drew her to the window and thrust it open, letting the backglow of moonlight illuminate her face. Soberly he gazed at the fine, intense features, loving them. He pushed a lock of hair from her forehead and touched her cheeks and lips with his fingertips, and then abruptly caught her to him once more.

"Why, Ross!" she laughed, softly. "I don't think you've ever had a girl before!"

"Not one I couldn't give up, before," he told her. "Do you care?"

"I hate every girl you ever kissed," she told him. She pulled back to look at him. Her eyes would not rest. They went from his lips to his eyes to his unshaven cheeks. Her face became very sober, as she said, "I love you so, Ross. But—but what are we going to do about it?"

Ross looked into the moonlit yard. "I don't know. That's what we've got to decide between here and Amargosa. We ought to leave soon. Shelton's out looking for you. He came to the horse camp this morning and told me he'd been here. Where were you then?"

She glanced at an Indian rug in the middle of the earth floor. "In the colonel's root cellar," she said. "With his Bible in one hand and a gun in the other. I heard him tramping around for a while, and then he went away."

"Why did you stay here?" Ross asked her. "I told you to go back to town."

"Lamar's moved all the horses off. It was too far to walk without the chance of being seen. It'd have been daylight before I ever reached town."

"Well, we've got to hurry or the same thing will happen. I've only got one horse. Get your things."

He went to the door and retrieved his carbine. He looked the yard over, the silver-and-black riddle nothing but daylight could solve to a nervous man's satisfaction. Returning, he watched her slender shadow at the table near the sink. "Laurel," he said.

"What, darling?" She looked up. She was so like a bride, somehow, beautiful and provocative and radiant, but the men in her life were a husband who was hunting her with a whip coiled about his saddle horn, and a lover who was a fugitive.

"Something I want to tell you," Ross said. He sat on the cot and drew her down beside him. She smiled at him with a tuck of curiosity between her eyes.

"See here," she said, "are you sure it's talk you want? I thought you were in a hurry."

"I've been thinking that you shouldn't go into town with me, because there may be a price on my head by now. If there is, I don't want you dragged into what may come of it."

"A price? For what?"

So Ross told her about the death of Gunlock, but for a while she did not comment at all. He looked at her fine, still silhouette as she gazed out the window. "I know I should have told you last night, but I—I was afraid of what you might say."

"What is there to say? It's a terrible weapon for them to have over you, that's all."

"Maybe, maybe not. They tried to use it last night. That's what they were doing when they followed me. I'm only guessing, but I believe Coles issued a warrant for my arrest, and they were going to kill me while 'resisting.'"

"But if that's true, you can't go back into town!"

"I don't think they'd serve it in town. I think the idea is to hold it back as a hole card, to be used when and where they have the chance."

"But you don't know whether they would or not! Ross," Laurel exclaimed, "this changes everything, don't you see? You can't take the risk of their seeing you in town. You'll have to stay right here. There's plenty to eat, and you can either ride away from the cabin or hide in the cellar if anyone comes."

Ross shook his head. "The one who's going into hiding is you. Your husband's on the warpath."

"So is Laurel. If he comes near me, after all that's happened—"

"Yes, and if you shoot him, there'll be two of us on the wrong side of the law!" Ross pulled his hands from hers and stood up. "We're going in together. Henry will put you on a train to El Paso. You can stay there until he gets things straightened out."

Laurel kept looking at him without expression. "And what about you?"

"I think the best thing for me to do is to get Henry started on squaring things for me, and then take off for Mexico for a while."

"I'll go to El Paso, and you'll go to Mexico: Is that it?"

Ross nodded, and she suddenly shook her head in exasperation. "I was right. You've never had a girl before. You just don't know the first thing about one, do you?"

"I know I wouldn't carry one around with me while a crooked marshal took shots at us."

"You seem to have the notion that a woman is necessarily a handicap. It's just possible she could help you, isn't it? For instance, I'm going to put all the income from the Tecolote ranch into getting you cleared, if I have to."

When she tried to rise, Ross laid his hands on her shoulders and smilingly shook his head. "There aren't two like you," he said. "But I'm not going to let you lick all the paint off this toy and see what's underneath. We're going to keep it new till everything's right. You—you just don't know how crazy you are, to talk about going with me."

Laurel held his hands and stood up. She turned her face to his, pale and smiling and exciting. "You just don't know how crazy I am about you," she said.

Ross's hands clenched her arms. "Don't, Laurel!" he pleaded. "I'm trying to keep first things first. Don't you see?"

"Love is a first thing, isn't it?"

"Yes, and it seems to me it ought to be taken care of. I want to protect you, the only way a man in my position can, don't you see? I'm trying to be practical, because if anything happened to you, that'd just about finish me."

"What's more practical than people in love staying together?" Laurel asked. But when he shook his head, she pulled him down on the cot by her again and said, "I'm not trying to joke you out of it, Ross. It just seems to me that it was meant for us to be together a long time ago. Our fathers being close, and both dying because of the same man, and then the way we met . . . I knew that very minute we were going to be in love."

"Crazy," Ross said, shutting his eyes, but clutching her with an arm about her shoulders.

"Yes, but perfectly logical," she said. "Men are just amateurs at love. Women are the authorities. And I have the feeling that if we let them separate us now, we'll never get back together. It just won't ever be right again. Your old practicality will get into both of us."

He looked at her, for her voice had become grave. Her smile was gone. She was perfectly right; he knew it. But he knew that, either way, it was probably spoiled for them. He could see ahead to the lonely, furtive life in Mexican hotel rooms, while the letters from Henry Lyman became less and less hopeful, less and less frequent. But at least, her way, they would have had each other for a while.

"You know I'm right, too, don't you?" she said gently, her smile coming again.

He did not answer, except to turn to her, kissing her throat, and pressing her lips roughly.

25

WHEN THEY LEFT the cabin they found the horse a short distance from where Ross had left him. Ross mounted first, then reached down to help her up. He held her to him for a moment and kissed her, before he seated her behind him. Because she could not ride sidesaddle, she had to pull her skirts up and tuck them about her knees. Looking at the dark little cabin, he discovered he had an entirely different feeling about it. This was not a line camp where an old man had come to his end. It was a place where something very wonderful and important had started.

Laurel rested her head against his back as they started off.

By various trails Ross knew, riding and resting, walking occasionally to rest the horse, they came in the gray fag-end of the night to the outskirts of Amargosa. Already, in the little Mexican farms, a few lights showed. Woodsmoke lay in a thin gray stratum over the village. They crossed the canal on the Acequia Street bridge across from Tomás Archuleta's home. Looking at it, Ross thought, *You ought to burn candles for the colonel, you old sinner!* They rode another two blocks on a potholed sidestreet, and turned toward the plaza. During the last hour of the ride Laurel had dozed, only her arms awake as she held to Ross. It filled him with a feeling of tenderness and responsibility toward her. From this moment on, everything must be done with the aim of protecting her.

He heard her ask sleepily, "Are we there, Ross?"

"We're a block from the plaza. You know what you're going to do now?"

"Love you," she said.

"Yes, and besides that you're going to stay in your room," he said sternly.

"Until you or Henry come for me. All right," she agreed.

"Don't leave on any account, you hear?"

She stirred, and sitting up began to fuss with her hair. "What kind of man do you think Lamar is?" she asked. "Do you think he'll carry me off under his arm, or something, right in broad daylight? Or scalp me like an Indian?"

Fearing to upset her, he had not told her what Shelton had said. He had not mentioned the whip on his saddle nor the way he had said, his eyes cold and depthless as those of a statue: *"With a horsewhip . . . down the main street."* But now, wanting to force comprehension upon her, he said:

"Yes—scalp you, like an Indian. He told me he was going to cut your hair off when he found you. They do it to women caught in adultery, in Mexico."

He felt her stiffen. "I—I'd kill him," she whispered.

"But he's not going to try, because he won't find you. We're going straight to the hotel, now, and get you an unregistered room. Your meals will be sent up. In a day or two—I don't know how long—it ought to be safe to come out."

They had come to the northwest corner of the plaza, down the street from the Gadsden Purchase Hotel. Smoke lay like a gauzy wafer above the bandstand and the tired-looking desert trees. A rack-jointed hound sloped along a path. A few *reboso*-wrapped women carried ollas of water from the well. Nothing was open yet; the saloons, the mescal shops, slept. It was the perfect time to arrive.

In a low voice, Ross recapitulated the plan to her.

"I think I had enough from Pard and Blade to put Shelton in jail. If we can operate without their affidavits, we'll go after him. Once we get hold of Pard, I think we can make him talk. In the meantime, I'll leave it in Henry's hands. Your husband may try to have me jailed for Gunlock's murder, but the fact that he's waited this long before talking may make his story look bad. That's all I can hope for."

He told her it would be better if she walked ahead and he followed, and so she let him lift her down. Her face looked tired, but he thought he had never seen a woman so beautiful before; never had such lovely, sleepy eyes smiled at him. They kissed decorously, then she turned and walked confidently down the street to the hotel.

Ross waited until she had almost reached the large galleried building before he rode on. He reached the hitch-rail before Laurel. After tying his pony, he ducked under the rail, and they gained the door together. "Maybe," Ross suggested, "you ought to wait here. I'll register you under some name and you can march right past the desk without being recognized."

"No, I'm famous," she said, with a rueful smile. "Famous for my overdrawn bank accounts and the number of my gowns. That was one way I could make him suffer."

They entered the large, cold lobby. A Mexican porter was asleep in a chair near the front window. There was an atmosphere of dead cigars, newspapers, and dust.

"Wait by the stairs," Ross told the girl. He went to the desk, waited for her to reach the stairway, and tapped on the counter with a coin. The desk clerk, asleep in a chair, started. He was automatically on his feet and starting forward, his hand reaching for the pen.

"Yes, sir! Early train, eh? How many?"

He looked confused and cheerful and nine-tenths asleep. Ross told him, "One. A lady. She'd like a nice room over the plaza."

The clerk, glancing at Laurel, who stood with her back to him, said: "The luggage is where, sir?"

"No luggage. It'll come up later."

The face of the hotel man began to harden. "Sir, we have a rule—"

"Everybody's got rules," Ross said, laying a gold piece on the counter, "but sometimes they're only fit to break. The room will be occupied by the lady alone. She's ill. She won't have any visitors, and she'd rather not register."

The clerk's finger touched the coin. Again he peered at the girl, and recognition lighted in his face. "Why, that's—isn't that Mrs.—"

"Maybe," Ross interrupted. "Whoever she is, you'll keep quiet about it. I'll make it right with you, you understand. If you've got to have a name for the register, try one from last month's book. This isn't a joke, and it's not the usual shenanigans you're frowning about. Do you know Henry Lyman?"

"Certainly; very well."

"Henry will vouch for her later today. He'll make it plain, if I haven't, what will happen to you if she's disturbed."

With a shrug, the clerk placed his right forefinger on the coin and slipped it from the blotter onto his left palm. "Yes, sir," he said. "I'll show Mrs. Smith to her room."

"That's as good a name as any," Ross smiled. "Give me the key. I'll find it."

"Two-oh-four," said the hotel man. "Head of the stairs. I'd lose my job for this, you know," he complained.

Ross accepted the key. "I'll bet we can keep as quiet about it as you can."

Taking the girl's arm, he escorted her quickly to the second floor. The stairs ended at the west end of a hall running the width of the building. Two-oh-four was directly facing the landing. Ross unlocked it and Laurel slipped inside. He followed her. The room had a ten-foot ceiling, an oiled wooden floor, and the smell of mothballs. There was a dark mahogany clothespress, a commode topped with a porcelain pitcher and washbasin, and a bed as large as a wagon. Ross raised the stiff green blind. He recognized the view immediately; the bandstand and trash-littered plaza looked just as they did from Henry Lyman's office, which was at the end of the hotel building, only two or three rooms away. Laurel gazed down at the street and made the same discovery.

"Why, it's only a few rooms from Henry's window!" she exclaimed. "We're on the same balcony."

Ross nodded. "But Henry's got a door onto it, and you've got a window."

She held his arm. "Just the same, I can hear the band play tonight. It's Saturday. The Amargosa Grays will march today and tonight the band will play."

"And the Mexican dandies and girls will walk up and down ignoring each other," Ross smiled. "And for a few hours, I'm going to ignore you."

Laurel turned to him, slipping her arms about his neck. "I'll die," she said. "I almost died the morning you came in on the train, when you wouldn't speak to me. You wouldn't even look at me."

"And now you know why."

"I guessed then," Laurel said, "but I felt just as bad."

Ross turned her to the window. "You can see out, but don't forget people can see in, too."

"I'm going to worry about you every minute until you come for me," Laurel said. "What will you do, now?"

"Six o'clock..." Ross pondered. "Nobody's going to be up and around for a while. I'll get a shave when the barbershop opens. Then some breakfast. By then Henry ought to be down. There's no use rousing him at his home. After that, I'll steer by his compass—whatever he says."

"At twelve o'clock," Laurel directed, "I want you to sit on that bench behind the bandstand. I'll be at the window, but I'll be careful. I'll raise the blind a little.—Ross!" Laurel exclaimed suddenly, staring at the west end of the plaza, where the Chihuahua road came in. "Isn't—isn't that...?"

With a jolt, Ross recognized the horsemen coming along the far side of the square. Though the light was still cold and gray, he knew Pard Mallet at once, and realized a moment later that the other rider was Lamar Shelton. His first thought was of Blade Ramsey's horse, tied at the hotel hitch-rack. He drew the shade down and turned away.

"I'll have to get out! They'll see my horse at the rack."

"But you can't go now! He might—heaven knows what he'd do."

"If he sees the horse at the rack, he'll know what we've done. I'll go out the back way and circle around through the alley. I don't want to be seen leaving here."

Quickly, he bent to kiss her. But Laurel embraced him tightly, and after a moment he had to tug her arms away.

"Now, don't worry! As long as you keep out of sight, everything else will go all right. *Sabes?*"

"Yes, but—Oh, do be careful, Ross. If anything happens to you—"

Ross descended rapidly to the lobby, signaled to the clerk that everything was arranged, and left by the rear door to the guests' livery stable. The yard, surrounded by a high adobe fence, was being sprinkled with water from a bucket, by an old Mexican who glanced up at Ross and removed his sombrero. "*Buen' tiempo*," Ross said. Glancing around, he saw a large woodrick at his right, a line of slop barrels to the left, the long horseshed before him. There was an alley between the hotel and a bank at the right. He walked quickly to it and passed between the buildings to the street. Glancing downstreet, he saw Shelton and Pard Mallet riding slowly toward the hotel, still a hundred feet away from it. He walked out, turned left and strode to the front of the bank. He stepped into the alcoved entrance and almost fell over a Mexican watchman who sat cross-legged, nodding, at the door. The man looked up, inquiringly. Ross took a cigar and a match from his pocket.

"*Mucho viento*," he said, nodding toward the street. He struck the match and touched the flame to the cigar.

"*Sí patrón, mucho viento!*" said the watchman. Ross stepped back into the street.

Shelton and the other man were now approaching the hotel. Ross saw Pard quickly pull in his horse. The blacksmith stared at the tied pony. Shelton's voice came curtly.

"What's the matter? Do you know it?"

Pard shrugged. He would have ridden on, then, but Shelton put his hand out to stay him. "Wait a minute! Is that one of the horses you and Ramsey have been using?"

"Thought it was, at first."

"You know damn' well it is!" snapped Shelton. Ross saw the swift lighting of his face as he rode over to the pony and inspected the saddle. He saw him draw the carbine, look at it and ram it back into the scabbard. "What's Ramsey doing in town?" Shelton asked Pard.

Then Ross knew that Pard had not told him about Blade's death. Still he did not understand their coming in together. All he knew was that he must handle this well. As he walked toward the men, he kept his eyes on Pard, not knowing what to expect. Pard's face looked ill-tempered and dull. His hat was tilted down over his left eye. Shelton discovered Ross first, and involuntarily pulled rein. Ross noticed with a frown that the flanks of Shelton's pony were striped with deep spur-gashes. Then he saw the man's free hand go to the Colt at his hip. Ross stepped short and stared at him, his own hand close to his gun. Then he walked slowly to the rail.

"Have you boys teamed up?" he asked them.

"God forbid!" Shelton said. He scrutinized Ross, glanced up the street as though to determine where he had come from, and then said in a hard, low voice: "You move around quite a lot, for a mustanger."

"You find wild horses in the damnedest places," Ross said.

"Yes. And sometimes we have to snaffle them down pretty snug to bring them around."

Shelton's voice had risen as he spoke. Ross did not think he was aware of it. About him there was something so tense, so rigid, that Ross thought, *He's at the breaking point*. He thought of the girl in the room upstairs, watching them and listening, and for the first time he perceived something about Shelton: Shelton's need of Laurel was ruthless and compelling. He had got her the only way he could—at forced sale. But the core of him was so tortured by the loss of her that you could see it in his eyes like a madness. You could hear it in his voice when he said:

"Be sure I'll have her back, Chance! This country's not big enough for her to hide in. Tell her that when you see her."

He lifted the reins and let the pony move a few strides, but halted to say through set teeth: "And tell her this. If she comes back, we'll forget everything. Including you. Tell her that."

Ross said sadly, "You won't get it out of your head that I've hidden her somewhere, will you?"

Shelton's tongue touched his lips. He shook his head slightly. "No. No. I won't," he said.

"And I won't get it out of my head that I owe you a crack over the head with a gun barrel," Ross said as Shelton started on. But the rancher did not reply.

Pard remained there, gazing with dull melancholy at Blade's horse. Ross spoke quickly, then. "Where's he going?"

Pard kept his muddy, stupid gaze on Ross. Then he looked at the saloon entrance a few feet from the hotel. "Christ, ain't that *cantina* open *yet?*" he said.

"What were you doing with him?" Ross demanded.

"Run into him on the way in. Seemed like neither of us wanted t'other behind him. So we came in together."

"All right," Ross snapped, "what did *you* come in for, then?"

Pard tilted his head down a trifle to stare at him. Between them lay the memory of their last meeting—over rifles. Yet the old man's eyes, those whiskey-shot eyes which could look mean as a sidewinder's, were somehow fogged with bewilderment. Suddenly he pulled his hand from his pocket. Ross flinched and had thrust his shoulder behind a scarred white column when he saw that all Pard held in his hand was a couple of coins.

"What'd you do it for?" Pard asked. "Like a God-damned undertaker layin' him out for burial. Pennies over the eyes! Why'd you do it?"

Ross rubbed his nose. "I don't know, Pard. Just something I felt like doing. What's it to you?"

Pard threw the Mexican coins into the dust. "You go to hell!" he said, racked by an emotion Ross could not fathom. Ross said quietly:

"*You* made me kill that kid."

"Like hell! Trackin' you was Blade's idea. You can't whip a man and walk out on it thataway. Look what that fella, Hackley, done. Sometime you ought to think it over."

"Sometime I will. When men like Hackley and Blade give me the time."

"*I'm* givin' you all the time you need, Ross," Pard said, his face breaking oddly. He massaged his eyes, as though his weariness were about to overcome him. "Listen to me, boy. Blade's gone now. And Gunlock's gone. This thing's going clean to pot, if you and me don't hang together."

"It never was any more than a nightmare," Ross said.

Pard fashioned a grin. "That gal, Francie, is still out there. Jesus, Ross, she's a piece for any man! And she took to you, she shore did! You come on out with me. Shelton's good for one more shakin'—it's going to be the Tecolote ranch, and then quits. Couple of thousand apiece if we decide to sell it. Two thousand and a gal like Francie! And you a young buck. If I was your age..."

"So long, Pard," Ross said. "Give me plenty of room next time you see me coming. Maybe you'd better take off somewhere. As soon as I can get this all down on an affidavit, some warrants are going out. I wouldn't fall dead of surprise if one of them had your name on it."

"I'd fall dead," Pard said viciously, "if they ever took me before I took three of them!"

Ross laughed, mounted the horse, and jogged down the street.

26

THE HOTEL DINING ROOM opened before the barbershop. Having
stabled his horse behind the hotel, Ross ate at the tall counter
among well-dressed travelers and businessmen who glanced
curiously at him. It seemed to him he had not worn decent
clothing nor kept a shave on his jaws in years.

He had four cups of coffee from a big percolator surmounted
by a brass eagle. He ate a breakfast steak, three eggs, and some
Mexican *pan dulce*, and took pleasure in letting his belt out as he
sauntered from the café. The barbershop was open now. Four
barbers in white aprons were shaving the well-to-do jowls of
Amargosa. As he waited his turn, Ross gazed out on the
wakening activity of the town. The morning procession of
water-bearers was well under way. Someone was burning leaves
in the plaza. Buggies rolled by on jouncing leather springs.
Across the square he saw a water wagon sprinkling the street.

Ross mounted a chair, gratefully stretched his legs across a
red plush stool, and lay back while the barber whipped up lather
in a community shaving mug. He reclined drowsily under hot
towels. The bell over the door tinkled. A customer entered, and
Ross's barber said cheerfully:

"Little wait, Marshal. Ten minutes."

A tingling started in Ross's hands, and ascended to his
shoulders. He lay stiffly under the polka-dot apron, half
suffocated by the towel.

"How early," asked the querulous voice of Marshal Will
Coles, "does a man have to get up to beat the wolf pack?"

"Earlier'n this," chuckled the barber.

Ross could hear the razor whispering on the strop. It went
briskly, hesitated, stopped. Then, as Coles's boots passed before
the chairs, it resumed. A little too fast, thought Ross.
Something's going on. He wanted to tear the towel away and sit
up. This damned spaniel of Shelton's! He'd shoot a man before

he'd risk taking him alive. Coles stopped before his chair. Ross visioned the sage-colored eyes peering fiercely at him through their stell-rimmed spectacles. Coles said something Ross could not hear.

The towel was suddenly whipped aside. The barber placed the razor-blade against Ross's throat. "Now, then, mister," he said, "just lay quiet. And nothing will happen."

Coles was standing beside the chair. He looked unnaturally tall and thin with his high-crowned Stetson set squarely on his long head and the ragged sideburns coming past his ears like dewlaps. He held a gun in his hand and was smiling a thin bloodless smile with a gold tooth at the corner of it. His collarband was as dirty as ever; the gold button shining in the middle of it only emphasized its dirtiness, thought Ross. His face was exactly the color of mountain granite.

"Don't move, Chance!" Coles said dramatically. "Until I git your gun. And manacle you."

As Coles took the Colt from him, Ross asked loudly: "What the hell is going on? Get that razor away, God damn you! Coles, what are you trying to do?"

He gave the barber a shove and sat up. "Look out!" a man said tensely. Customers reared noisily in the chairs. But Ross stayed in the chair, confronting the marshal angrily.

"You know what this is fer," Coles stated, as he locked a manacle on Ross's wrist.

"How would I? I'm not a mind reader . . . assuming there's anything here to read."

Coles flushed with anger; Ross did not know why he could not leave this male old maid alone. He brought out the meanest in him. Coles jammed the other cuff on so tightly it pinched, and Ross swore. Coles stood back, the Colt level.

"This is for the murder of George Gunlock," he declared.

Ross's face sobered; then he suddenly began to laugh. "Oh, so that's it! The boy detective, eh? Is this according to the instructions they mailed you last month, Will?"

A stranger in the chair next to Ross began to grin. Coles, whose dark star it was never to be taken quite seriously, bristled. He tensed forward. "Listen, you—you worthless horse-catcher! This is as bad a mess as a man could get into! Unless you've got God, luck, and the best lawyer in the Territory o' New Mexico on your side, you'll hang within six months! Git up, now."

Ross rose. He took his jacket from the antelope prong on the wall, and slung it across his shoulder with his manacled hands.

Without a word, he walked to the door. But here he paused and turned back. The faces watching him—pink-shaven, half-shaven, snowy with lather—were rapturous with excitement and the story they were going to tell their wives later.

"No, sir," he said. "A man could get into a worse mess than this, Will. He could get up to his eyeballs in something a lot worse than this."

Coles marched him to the cathedral end of the plaza and brusquely turned him north to the jail two blocks up, in sight of the railroad station. *I bungled it!* Ross realized. *Henry may not know I'm here until it's too late. God knows what this fool would do to save his own bacon.*

He was thinking this as Coles prodded him into a cell. The first thing Coles said was:

"Where's Mrs. Shelton, Chance?"

Ross extended his hands toward him. "Take these off and maybe I can talk."

After removing the irons, the marshal repeated his question. "Where is she? Because somebody I know will shoot the guts out of you if you don't tell us."

"Somebody you know too damn' well," Ross cut in.

Coles's prim granite-like face stiffened. "How so?"

"I've been hearing things about you, Will. You were Shelton's lawyer on the sale of my dad's land to him, weren't you?"

Coles wore so little expression that it was difficult to tell when something scored on him. But his fingers made a convulsive movement with the manacles; they jangled softly.

"Yes, I represented him."

"What'd my father get for the land?"

"Twenty-four thousand, as I recollect."

"What'd you get," Ross asked, "for keeping quiet about the fact that he didn't get anything—let alone twenty-four thousand?"

Coles's pale eyes watched him. "Sometimes you talk like a maniac."

"You're not denying anything," Ross pointed out.

"I deny that there was anything irregular about my part in the deal," rapped the marshal.

"You still aren't denying that it was blackmail," Ross said.

"How do I know whether he collected the money or not? I represented Shelton—not your father. It wasn't my lookout whether he got paid. Although I assume," he said stiffly, "that he received his money in good order."

"No, you don't," Ross said. "Or you wouldn't have tried to murder me, night before last."

With a savage gesture, Coles jarred the door closed. "Do you want to make a statement?" he asked. His face was frozen, his lean rack of a body stiff, and his terror as plain as the trembling of his lips as he set them together.

Ross frowned at him a moment. "Yes. I'd like to go on record as thinking that my father was not only robbed, but murdered."

Again Coles challenged, "How so?" but so dully that he hardly seemed to make it a question.

"I had it from a man who ought to know. He claims the colonel got pestiferous when he saw he was going to lose the rest of his ranch for taxes. He had nothing to lose anyway, so he was going to expose Shelton's whole plan. Of course that would have wrecked Shelton, too. So he was beaten to death near Tecolote camp."

"Who does your informant say perpetrated this crime?"

Ross walked to the cot and sat down. The supporting chains creaked. "I'd like to talk to my lawyer," he announced.

"You go to hell!" Coles raged suddenly. He pressed his face against the strap-iron grille. It resembled the face of a mountain goat. "You come in here mouthin' lies like that, you can keep them to yourself a while! Sweat you down to size in a few days, Chance. You ain't so—" His voice broke.

"What's the matter, Will?" Ross prodded. "I wasn't talking about you, was I?"

Marshal Coles pivoted and walked rapidly down the corridor.

An hour later, he returned, surprisingly, with a tray of breakfast. Wordlessly he passed it into the cell. He had adopted a gruff-but-fair manner. An iron tension was on him.

"The charge—" he began, but he was forced to clear his throat. "The charge against you is that you killed George Gunlock in a brawl on the train. Lamar Shelton is the complaining witness. He states that he was forced to corroborate your story earlier by threats of retaliation. As proof of the fight, we have Gunlock's gun, found in the caboose, with a shell fired in one chamber, and a bullet hole in a cupboard of the same caboose. Do you deny this?"

"No," Ross told him. "It proves he threw down on me."

"Then you admit you were lying before?" Coles's eyes glittered triumphantly.

"Sure. Both of us were. But I wonder how you'll ever prove which one of us knocked Gunlock off the train!"

"The burden of proof, at present, seems to be on you," the marshal pointed out.

"Gunlock," said Ross, "will be a forgotten man, after I open up in court.—When will I be arraigned? I've got a lot of things to talk to the justice about."

From his pocket, Will Coles took a rum-soaked cigar, started to light it, and then offered it to Ross with something resembling a smile.

"Not after you've handled it."

Coles looked away. It was killing him, Ross knew—having to take all this from him. But he was under the gun, and he knew it. "Listen, Chance," he said. "This is irregular, but—I'm going to give you a chance. You stand trial and you'll swing, sure as hell. You work for me, and I'll work for you?"

Ross closed one eye. "How's that?"

"That sale. . . . I knew it wasn't right, somehow, but I figured it wasn't any business of mine. So I didn't puny around in it, just wrote the papers and forgot about it. If you go dragging me into it now, I'll be in a mess, don't you see?"

"I sure do."

A plaintive note crept into Coles's voice. "I worked like hell to put myself through law school, Chance. It was hard going—never come easy to me, since I had to shave spokes to make expenses. And then the clients I got were always drunks or somebody wanting a divorce. I always did have the God-damnedest luck. The deck's always seemed to be stacked again' me."

"Mmm."

"So I took this job, when it was open. I've done an honest job, too. Chased the tarts out of the saloons and threw the fear into the crowd that used to raise hell in the plaza—the Spiks, you know."

"What's that got to do with me?"

"What I said—you go opening up that old business, and how'll I look? 'He chased out the whores,' they'll say, 'but he was no better'n a whore himself.' That—that'd kill me. I don't figure I merit it."

"Why not? You took that chance when you helped rig my father."

"I didn't rig him! I—I told you how it was."

"No," Ross said, "that land transaction was just how it started. But you were into it, then. And when Shelton needed a man for a job, you were it. If I knew for sure you helped him kill my father, do you know what I'd do to you?"

Coles watched him sop the blue-black coffee. "I'd beat your face off," Ross said. "Then I'd drag you up on the bandstand and tell them all what kind of a marshal you've been to Amargosa. Murder the men you're paid to protect . . . like myself. And I'd testify against you, and come to the hanging."

For a moment the marshal was wordless. He looked down. Slowly he began to speak.

"Just as sure as you're in here, you're going to hang. Unless you let me help you. And I will, to protect my name. I'll give you a hundred dollars and leave a horse out back, where you can find him. But you'll have to do one thing for me before you leave."

Ross shook his head. "No, I can't tell you where she is. How should I know?"

"Then we can't make a deal. Shelton would raise hell if I let you go without finding that out."

Ross smiled. "I guess it seems pretty foolish to you, eh? Passing up a chance to get myself bushwhacked again at Clear Fork. But the minute I come up before the justice, I'm going to have my say. And it'll be over for you and Shelton."

Coles's green eyes rose solemnly, full of pain and menace. "There's just one hell of a good chance," he said, "that you won't come up before no justice. There's a good chance that you'll be shot while escaping."

He went away with a soft jingle of keys.

27

Ross's CELL WAS at the rear of the jail, on the south side. Past a vacant lot he could see the stage depot, and beyond that a store on the northeast corner of the plaza. Between these two buildings was discernible just a wedge of the square itself.

Ross gazed out the window for some time, striving against the agony of impatience in him. He took a cigar from his pocket, but remembered the marshal had taken his matches. He held it in his teeth and turned back into the cell pondering desperately....

That damned hotel clerk. If I scared him into the thing, he reflected, Shelton could scare him out. He'd give her up for a dollar.

As he sat there, Ross seemed to hear his father lecturing him, as he always had, irate and red-faced, savage with contempt, disappointment, and love.... *Never did a thing right in yo' life! Bungled every last thing you ever laid a hand to! Pick yo'self up, now, Goddamit, and quit yo' whinin'*. But perhaps he had not been the feisty little top sergeant because he wanted to injure. Perhaps he had a fear of being injured himself. And this son of his, this lout who stood inches taller than he and behaved like a cub—he was the supreme pride and shame of his life. The best horseman in the county, and a stockman in his own right—and by God if he didn't make an ass of himself in a saloon and get in a fight in a whorehouse!

Somewhere in the jail a man was talking in a high, nasal voice. The words were indistinguishable; the tone was plain. This person was telling another how it was going to be, and Ross, his face slowly coming up, recognized that it was Henry Lyman. In a moment a door opened and Marshal Coles and the lawyer came down the corridor. Coles unlocked the door of Ross's cell.

"Have to lock you in, Lyman," he said.

"All right," the lawyer said. "But be back in fifteen minutes or I'll sue you for your eye teeth."

Ross watched the little dandy of a man enter and in some distaste inspect the cell. Henry Lyman did not acknowledge the large roach-haired man on the bunk. Lyman, as always, wore a fresh pleat-front shirt and frock coat. His boots were square-toed, the color of polished rawhide. Everything about him was neat, ordered, and reassuring.

As Coles departed, Ross went forward and slapped him on the shoulder, smiling with relief and affection. "You know," he said, "I had the funny idea you might not know I was here for two or three days. Who told you?"

"What kind of a town do you think this is?" Lyman retorted. "A community of deaf-mutes? I knew you'd been arrested ten minutes after Coles put the manacles on you. I've been over at the courthouse ever since, trying to get a writ for your release. Couldn't swing it."

He placed his elbow against the high sill of the window. "Two days," he frowned. "Two days and where the hell have you been?"

Ross went back to the cot and lay down, one leg propped across the other. "In heaven, for a while," he said, "and in hell the rest of the time. I killed Ramsey, Henry, when he and Pard jumped me in the hills. And Coles and Lamar Shelton tried to bushwhack me, too. I've been pretty busy. And now Shelton's hunting for his wife, with a whip in his hand. God knows what the fool will do if he finds her."

The lawyer received this news with fatalistic lack of expression. "You can kill all the pardners you want, as long as you do it out in the hills," he said, "but I wish you'd leave other men's wives alone.... Do you think Shelton will find her?"

"I don't know."

"Do you know where she is?"

"In the Gadsden Purchase, under the name of Mrs. Smith. I just left her there."

"My God, man! How long do you think it'll be before the town's talking about *that?*"

Ross told him about the early-morning registration, but Lyman did not reassure. He lighted a cigar and threw the wax wick of the match through the window. "How far have things gone between you and this lady? Is there any reason you can't forget about each other?"

"Just one," Ross said, with a smile.

Sadly, Lyman contemplated him. "The fact that she's married doesn't cut with you?"

"Three days ago," Ross reminded him, "*you* were telling *me* her marriage wasn't on the level. Now you're going preachy on me."

"I'm not preaching," snapped the lawyer. "I'm just— Well, God Almighty, what's her husband going to be doing while you two carry on?"

"We aren't planning to carry on. She's going to get an annulment—you're handling it, you ought to know. Then we'll start in as though he'd never existed."

"Let me get this clear." Lyman held the cigar precisely between two fingers. "First you oust Mister Shelton from his land and throw him in the plaza without a nickel. Then you steal his wife.—One thing about your father," he declared. "He knew men from the spurs up. You seem to have mistaken Shelton for a flash-in-the-pan."

Ross shook his head. "No. But I got enough from Pard to know where to start on recovering the ranch. The tax angle—I don't know about that. Maybe we'll lose it all over again to the Mexican government. But in the meantime, Laurel's going to shake him off. You know yourself the man forced her into the marriage."

"And a man who'd dragoon a girl into marriage that way won't give her up to anybody. As long as Shelton's alive," Lyman stated, "he won't see her in any other man's arms. You ought to know that."

Ross glanced at the floor. He said, "Yes. I guess I do."

"Then what are you and Laurel going to do?"

With an impatient gesture, Ross walked to the window. "I don't know. That's what I thought you might be able to tell me."

Lyman's voice softened. "Ross, if you weren't playing with gunpowder, I'd tell you everything was going to be all right— don't worry about a thing. But in the first place, you're in jail on a murder charge, and who knows how *that's* going to come out? And in the second, you've set out to violate one of the basic precepts of community living—leaving other men's women alone. And in the last place, Lamar Shelton is probably the toughest, trickiest, rock-hardest man either of us ever knew."

Ross did not speak. He continued frowning at the floor.

"Don't you see, Ross, what you've taken on?" Henry said. "Only a certain kind of man would send an old man to ruin to steal his land. Only a certain kind would railroad an honest lawman into prison to get rid of him. And then buy his daughter on the proposition that he'd get the old man out of jail, when he hadn't the slightest intention of doing it. It's a man with a knife where his morals ought to be. It's a man who'll take chances that would send anybody else running for cover. He'd make a hell of a fine general or a marshal, because coming out on top is all that matters a damn to him. He isn't capable of quitting even when he's licked."

All this Ross knew, but he found himself still arguing against it. "But even a man like that can be hanged, can't he? And Pard Mallet all but admitted to me that Shelton had something to do with my father's death."

Lyman's eyes showed a mild surprise. "I'd often wondered about that," he said, "but I never heard it suggested before. Now that I've heard it, I can't see where it changes anything much. If Pard's the Territory's witness, it's only his word against Shelton's, ain't it?"

"I don't know. I don't know whether he had any proof or not. And he and I aren't testifying for each other right now, anyway."

It was quiet in the cell. In the distance a drum boomed; a horn could be heard, its notes short and brazen. It made Ross wonder how a man's life could be so uncomplicated that he joined a marching club for something to do. The cell was full of the blue-gray sharpness of the lawyer's cigar. And now Henry began speaking in his dry counsel's voice, and Ross tried to follow him. But all he could concentrate on was a gray-eyed girl in a room a few blocks away—a few blocks that were more remote than the moon.

"Yesterday I run down to El Paso on the morning train and had a talk with a government lawyer I know there. I had to talk all around the subject, of course—*if* this, and *suppose* that—but he promised to look up some things for me. About the government's responsibility for international lines, and so forth. . . . Well, no use worrying you about it now. He's going to wire me what he finds out."

A lock jangled, and Marshal Coles's spurred tread sounded on the packed earth floor of the hall. Lyman spoke rapidly, then.

"Here's our defense, Ross: Gunlock's gun had a burned shell in it. That proves he fired at you. It was self-defense, savvy? You were driven to hitting him."

Ross nodded. "That sounds good enough to me."

But after that it was a day of waiting, again.

Around the plaza, the Amargosa Grays marched to drum, fife, and horn, and afterward there were ragged volleys of shooting in the field next to the slaughterhouse. It was noon; it was past one; Laurel would know by now that there was trouble.

At two-fifteen, Marshal Coles unlocked the door. He was grinning, this time. He looked unconscionably happy. There was an odor of brandy about him. "How'd you like to walk out of here for a while?" he said.

"Great," Ross said sourly.

"Serious!" Coles said. His smile showed his bad teeth and made him appear foolish. He was more pitiful drunk than he was sober. "Somebody's went your bail."

"Bail on a murder charge?"

"So far as we know now, it's only assault to commit same."

Ross scrutinized him suspiciously. "Yeah? Who went it?"

"Party didn't want to be mentioned."

It struck Ross that Laurel might have done something this idiotic. Hearing of his arrest, she might have risked being found by her husband to get him out. But he did not dare suggest it to the marshal.

"Okay," he said. "Let's go."

When they entered the marshal's office, he perceived that another man was here. Hands on hips, he stood gazing at the shelves of patent medicines left by Laurel Shelton's father, but as Ross entered he glanced around. It was Lamar Shelton. At once Ross saw that the pressure was off him. He looked quite easy in his mind; his face was relaxed and he smiled faintly. A slow fire of alarm began to burn in Ross.

"Hello, jailbird," Shelton said.

Ross turned to Coles. "Where's my things?"

Coles laid them out on the desk—a little money, a pocket knife, a comb, a handkerchief, a block of California matches.

"Where's the gun?" Ross asked.

"In my safe. You'll get that when you're cleared."

Ross coolly lighted a cigar. He restored his belongings to his pockets. He was at the door when Shelton said:

"No hurry, Chance. She's left."

Ross halted, staring into the sunlight, his face set. "She's left where?" he asked, not looking around.

"She left the hotel where you left her," Shelton said.

Ross turned. Flames of joy burned in the rancher's eyes. He stood with an elbow against the wall, his coat flipped back to expose his gun. Ross was sick with wondering.

"What hotel," he inquired sardonically, "did I leave her in?"

Shelton shook his head. "She's not there, anyway. I moved her to a new place." Then, seeing Ross brusquely turn away, he added, "What's left of her."

28

OUTSIDE, THE SUNLIGHT was lemon-yellow, the shadows were sharp, but everything seemed off-center. Ross was frightened; he wanted to ask help of someone. He felt he had come as far as he could; now it was up to someone else. If Laurel were hurt, he would kill Shelton, and after that it did not matter one damn bit what they did about this world.

He did not think he was capable of carrying the bluff any further. He had to know whether Shelton was telling the truth. He turned back.

But as soon as he looked into the rancher's face, the conviction struck him that Shelton was playing a smart card to see what it drew out. He looked too intent. He looked like a coin balanced on edge.

"You don't play enough poker," Ross told him. "I can see your hole card from here."

"Then you ought to be able to see my aces."

Ross lingered, tormented by the fear that Shelton was telling the truth. But all Shelton betrayed for sure was satisfaction at causing pain. True or not, he knew what he had said was torturing Ross.

Ross turned away. Coles's voice followed him. "Where to, Chance?"

"I'm going to get that shave you broke up."

"Well, don't try leavin' town, or I'll lock you up again."

In the chill sunlight, Ross walked to the plaza. The marchers had cleared away, but many people, Mexican and American, roamed the plaza. Children threw rocks, baited dogs, hung to their mothers' skirts. Ranchers from out of town were in to buy supplies. The racks were crowded before saloons and *cantinas*.

Ross walked behind the bandstand. But the bench Laurel had indicated was occupied by a picnicking ranch family. He stood near it, but for a long time did not risk looking up at

Laurel's window. Then he shot a quick glance at the green blind near the end of the gallery. It was drawn. He looked away. He had told her not to give herself away; yet now he prayed that she would give him some sign that she had seen him. He did not dare stare too long. If Shelton had set the trap, he would be watching him.

When the cigar was burned out, Ross gazed once more at the window. The blind seemed to stir; but other blinds stirred in the same breeze. There was utterly no sign that she watched behind it. At last he left the plaza.

It was necessary, he realized, to follow his own orders to Laurel: to give no clue whatever that she was in town. He returned to the barbershop. There was a long wait before he got into a chair. He was recognized, but no one spoke to him except the barber, who said agreeably:

"Reckon we'd better soften them whiskers again, eh?"

"I reckon," Ross said.

He had everything but a manicure. He still felt ragged and nervous when he left the barbershop. He glanced up the street. He did not see anyone watching him, and now he walked quickly into the lobby of the Gadsden Purchase Hotel. It was full of cattlemen and drummers, and a few ladies who occupied most of the chairs. He walked to the desk, without fully knowing what he was going to ask. A clerk glanced up—not the man who had registered Laurel.

"Has Mrs. Smith checked out?" Ross asked him.

The man smiled. "I don't think we have a Mrs. Smith registered. Though," he added, "we may have had. The Mrs. Smiths don't generally stay long."

Ross grinned sheepishly, as though he were privy to the joke. *Do I dare pump this fellow?* He threw a glance at the entrance. The muscles tightened down his back. Will Coles was tying his pony at the rack. He said hastily, "Thanks just the same."

"Don't mention it. Maybe someone in the bar can help you find Mrs. Smith."

Coles had tied the horse. Appearing more relaxed than usual because of the liquor in him, he was drawing off his gloves as he peered into the lobby. But it was crowded, and dark, and Ross did not believe he had been seen. He walked quickly through the entrance to the bar.

The saloon was crowded. At a table near the lobby entrance, a burly old man sat with big Tom Bailey, who ran the mercantile across the plaza. A joking crowd of men surrounded them. Ross noticed that they had their chairs sidewise to the table and each had one elbow planted on the table; they faced each other with their hands locked, arm-wrestling style. It was a moment or two before Ross realized that Bailey's opponent was Pard Mallet. Both men looked intent and a little irritated; they were waiting for a signal before trying to force each other's arms back.

A man thumped a gold piece on the table. "Five dollars Pard takes him again!"

Someone covered him. Other bets were made before Pard challenged: "Twenty-five too much for you, Tom?"

Bailey bristled: "Not if you keep that elbow on the wood."

Pard bristled. Ross read his complexion—purplish and sweaty, it showed that he had been drinking all day. "Are you saying I tinhorned you?"

Tom Bailey—old enough to know better, but obviously in his cups also—thrust out his chin. "By God, you keep your elbow down, or I'll say it!"

"Get to it!" the man who had put the first gold piece down called. "One—two—!"

On the signal, both men lurched slightly in their seats. The stout forearms corded. Pard's face thickened with tension, the rutted brow glistening with perspiration. They thrust and parried, feinted and powerhoused; at last Bailey's arm wavered and went backward. The back of his hand touched the wood as he went off-balance.

Pard shouted his laughter. Tom Bailey paid. The other bets were adjusted, and Pard was about to suggest another round when his eyes found Ross's watchful face. He seemed to start. The beery good nature drained out of his features. The man who had won on him said:

"Come on, Pard—rub this for luck!" He was holding out a good-luck piece.

Pard rose, finished his whiskey, and shook his head. "Later on, Ed. I'm goin' out back."

Ross observed him come through the crowd, which began to break up. Pard came to him and without looking at him muttered, "Want to talk to you, Ross." At a lurching roll, he passed the roulette table, rested a steadying hand on the mechanical piano, and went out the back door. Ross was certain that something new had occurred to upset him. He followed into the yard. There were privies across the yard, but Pard was waiting by the door. He looked very drunk, very old, and very worried. He peered at Ross with a murky frown, put out a hand to the pebbly adobe wall and steadied himself.

"What are we going to do about him, Ross?" he asked.

"About who?"

"Jesus God, man, who do you think I mean?" Pard said thickly. "Shelton! Gunlock's gone, Blade's gone—I thought you was gone, when I heard they'd locked you up. That'd only 'a' left me. He'd 'a' got me soon enough."

"You're drunk, Pard," Ross said. "I don't know about Gunlock, but I know he didn't kill Blade."

"He set us to wrangling, though, didn't he? He knew we'd argue over whether to keep after him, if he showed fight. *He* knew what he was doing!"

The drunken logic escaped Ross. "That's cutting it pretty fine."

Pard's swollen features squinted. "Too fine for that fox? Listen—I'm going to tell you...No," he said, with a pained frown. "I can't tell you."

Ross gripped his arm. "What is it, Pard? Is it what you started to tell me before? About my father?"

Pard Mallet brushed his hand away. He gazed at the privies. He began moving uncertainly in that direction; Ross paced him.

"You said one thing that's right: he'll get to us soon enough. If you've got anything to tell me, you'd better make it now."

Pard stopped. Ross's hand steadied him. He saw tears in the old blacksmith's eyes. "Jesus, boy, things shore do get out of hand, don't they?" Pard whispered.

"Sure do, Pard."

"This—this thing I was going to tell you...Well, look," Pard said, "if you can git Henry Lyman to his office, I'll come up and give a depo—What do you call it?"

"Deposition."

"Yeah. I ain't told anybody this before. It'll set some people right on their tails in this town! I done it once, and I'll do it again. You git Henry up there, and I'll come in about fifteen minutes."

"Is that a promise?"

Pard raised his hand, grinned in a pained way, and lurched on toward the privies. Watching him, Ross thought that if there were a picture to chouse a man into the Christian life, it was this: an old man with tears on his face, tottering toward a saloon privy. Misery rampant on a field of whiskey bottles.

Fifteen minutes...He knew that Henry worked every afternoon except Sunday. And now a desire possessed him that he could not put down. He had to know whether Laurel was all right. If she were not, then there was no use wasting time with Pard.

The next thing would be to get his carbine from the stable and go after Shelton.

He returned directly to the saloon, walked through the door into the hotel lobby, and stood by the desk. He saw that Coles had either gone on or not come in after all. Shelton was not in the room. Ross pivoted and strode to the rear stairway. He went up quickly, turned at the landing, ascended to the second floor. Standing tall and straight, he glanced up and down the hall. He could hear faint sounds from the saloon.

There was only the width of one room to the blind end of the corridor at his right. The uncarpeted hall ran, unlighted, for some distance to the left. But no one was there. Ross quickly crossed to Laurel's door. He rapped with one knuckle. He whispered the girl's name.

For a few seconds there was no answer. Ross raised his hand to knock again, but suddenly he began to perspire. He was shaken and sick. If she were gone . . . Then he rapped again.

"Laurel!" he whispered. "Laurel!"

Bedsprings creaked, and he stood there with a hand braced at either side of ther jamb, wondering if it would be a strange face he saw: a man, perhaps, or another woman, a new occupant for a recently vacated room. Footsteps came to the door and halted. There was an interval of silence.

"Ross?" a voice whispered.

"Yes! For God's sake, are you all right?"

The lock scraped, the door opened, and she stood there in the dusky room, her hair rumpled with sleep, her eyes drowsy, her body slender as a candle in her white petticoat. "Of course I'm all right!" she said. "But where were you?"

Ross moved her out of the way and closed and locked the door. He leaned back against the door, gazing at her. "I was in jail," he said. "But Coles let me out. Shelton said he'd found you and moved you. I fell for it. I came straight to the hideout, and they probably aren't far behind me. I was a damned fool, honey. But that's what comes of being in love."

She came to him. Ross's arms enclosed her with desperate need. His fingers pressed the flesh of her back, feeling the slender bones under the thin garment, and a terrible vision came of Shelton tearing the clothes from this thin, precious body and violating it with the fury of frustration and vengeance. He buried his face in her hair and held her with all the strength of his body.

At last she was drawing him to the chair by her bed, and seating him there she sat on the bed by him. "You weren't in the plaza," she said, "so I knew something had happened."

Ross told her about it, but his attention was as much for sounds in the hall as for Laurel. He wished he had stopped in the hotel stable for his carbine. He tried to think ahead, but his mind was sluggish.

"I knew it was something like that," she said. "I waited until noon, and then I was so tired I lay down. I didn't know another thing until you knocked on the door. Oh, Ross—" she said, touching his face and smiling, "don't worry. It'll be all right."

"I'll stop worrying when you're in Tucson," Ross told her. "There's a ten-o'clock westbound tonight. You'll stay there until your husband is behind bars."

Laurel's eyes, the last of the drowsiness gone from them, watched him. "On what charge?"

"Fraud, for one thing," Ross said.

"How long would that give us?"

"Maybe a couple of years," Ross said.

"Do you think that will be long enough? Wouldn't he be the same when he came out?"

"You know that better than I do," Ross said. "Would he?"

Slowly she shook her head. She reached up to press a crumpled lock of black hair away from her brow. "He'd never forgive me for what I did to him—nor you for what he thinks you've done."

Someone was coming up the stairs. His boots were placed quietly and carefully on each riser as he mounted. Slowly, Ross came to his feet, gazing with stiff features at Laurel. She looked steadily at him. The footsteps were a man's, heavy, with a faint chime of spurs. They reached the top and Ross could see him in his mind standing rigidly with one hand on the newel post, gazing up and down the hall.

Then the footsteps came toward the door.

29

Ross laid his hand on Laurel's shoulder. Lying on the floor beside the bed was her small nickeled revolver. He bent to pick it up. A hand took the porcelain knob and twisted it gently. Ross faced the door with the gun in his hand. It felt like a toy; the trigger-guard pinched his index finger. He could see the knob turn slowly to and fro. Then it was silently released. They could hear the man move quietly down the hall.

Neither of them said it—but they both knew it had been Shelton.

Ross stepped to the window and pressed the blind aside. The plaza was still crowded, but the shadows were long, blurred by dust. He searched for any sign of Marshal Coles. When he did not find him, he turned back.

"Are you afraid to stay alone?"

She still sat on the bed, the pistol in her lap, where Ross had placed it. She shook her head.

"Then I'm going to crawl out the window to the gallery. Henry's office is at the end of it. I don't dare leave by the stairs, now, because they'd see me."

"But why must you go?"

"Pard Mallet's going to be at Henry's in a few minutes. This could be the most important thing that's happened since Shelton ruined my father. Pard's tying one on, and if I don't get him now, I may never have another chance."

He raised the lower sash of the window, keeping the blind over it still. "I'll leave the shade down. If he tries to force the door, come onto the gallery and down to Henry's office. But I don't think he'll dare. He can't break down every door that's locked."

He strode back to her and tilted her face up with a finger under her chin. "Believe me, I wouldn't leave you if I dared to stay. But I'll be back with Henry—by the window, understand—

a little before traintime. Then you can sit back and relax for a while."

"Never," she said, "until you're with me."

In the corridor, the man walked quietly, slowly, back to Laurel's door. He hesitated here an instant. Then he was heard descending the stairs. Quickly, Ross kissed her and hurried to the window. "He'll be watching the gallery. Remember—if he comes back, come to Henry's office; don't hang around."

He stepped onto the gallery. He felt vulnerable as a fly on a wall. Though other rooms had doors onto the railed porch, he was the only figure on it. Below him was the soft dusty turmoil of the street, a moving pattern of horses' backs and riders' hats, of the long dark gowns of women and quick-moving coveys of children. In the dusty heart of the square, he saw gray-uniformed men with the green sashes of the marching club.

Ross turned quickly to the right and walked to Henry Lyman's office. Standing at the screen door, he gazed in. He could see the racks of tawny cowhide books along the left-hand wall, the desk with its back to the gallery, the map of Doña María County on the far wall. A man sat in a chair facing the door, while another stood behind him, talking animatedly. The man in the chair was Pard Mallet. Glancing up suddenly, he saw the figure of Ross, and started to lunge from the chair, his hand groping for his Colt. Ross pulled the door open and stepped inside.

Seeing Ross, Henry Lyman grasped Pard's hand. "Now, cut that out!" Pard's face was choked with unhealthy color; the mottled spots of gray in his cheeks looked like frostbite. Recognizing Ross, he sank back.

"Why the hell didn't you come down the chimney?" he panted.

Lyman, too, appeared puzzled. Because he did not trust Pard, Ross did not wish to explain before him that Laurel was only thirty feet from them at this moment. He told Pard with a grin:

"I took a shortcut."

"Pard says he's got something to tell us," the lawyer said.

Pard rolled his weight against one arm of the chair. He looked preoccupied with his misery, an old giant with a rotten body. "You got anything to drink?" he asked Lyman.

Henry glanced at Ross. "After the other day, I put in a supply." He brought Pard a third of a tumbler of brandy. "This stuff is going to kill you, Pard," he warned.

Pard absently raised it in a gesture of salute. *I'll bet he does that when he's drinking tap-water*, thought Ross. "Everybody," Pard said, "gits killed by something. Do you think a lunger gets any more fun out of t.b. than I do out of whiskey?"

Henry pursed his lips. "I feel like there's something wrong with that thinking, Pard, but I'll be blessed if I know what. Now, get to it."

Ross walked to the safe, where the liquor was kept, to pour himself a drink from a glass on top of it. He heard Pard sigh windily. He heard him ask, "You're a notary, ain't you?"

"Certainly."

"Put this down over your seal, then: Pard Mallet, being of as sound a mind as he ever was, saw Lamar Shelton kill Colonel Bob Chance on the twenty-second of April, eighteen eighty-one."

Ross turned, the neck of the bottle still against the rim of the glass. He stood that way a moment, conscious that they were both watching him. Then he finished pouring the liquor, drank part of it, and walked to the screen door above the street, still holding the bottle and glass—a solemn, dark-haired young man, his jaws smooth with recent shaving, and no emotion in his face except regret.

"What do you think of that?" Pard asked.

"I think I ought to be horsewhipped for leaving here," Ross said.

"Rot," said Lyman nasally. "You couldn't get along with him a week, even now. It's one thing to know a man, another to be able to live with him."

Ross looked at him as he raised the glass, hesitated, and took the wisdom with the brandy—both felt good inside him. "You know, I reckon you're right," he said.

"I know I'm right. It's the curse of a man like the colonel to end his days alone—with two or three friends who've learned to love him in spite of himself, but everyone else driven away."

Pard looked disappointed that he had not created more stir. "I suppose I ought to grab a gun and run out into the street yelling," Ross said. "But I don't feel that way. I feel like what happens to Shelton should be slow."

Pard grinned. "Apache style, eh? Head down over a slow fire... Man! I hope I'm there."

Ross looked sadly at the lawyer. "It seems like he had to die to please a flock of strutting buzzards, doesn't it? Everybody got something out of Rancho Pacheco at the last but him. Shelton got big spending money and a young wife, and Gunlock finally got a lottery that paid off. Even Will Coles got something—prestige. Silver plating over his tin badge."

He gazed drily at Pard. "And you got the most of all. You got to see a man squirm that you didn't have the guts to stand up to yourself. You hope you're around when I fix Shelton's plow—but you don't have the guts to do it yourself."

"I'm prepared to testify again' him—*that's* standing up to him, ain't it?"

"You mean you've been scared into testifying against him. Now that he's backing you into a corner, you're ready to tell what you were afraid to before."

"No," Pard retorted. "I wa'n't never afraid to. But I couldn't get much out of him dead, could I? So I let him be."

"If that's the way you see yourself, then you'd better sober up sometime and take a good look. You never were worth a damn, Pard. You took money to change an international boundary. Then you retired on an annuity of what you could do to other people if they didn't keep you happy."

Henry broke in briskly—smoothing it over while Pard was still of a mind to talk, Ross perceived. "Well, Pard, maybe we're all the way we are because the Lord willed it. . . . Now, how about it? What was the way of Shelton killing Colonel Chance?"

For a moment it seemed that Pard Mallet was through talking. But he continued for the same reason he had begun—for reasons of personal safety.

"It was out at Paso Redondo," he said. "I'd done a little day work for Shelton there. I didn't work for him regular, you know. There was leaks in the water tank, and I drove a wagon out with a barrel of cement. I drained the tank and worked inside. I was plastering over the leaks when I heard them talking. I never did hear them ride up. I clumb the ladder and looked out and they were at the other side of the pond."

"Could you hear what they were talking about?" asked Lyman.

"No. Mostly they was cussing each other out. They were on horseback, facing each other. All at once the colonel swings on Shelton with that bull-pizzle quirt he carried. Shelton tore it away from him and pulled his Colt. He clubbed him with it a couple of times and the colonel's horse took off. The old man fell out of the saddle, but his foot caught in the stirrup. The horse was still running, the last I saw of it."

"Did Shelton make any attempt to stop it?" asked Lyman sharply.

"Hell, no! After a while he looked around. He stared at the camp. I was afraid he was going to come over and see if I was there. The wagon was out of sight behind the tank, so I reckon he didn't know I was around. Pretty soon he left. But he pumped me about when I'd finished, next time I seen him. I put him off, though. To this day, I don't think he has any idea I was there."

"What do you want us to do about it now?" Lyman asked harshly.

"Jail the son-of-a-bitch! Ain't that what you do with murderers?"

"Yes, and Coles may jail you, too—as a material witness."

Pard frowned, dug at his ear, and shrugged. "That's all right. Shelton won't be sniping at me, at least."

Lyman looked at Ross, who was smiling faintly as he recalled Coles's warning: *You may be shot while trying to escape....*

"I think it better," said Lyman, "for you to hide out somewhere, however. There are safer jails than the one Marshal Coles keeps. One of the Grays might lob a shot through the window while practicing—according to Coles."

Ross took another drink of the brandy, contemplating the blacksmith. "Are you going to stay with this story, or back out when it comes to trial?"

"I'm with it all the way, Ross. To tell you the truth, I wasn't shook up much by the colonel dying; but it's time justice was done."

Henry Lyman plucked his hat from an antelope prong on the wall. "Then let's get over to the marshal's office and put it in writing. I'll see that you aren't locked up."

It reminded Ross that Laurel was still in danger, and he wanted to clear things with the lawyer before they left. So he told Pard, "Go downstairs and have a drink. We'll meet you at the bar."

Pard went out. Ross explained what he had done. The lawyer shook his head. "I don't like this, Ross. It's like walking around with a diamond in your hand, daring anybody to take it. The minute we take our eyes off it, Shelton's just likely to take it."

"Then I'll stay here," Ross said, "and you get Pard squared away."

"All right. I think that would be safest."

He was at the door when they heard the noise in the street. It sounded to Ross as though a fight had broken out in the plaza. It grew, coming closer to the hotel—a clamor of men's voices shouting something: a single word seemed to be repeated. At last it came to Ross what they were saying, and a slow process of freezing began in his spine. He looked steadily at Henry, waiting for confirmation in the lawyer's face. It struck the sour-eyed little lawyer very suddenly; he stared at Ross.

"Aren't they saying 'Gunlock'?" he frowned.

"It sounds like it, don't it?"

Abruptly, Lyman rushed onto the gallery. Ross turned to watch him as he stared down into the street. He heard a wagon approaching slowly, a mournful clop of hoofs, a patient grind of tires. Lyman said, "Yes. It's Gunlock."

Ross drifted onto the gallery. Upstreet, just passing the bank, a yellow spring wagon was moving with difficulty through the crowd of men, boys, and dogs that surrounded it. From all parts of the square, others were rushing toward it, jumping benches, dodging shrubs. Will Coles, mounted on his bony gray, went ahead of the wagon, trying to open a path for it. Behind the driver of the wagon, a man knelt beside a blanketed form on the bed.

Lyman began drawing Ross back into the room. "You'd damned well better stay here! There's no bail for murder, Ross. They've found out what they wanted to from you, and now they'll be ready to lock you up again."

But Ross pulled his arm away. He went forward to lean on the railing, his body tense. "Henry!" he said. "Look at this . . ."

Lyman came up beside him. He drew a quick windy breath. "For God's sake!" he exclaimed. "He's moving. He isn't dead a-tall!"

30

THE RAILROAD MAINTAINED a small hospital for its employees on Hidalgo Street, behind the courthouse. Marshal Coles was explaining to the crowd—the wagon having been forced to stop—that they were moving George Gunlock there, when Ross and the lawyer stepped from the hotel. Coles at once spotted them in the crowd. He leveled an arm at Ross.

"Chance!" he said. "Come here."

Heads turned toward the tall man by the shriveled lawyer. Lyman snapped at Ross, "I'll talk to him," and pressed ahead. But Ross followed him.

They stopped at the rear of the wagon, where Coles was. The man with Gunlock was Doctor Hangos, the little Greek railroad doctor. Ross remembered him from long ago. Hangos was sitting on the wagonside, now, gazing thoughtfully at the former Pacheco ramrod. When Ross saw Gunlock he set his jaws together sharply.

Gunlock was regarding him with tranquil brown eyes shining beneath a turbanlike bandage. He was as pale as tallow. He wore a cheap serge suit evidently provided by the railroad, and a blanket was tucked about his legs. His scimitar-cut sideburns, coming below the bandage, were a false note of cocksureness, for the face was the mild, ascetic one of a dying monk. Gunlock's body was here, but he gave evidence of having left some of his mind in the Rio Grande.

Coles's nose tones came stridently through the inquisitive, noisy quiet of the gathering. "The doc don't know whether he'll live or die," he said. "If he dies, Chance, you see where that will put you. If he lives—well, he can sue you for your socks. *After* you get out of prison."

The doctor threw an angry glance at the marshal. "Will you be quiet?" he said sharply.

175

Gunlock's hand stirred from under the blanket. He reached it toward Hangos, shaking his head very slightly.

"Has he signed a complaint?" asked Henry Lyman.

Coles shook his head. "He can't be questioned yet, the doc says."

"Then why all the big talk?"

Coles said pointedly, "There's another complaining witness, Lyman. It don't matter whether George talks or not."

"I wonder if it could be the same man I was coming to your office to see you about?" Lyman smiled.

Something changed in Coles's face. "Who's that?"

"I'll tell you in your office. But for the time being, don't you think it would be a mercy to get this man to the hospital?"

Doctor Hangos nodded and spoke to the driver. "Go ahead, man."

"No. Wait."

It was Gunlock's voice. Rather, the voice came from Gunlock's lips, for Ross had never heard it before. It was low and distinct, though feeble. Ross's hand closed slowly on the gate of the wagon, as he gazed dumbly at the foreman.

A man stood on the hub of a rear wheel to stare at Gunlock. The wagonsides were lined with faces. Except on the fringes of the crowd, there was silence.

"Don't make trouble for him," Gunlock said, with a little wedge of silence between each word.

"How's that?" Coles bent over the saddle horn to scrutinize Gunlock.

"Don't bother him, I said," Gunlock repeated. "I say I started it."

"Tell us about it, George," Lyman suggested.

"We had a fight. I don't exactly remember. . . . I pulled my gun. He hit me. And I fell off the train."

"Don't you remember why we were fighting?" Ross asked him.

Gunlock's white face frowned. "No. I—"

"You and my partner cheated me out of some money."

"I reckon—yes, that was it."

The man standing on the wheel hub spoke breathlessly. "What happened to you, George?"

"I fell onto the bridge and rolled off. I drifted a long time. I was holdin' onto a log."

Coles came in again, acidly. "And if it hadn't been for that log you'd be a dead'n, now."

Gunlock's mild, far-off manner hardened as he looked up at Marshal Coles. "But if Ross hadn't hit me, he'd be the dead'n, Will. I was drunk. And crazy." He was quiet for an instant, and then his eyes turned up to the sky. "I reckon I've been crazy for a long time."

Doctor Hangos winked at the driver. "Drive on, man."

As the wagon stirred ahead, a man asked: "What's a-matter with him, Doc?"

Hangos pressed his palm against his own back. "Broke," he said.

In the gauze of dust raised by the wagon there remained after a moment only the marshal, the lawyer, and the mustanger, as the crowd moved with the wagon or hurried off to pass the news. Coles looked down in perplexity at the lawyer, and Lyman said:

"Go on. We'll pick a man up and meet you at your office in fifteen minutes."

Pard Mallet had remained in the saloon while the ramrod made his brief halt in the street. He and Ross hurried him through his drink and went onto the walk. Ross told him that Henry would handle the deposition, and Pard shrugged and started toward the jail with the lawyer. Ross hurried upstairs to the lawyer's office.

The clock now said three-ten. Ross lighted one of Henry's bitter cigars and stood at the gallery door to smoke it. For some time he stood here, thinking of Laurel, only a few yards away. He wanted to return to her; to call her name and be reassured that she was still in the room.

It struck him abruptly that he was still unarmed. If Laurel came to him and Shelton followed her, he would be helpless against the rancher. Making a sudden decision, Ross left the office and went to the hotel stable. He procured his rifle and returned.

He finished the cigar and lighted another one. He sat at the desk and leaned back in his chair, trying to deceive himself into relaxation. He filled his mouth with blue smoke and let it rise to the ceiling. At this moment, Coles would be taking Pard's affidavit regarding the murder. Then the warrant for Lamar Shelton's arrest would be sworn out, and Marshal Coles, goaded by Henry, would go out to find him.

I'll bet he hasn't the guts, thought Ross. Shelton would never let himself be jailed. You could not blame even a straightforward marshal for hesitating over such a job—let alone a man like Will Coles.

At three-forty-five, Ross paced to the door and stepped onto the gallery. Early dusk was coming over the plaza, slanting its long brassy bars of light through the chinaberries. Ranch wagons were rolling from the village; out-of-town cowboys began to drift in for their infrequent Saturday nights. But there was no indication of Lyman on the walk.

Thinking into it, Ross did not know what he expected Shelton to do. Of Shelton, you could expect only the unexpected. He would not submit to jailing, he was sure. On the other hand, Coles might be enough of a lawyer to predict that Pard Mallet's testimony would be poorly received.

They had not discussed the effect of such a trial on Rancho Pacheco. Of course it would blow things wide open: to establish the motive, it was necessary to expose the fraud. Amargosa would be a nine-days' wonder. Government surveyors, lawyers, and hordes of curious would move in to look at the disputed land and argue about it.

At four-fifteen, Ross knew something had gone wrong.

He laid the carbine on the desk and drew the loading tube. It was full. He snapped the hammer on an empty chamber. Reloading the gun, he worked the lever once and put a shell under the firing pin. Then he laid it down and walked onto the gallery. He inspected the street carefully before he called quietly:

"Laurel!"

Almost instantly she answered him. "Yes, Ross!"

Ross said, "I'm going out for a few minutes."

"All right," she said.

Ross backed into the office, turned to the desk and scooped up the gun as he hurried by.

31

AT THE CORNER by the cathedral, he ran into Henry Lyman hurrying along with his coattails flipped back and his hands buried in his hip pockets. A red anger glazed Lyman's face. He did not see Ross until Ross seized his arm and held him from passing.

"Oh, that God-damned billy-goat of a lawman!" he groaned.

"What's wrong? Where's Pard?"

"In jail! As a material witness...."

Up the cold autumn street with its traffic of leaves and dogs, Ross could see the jail, crusted with scabs of old plaster. "We've got to get him out, Henry! He's the only leverage we've got on Shelton."

"You don't have to tell me my business, boy," Lyman growled. "I've been with the justice of the peace for a half-hour, but he won't give me a writ. He says it's for Pard's own protection."

"What about the warrant for Shelton's arrest? Will Coles serve it?"

Lyman kicked some adobe from the broken corner of the building. "They wouldn't even issue one. And the hell of it is, the justice is right. He won't issue one until Pard comes to him, cold sober, and tells him the same story."

"In the meantime, Pard's apt to sober up with a bullet in his belly."

Lyman grunted. "I've done all I could. It's about five hours till traintime for Mrs. Shelton. I suggest you hike up and get her a ticket. We don't want to have to stop for anything when we put her on her train."

"All right. Are you going back to the office? Somebody ought to be there."

"I'm on the way right now.... By the way, check at the telegraph office and see if there's anything for me."

179

At the station, Ross bought Laurel's ticket. He checked the traintime: ten-ten. An eastbound was taking on coal and water; her passengers strolled the tracks. In a few moments that brief, sooty string of cars would be gone. Ross thought of the beautiful simplicity of going away on a train, of slipping painlessly out of the intolerable—turning off the light in one room and turning it on in another. He had done it once himself. He knew the clean feeling of stepping down on a new range, finished with the old.

But you had not killed the men and events that had driven you away. Sooner or later, they called you back. Looking down the darkening street, he knew it: *I couldn't leave again if I wanted to.* He had taken one step toward Amargosa, and been swallowed up. He was part of Amargosa now, and it was part of him.

He took a side street back to the hotel, cutting through the hotel barn, and then passing through the saloon to the office stairway. In the office, Lyman asked him, "Was there a wire for me?"

Ross sighed. "I've been wool-gathering, Henry, I didn't ask."

"Sometimes I think you care less about that land than I do," Henry said sourly. "I ought to hear from that government man pretty soon, if I'm ever going to." He spun his chair and gazed out the screen door. The blood of sunset spilled across the sky; the smokes of Amargosa washed over it.

"I remember," he mused, "the first day he came to me, a little, banty-rooster of a man with a chip on his shoulder. 'I'm looking for a lawyer with some brains,' he said. 'My name's Chance.'"

Half-listening, Ross heard Henry going on, detailing with a lawyer's pride how he had stalled creditors for years during the rough times, to pin those little rags of land together on a map called Doña María County, and when it was all finished, it was the finest ranch between El Paso and Lordsburg.

All at once, finished with reminiscing, Lyman rose, took a pistol from a drawer, and shoved it under his belt. "I'm going down now and have some dinner," he announced. "Then we'll put Mrs. Shelton on the train. After that we'll buy a gallon of coffee and set about sobbering up Pard Mallet. The minute he makes his statement and I get a warrant for Shelton, I'm going to see that he's jugged."

Lyman stepped to the gallery door. "Every night at five-thirty, for the past twenty-five years," he said, "I've stepped onto this gallery and dropped my final cigar into the street. People have got into the habit of watching out for sparks. It won't look unusual if I discard my cigar five minutes early—and check on Mrs. Shelton at the same time."

Ross watched him step outside, draw on the cigar as he strolled down the railing, and pause to look over the plaza. He spun the cigar into the street. Then he called softly:

"Mrs. Shelton."

Ross waited by the door.

"Mrs. Shelton!" Lyman said again. When there was no reply, Ross saw him walk farther toward the girl's window. A ripple of tension went up Ross's back. Again he heard Lyman call Laurel, but there was no reply; and suddenly Lyman came striding back to the door. He looked at Ross out of a face rigid with shock. His hand gripped the edge of the door. Without a word, Ross thrust him aside and strode up the gallery. He halted at Laurel's window and raised the green blind with the barrel of his carbine. The room was dim. While his eyes adjusted, he made out the white bulk of the bed, the shapes of the chair and chest of drawers. At last he saw that the door was open into the hall.

He stepped through the window. Standing in the silent room, he looked at the rumpled bed. Nothing gave the slightest sign that a girl with black hair, and lips that had whispered his name in ecstasy, had ever been here. The prayerlike thought seized him—maybe it's the wrong room! Then the odor of lavender reached him.

Sitting on the bed, Ross hunched over with his forehead gripped in his hand. Suddenly he thought he heard her voice, and he sat up stiffly, looking about. But the room was empty. There was no closet, nothing but the large commode, which yawned open.

He crossed to the hall door and stared up and down the shadowy corridor. He turned back, but with sudden weariness leaned against the jamb and regarded the empty room helplessly. He heard Henry Lyman coming to the window and now the shade was raised and a yellow cowhide boot was thrust through. He did not seem to be able to stir his mind from this room. When he tried, mentally, to follow her, he immediately stood at the crossing of a hundred trails.

Lyman scratched a match and deposited the small flame on the oily wick of a lamp. Replacing the chimney, he glanced around. At once he saw something else which had escaped Ross. He lifted a paper from the foot of the bed and read it. He raised his eyes to Ross's, then, and said slowly:

"This is how he did it. 'Laurel,' it says: 'We've got to leave at once. Follow the boy who brings this to the stable. Horses are waiting.' Signed..." He cleared his throat. "Your name," he grunted.

Ross snatched the letter from him. It was written on plain paper; the writing was unfamiliar. "My God, Henry, she ought to have known I didn't write it!"

"Had she ever seen any of your handwriting?"

Ross frowned, and shook his head. "I guess—I guess you're right. But why didn't she check with us?"

"Maybe she tried to. We were both out for a while, you know. Personally, I don't think there was a boy. I think Shelton shoved it under the door himself. When she opened it to look things over, he—"

Ross tore the paper savagely. "Where do we start? My God where are we going to start, Henry?"

Henry scowled. "It would help if we knew a few things. Did Coles pass the word to him that Pard's going to testify against him? If he did, then Shelton may be planning to take off with the girl. If he didn't, maybe he's holding her in some other hotel room...."

There was a shout in Ross which wanted to be released; there was an anger and a terror which kept expanding. He wanted to strike out, but there was nothing to strike at.

"The stable!" Lyman said abruptly. "He must have taken her out the back way. We can ask out there."

They went down to the stable yard. But there was only one groom in the barn at this quiet time of day, and he had not seen Shelton enter or leave the hotel, though he knew him. Lyman, who was acquainted with every hotel clerk, roustabout, and banker in Amargosa, made inquiries at the desk. The hotel manager told him no one had checked out within the hour, nor had any messages been sent up.

"Thanks," the lawyer said tersely.

As he pushed through the lobby to the street, Ross was aware of people staring at him. He reached the paper-strewn walk before the hotel and looked around with quick glances. Henry was at his shoulder.

"All right, let's start with the streets. I'll work from here up to the station. You nose around the plaza and work down to the canal. I'll meet you at the jail in forty-five minutes."

Ross nodded. But for a time after the lawyer marched east toward the church, he merely stood there. At last he crossed to the plaza and walked quickly from one side to the other, then from end to end. Then an urge to haste seized him, and he ran down the little street slanting west, past El Minuto Café into the scrubby Mexican-town. But he halted, panting, in the dark, smoky village with its quiet sounds and soft laughter. He turned and ran south to the canal. He passed Tomás Archuleta's walled home. He thought of the remorseless progress of that ancient sin of his. Because he had bribed Pard Mallet to change the international boundary, an old man had been murdered, a girl had married a man she did not love, a marshal had died in a Mexican jail—and a girl, perhaps, was undergoing a night of pain and terror.

It was dark before he finished his search. He had stared through uncurtained windows and cut across back yards, and at last, blocked and desperate, he came onto the southeast corner of the plaza, by the church. Though the night was glazed with cold, his body was drenched with perspiration. A few lanterns gleamed on the bandstand of the plaza, smoky halos of dust floating about them. The little desert square was almost deserted now, but in an hour the band would draw the crowd back.

Ross started toward the jail. Not far from it, a shadow separated itself from a tree. Henry Lyman's voice asked quickly:

"Find anything?"

Ross shook his head, and the lawyer said almost angrily, "I checked the station, too. No sign there. Not one damned sign anywhere! I think they're still in town."

Ross leaned against the tree. "It's all gone to hell, Henry! Everything. I wish to God I'd never met her. Then I couldn't have got her into this."

"There's a few hotels in this town," Lyman said. "Let's look over the registers."

Ross was past reasoning. He was grateful for an order he could follow. "All right," he said.

They split up again and Ross began a tour of the smaller backstreet hotels—the cheap one-night rooming houses where cowboys, hard-up drummers, and travelers put up between trains and stages. Lyman had given him a list of them. He asked questions, but listened less to the answers than to what the faces of the proprietors said. It was more than an hour before he met Henry again in the Gadsden Purchase Bar. They had a drink in the crowded Saturday-night saloon. Lyman set his glass down hard.

"Let's go talk to Coles now."

They walked to the jail. A thin coal-oil light illuminated the office, with its legacy of medicinal odors left by the late Marshal Henderson. But Coles was not there. Looking at the big nickel-plated clock on his desk, Ross saw that it was after nine o'clock. Lyman opened the corridor door with a ring of keys which lay on the desk.

"Maybe he's feeding the prisoners."

"There aren't any," Ross said. "At least there weren't when I was here today."

"Always a few drunks Saturday night," said the lawyer. "And there's Pard, some place or other." Lyman took the lamp from the wall bracket and peered along the short hall with its strap-ironed doors on the right, the blank wall on the left. Looking across his shoulder, Ross saw that the hall was empty. He started to turn away, but the lawyer started down the corridor. "There's the drunk tank, out back."

They passed through the jail to the windy back yard. In the feeble glow of the lamp, Ross saw a wind-scoured stretch of ground marked by a woodpile, a dusty heap of coal, boxes of ashes, and a privy. There was a small adobe shack near the back alley. It was windowless, had a flat, *viga*'d roof and a strong door. Before Lyman reached the hut, the wind pinched out the lamp flame.

When Ross came up, he was trying keys in the large bronze padlock. It snapped open, and the lawyer stepped into the cell. There was the sulphurous fizz of a match. "Ross—look at this!" Lyman said.

Ross looked down at the familiar, shaggy head of Pard Mallet. Pard looked like the prototype of a temperance deacon's drunkard. An empty quart whiskey bottle. He was crumpled limply with his feet under a cot amid a litter of old newspapers and tobacco trash.

Henry went on one knee by him. "This fellow's dying, Ross!" he said.

"Dying?—dead drunk!" Ross commented.

Lyman's match went out. In the darkness he stood slowly. "There is such a thing, you know.... There was a case in Tennessee when I was a boy, where two men made another drink a lot of whiskey, as a joke. He died from it.... I wonder if anybody's been playing jokes on Pard?"

Ross fumbled for matches. He found one, lighted it, and relighted the lamp the lawyer had set down. "Maybe somebody's been slugging him."

But there were no marks on the blacksmith. He breathed in a

deep, snoring fashion. His face was lead-gray. But at last his face distorted with effort and he seemed trying to raise his head. When he failed, Lyman said quickly:

"Stay with him. I'm going for a doctor."

Ross worked with the man while Lyman was gone. He got Pard onto the cot, but his head rolled loosely on the fat, unshaven neck. At last his eyes cracked open and he dragged an unfocused glance about the ill-smelling cell. Ross shook him.

"What's the matter, Pard?"

Pard's tongue slurred over some meaningless syllables. He went slack against the wall, staring glassily at his feet.

It was Doctor Hangos, the railroad doctor, who finally came. Henry, the doctor informed Ross, had stopped for a suds-pail of coffee. He was a swarthy, graying man of about forty, with curious brown eyes behind gold-rimmed spectacles. He deposited his bag on the floor and make a quick, frowning examination of the blacksmith.

"Just drunk?" Ross asked him.

"Among other things. His heart's running like a three-legged horse. This is alcoholic poisoning."

"What's that mean?"

Hangos, straightening up after Pard was lying flat on the cot, said: "He must have been putting it down as though he was afraid of a shortage. I'd say he's got over a quart in him. Honest to God, some men must be crazy!"

In the darkness, Ross heard running steps and the tinny clank of a lid on a pail. The lawyer brought a dripping beer-pail of coffee into the room, set a cup on the floor, and filled it. He and the doctor commenced trying to get some of the coffee into the blacksmith.

For a while, Ross's mind had been taken off Laurel. But now he stepped into the yard and felt his fear squeezing down on him once more. He gazed up at the frosted night sky, and tried to think. He heard a horse moving quickly toward the jail; a rider came into the vacant lot and jogged toward the shack behind the jail. As he recognized Marshal Coles's high-crowned Stetson, Ross suddenly moved to the corner of the woodpile and waited. The horseman rode along the side of the jail and dismounted at the edge of the yard. He came toward the hut, pulling off gauntlets, a stooped, tall figure with his Stetson set four-square on his head. He moved with nervous haste. Distant light glittered on the cartridges in his shell-belt. Ross stepped into his path.

32

"IN A HURRY, Marshal?" Ross asked.

Coles made a small bleat and took a step backward, raising one hand. "Oh—Chance!" he said at last.

"*Last* chance, Marshal," Ross said. "Where is she?"

"She? Mrs. Shelton, you mean?" Coles asked.

Ross made a swift move with the gun. The gunsight slashed the marshal's cheek, and he gasped in pain and moved away. Ross's voice stretched tight with savagery.

"Talk straight, if you're ever going to!" he said. "Because if you don't, you'll be laid out in rock salt tomorrow. *Where is she?*"

Coles dumbly shook his head. His eyes were large and wet behind his round spectacles. "Is she—still gone?"

Ross took a step toward him. The barrel of the gun prodded the lawman's belly. A fit of wild anger seized Ross. He heard his voice ringing from the hard walls of the adobe buildings.

"*Where is she, God damn you?*"

"I—I don't know," Coles said huskily. "I ain't seen her since..."

The gun swung again; the walnut butt thudded against the side of Coles's head. His knees loosened. He fell forward into Ross. Ross sidestepped and let him crash to the ground. He stooped to take the marshal's gun and thrust it under his belt. In a moment Coles recovered his senses. He looked at Ross, winced, and struggled to his knees. "Chance, for God's sake—!"

"Get up," Ross said. "Walk into the jail."

Staggering, the marshal crossed the yard toward the jail. They went into the dark hall. With the marshal halfway to the office, Ross ordered him to halt. He shoved open one of the cell doors. "Get in there," he said.

Coles entered the cell. Ross set the carbine against the wall outside the door. He went in and faced Coles.

"What did you do to Pard Mallet?" he asked.

"I locked him in the drunk cell," Coles said, "I was just coming back to see if any of his friends had brought him any whiskey. We've got to get him sober before he can make a statement."

"You mean you were coming back to see if he was dead yet."

"No! My God, Ross," the marshal exclaimed, "what do you think I am?"

Ross's hand ripped off Coles's spectacles and he threw them against the wall with a bright splatter of glass. He struck the marshal on the jaw. Coles reeled to the wall and slid down against it. Ross lunged after him, jerked him up by his shirt and sent him stumbling into the middle of the room. Sobbing in panic, Coles tried to push him away as he followed. A fist rocked his head. Blood was pouring from his nose. He looked old and sick and pitiful, but Ross could not see him: all he saw was Lamar Shelton, telling him what to say, what to do, in case this happened, or that. He hooked a left into Coles's head and when the marshal fell aside he arrested him with a smashing blow to the face.

Coles was down again. He lay perfectly still until Ross kicked him in the ribs. "Get up, you old goat! You can stop this when you're ready." Writhing, the marshal crawled away and used the bunk to raise himself. He staggered as he faced the big, angry man bearing down on him again. Ross slammed an overhead right into his temple, and now the marshal collided with the cot and fell across it. He lay limply upon it. Ross stared at him, breathing heavily.

"Pass out, and I'll dump you in the rain barrel till you're ready again. You've had your picnic. Now we're going to have ours. *Where is she?*"

When Coles continued to lie on the bunk, Ross seized him by the arm and pulled him to his feet. Coles's arms hung limply. He could not hold his head erect. The bloody, white old sheep's-face waited in dumb misery for the next explosion of pain. Then his lips moved.

"Shelton and the woman left on horses. An hour ago. For Mexico."

● ● ●

Ross ran into the yard. In the drunk tank, they were still working over Pard Mallet. Pard was speaking thickly to Henry Lyman.

"Kept pourin' it. Into me, Henry. Wouldn't let me—alone."

Ross filled the doorway, straight and tall, with the glitter of excitement in his face. "They've left for Mexico," he said. "Coming with me, Henry?"

Henry Lyman turned. "How's that?"

"I shook Coles up. He says Shelton sent the note in and they grabbed her when she came out. Locked her in another room on the same floor. Coles stayed with her till Shelton finished with Pard. They left at sundown."

"How about that, Pard?" Lyman turned swiftly to the old man.

The doctor held a cup of coffee to his lips, but Pard ignored it. "Slugged me. When I spit it out. Wouldn't—let me . . ."

"You won't get anything out of him tonight," Doctor Hangos said. "What was all the to-do about the marshal?"

"You'll read it in the papers, George," Lyman said, rising from the bunk. "Of course I'm going with you, Ross. And anybody else we can round up."

He gave the doctor instructions for moving Pard and setting a guard over him. Then he and Ross ran to the street. As he turned toward the hotel, Ross said: "Just the two of us, Henry. Coles said that Shelton told him he'd kill the girl if anybody followed them. That he'd shoot her and make his getaway."

The lawyer halted. He gazed at Ross. "But you're going to follow anyway."

"I've got to."

"Well." Lyman's thin shoulders stirred. "Well, I'm glad it's not my decision. It's not much of a choice, is it?"

For the first time in hours, there was a quietness in Ross, the shadow of a smile on his mouth. "Whatever happens, Henry, I'll be with her again. That seems like a pretty fair trade, to me."

Lyman always drove a polished black rig to the Gadsden Purchase barn, and at six o'clock it was inevitably ready for him, his appaloosa patient between the shafts, the reins tied to the whipstock. They found it like this when they reached the stable yard. A Mexican hurried from the barn as they entered the yard, removing his big straw sombrero to hold it against his belly. He began chattering Spanish.

"'*Sta 'ueno, 'sta 'ueno, Enrique*," said the lawyer impatiently. "I was held up. And now what I need is a saddle horse."

The holster gave Ross a look of silent reproof, as though he were leading astray an old and beloved friend. "Four years you are not on a horse, Meester Lyman. Seence you fall on the stairs."

"Well, I'm going to be on a horse tonight. What've you got?"

Ross interposed. "Hold on, Henry. You're not going to be able to keep up with me anyway. Why don't you take the buggy and follow me?"

"Follow you where? What road are you taking?"

"There's only one quick way to Mexico from here," Ross said. "And I figure he won't leave without a few supplies. I judge he'll stop at Paso Redondo and pick up blankets and food. Maybe even go by the ranch and take all the cash he's got. Though I don't think he'd risk the ranch hands getting onto what he's doing."

"So what do you plan to do?"

"Get to Paso Redondo first."

"And then wait? What if he meant what he said?"

Ross frowned at the rifle in his hands. "I don't know . . . I'll try to outfigure him between here and there."

"And what if you miss him there?"

Ross walked into the barn without answering.

He found Blade Ramsey's big bay gelding and threw blanket and saddle onto him. He thrust the carbine into the boot. He mounted and ducked under the lintel of the door as he rode into the yard. Henry was on the seat of the buggy. As Ross reined over to him, the horse restive, the lawyer told him wistfully:

"I never felt old before Ross—not handicapped, at least. But I wish to heaven I were on that horse and you were in this contraption. I feel like I've got a stake in this, too."

"Sure you have. I'll put a bullet in him for you, if I get a chance."

"I'll tell you something," Henry said gruffly. "Not being a woman, I can't speak with authority. But it might be a lot better from Laurel's standpoint if somebody besides you did the shooting, if there's any done."

The idea had lain like a minor irritant in Ross's mind for some time. But he did not comment, and Henry went on:

"Maybe it wouldn't matter to her, at first. I'm thinking about the effect of gossip, though. It might begin to wear her down—the eternal whispering that you shot the husband to get the girl. That's why I wish I was on that horse."

"I'll worry about the ethics of husband-killing later," Ross said. "Just now I'm worrying that I may not get a chance to kill him." He let the horse sidestep toward the high gate in the adobe wall.

"Good luck, boy," said Lyman. Then he added soberly: "*Y vaya con Dios.*"

"Adiós, Henry," Ross said.

33

FROM THE FIRST, there had been no possible conclusion for it but this. When Laurel smiled at him at the Las Truchas railroad station, an end had been established as well as a beginning. It was something too primitive to have a civilized conclusion.

There were such tales in the Bible. Two men, one woman, reducing, through violence, to one man and one woman. If the wrong man lost, the woman came to love the other man merely because he had fought for her. No one was ashamed to admit that it was possible for a man to love another's woman; nor that it had to end violently.

But civilization sometimes put chains on one of the men. As he crossed the bridge over the canal, Ross turned over what Henry had said, and knew it was true: *It might be better, from Laurel's standpoint, if someone else shot him.*

How did you handle a murderer with kid gloves?

According to Will Coles, the rancher had left about eight-thirty. It was nearly ten, now. Shelton and Laurel were more than an hour out on the dark apron of prairie sweeping up to the mountains. There was no certainty whatever that they had taken the route he was following. Shelton might ride east or west and try to catch a train at some water tank. But seemed to Ross that his first, instinctive thought would be to get out of the country.

Riding steadily, a man could ordinarily make Tecolote Camp in about five hours; another two to Paso Redondo. But a girl on a sidesaddle was a slow companion. An unwilling one like Laurel might retard him miserably—the trick would be to retard him without provoking Shelton's hair-trigger temper.

Ross worked through a rough scrape of hills and gained one of the small scythe-like valleys. By the light of a white paring of moon, he tried to find behind him a sign of dust on the freight road; but it was only a pale streak ascending the hillside. Fear fluttered in his breast like a blind moth.

He crossed the valley with the night wind on his cheek, a wind toothed with frost. He began making the sort of desperate pact with Providence which a frightened man made: Let her be all right, God, and I'll join the church. I'll learn to pray. But let her be all right now.

Life, which seemed so complex, was really a very simple proposition. A man was a damned fool to get agitated over the trivial things, when all he really needed was a woman—the woman. Take her away from him, and all his precious gather of possessions was trash.

Then he was breasting a roach of sagebrush along a ridge and seeing the broad, pale arm of a valley beneath him—windswept, tarnished with moonlight, the road deserted. He cut at the horse's rump with the ends of the reins.

After some time he realized the gait of the pony had become broken. Its hoof struck a stone and it nearly fell. Ross angrily pulled it in and dismounted. While it blew tufts of steam, he walked up the road, as if he could store up distance for use when the horse was ready to run again. On a sudden impulse, he knelt in the road and made a shelter with his hat. He struck a match and held it inside the hat, like a storm lantern, to examine the roadmarks. But there were many hoofmarks, a dozen broad stripes left by the tires of freight wagons. If Shelton and his unwilling bride had come this way, there was no way of telling it. He would not know their hoofmarks from any others.

Ross straightened to gaze toward the south, his hat hanging from his hand. At last he turned and walked back to the horse.

The night had rubbed thin when he came to the Tecolote camp turnoff. A man with imagination could detect the rust of daylight in the east. He could pray that dawn would be brief and brilliant. He could ride with anxious haste into the yard of the deserted ranch house and search for indication that anyone had passed there, and see nothing at all to cheer him.

But after Ross had sat the pony in the yard for a time, it occurred to him to look for hoofprints again, and this time, close to the cabin, he found where two horses had stood long enough to create twin, trampled patterns in the earth. He straightened. The muscles of his body snapped to tautness. He walked to the cabin and examined the ground about the stoop. Here he found a man's bootprints and the much smaller prints of a woman's boots. He crossed the porch and kicked the door open. Standing in the dark cabin, he struck a match. A candle, gnawed by camp rats, stood in a sardine can on the sink. Ross lighted it and began a quick inspection of the room.

There was a cigar butt on the floor near the round ovenlike fireplace in a corner. Ross picked it up. The chewed end was moist. He flung it into the hearth and pivoted to examine the room.

They had been here: he knew that, now, and he knew it could not have been long ago. He ran from the cabin.

The trail to Paso Redondo was up Clear Fork—the route Ross had followed yesterday. He crossed the creek and afterward let the horse pick its own way. The moon was deep in the west. The rimrock walls of the canyon were obscure on either side, but above the east wall the sky was lightening. On the brushy canyon floor the cold had packed down during the night. A windless dawn had commenced as he reached the stubbled willow growth at the confluence of Clear Fork and Turkey Creek.

A pink light as cold and pure as ice was spreading through the sky. It was not strong enough to form shadows, but its chilly glow made the trail plain, while leaving the rimrock marbled with darkness. Ross dismounted to study the trail where it split—left to Paso Redondo and the main freight trail it had splintered from miles back, right to some of the smaller and more distant ranches along the border. Shelton and the girl had taken the left fork. Ross was about to follow when he realized what this would mean.

A man being followed always heard the pursuer first: pursuers traveled with speed and noise. So Shelton would be waiting for him, unless he were lucky. At best, there would ensue the kind of meeting Ross did not want: a point-blank collision.

He stood by the horse with one hand on the pommel, hesitant. If Shelton decided not to stock food at the Paso Redondo camp, then Ross would miss contact with him completely. He would be waiting there while Shelton detoured around the camp and struck into the mountains.

Ross swung quickly into the saddle and took the right-hand trail to Paso Redondo.

The light was a full, claret flush over the mountains when he came to the foot of the mesa. Peering east, he saw the line camp in its lavender scope of bare cottonwoods. The dawn was mirrored in the pond. He could see the dimples left by striking trout on its still surface. A few horses roamed the upper end of the trap. A sudden recollection struck him.

Was the girl, Francie, still here?

Assuming Shelton came to the cabin, she could spoil everything. Pard would have told her of Ross's killing Blade. He had no way of guessing how she would have taken it. Ross searched for any sign that Shelton was already here, or approaching; but willows obscured the trail on the far side, and there were no horses in the yard. He quirted the tired horse with the reins' ends and it moved forward.

He dismounted behind the tank and left the pony there. Carrying his carbine, he walked to the corner of the feed shed and studied the cabin. The door hung open on its rawhide hinges. The chimney was smokeless. Through the unglazed window facing the water tank, he saw nothing. Still he waited. A girl with a gun could be as dangerous as a man—at short-range, at least. Then he remembered the old spring wagon which had stood in the yard. It was gone now.

He went to the cabin door and looked in.

A paper rustled. He pressed to the edge of the portal and kept the gun trained inside. Then he saw the ruby flash of a pack rat's eyes. He entered the cabin. He could tell by the odor that it was empty: the minute people moved out, the smells moved in—dust and deadness. The stove was cold. The cot had been robbed of blankets. Ross made a light and looked about. The trash of haphazard living was all that remained of the short love life of Francie and Blade Ramsey. A profusion of cans in a box by the stove, an inordinate number of liquor bottles, matchsticks everywhere, corpses of cigars and cigarettes. An old newspaper lying on the floor near him showed a bony-looking head cut up into segments, under the caption: *Noted Phrenologist Says Improve Your Chances.*

All right, Ross thought, but I'll take my chances this time with a .38-40.

He found coffee in a sack and threw a handful of beans into the grinder. He interrupted the job to stare out the east window. Then he ground the beans and poured the grind into a cup of cold water. He wished he could have risked heating it. Since he could not, he let the grounds soak until the water was a sickly amber, and drank this gratefully. He resumed his vigil by the window.

He had been there ten minutes when he heard the horses.

It was several minutes more before they came into view. Ross was on his knees beside the window with the gun on the floor by him. He saw the first rider come into view at the far end of the pond, where the crossing was—and even at this distance of a quarter-mile, with the sun in his eyes, he recognized the color of her gown. It seemed to him that that remembered teal-blue was the most precious color in the world. There was something miraculous about it, coming to him in the cold still dawn when he had thought he might never see it again. She was riding a sidesaddle, and just behind her rode Lamar Shelton.

Ross put the barrel of the gun on the windowsill and sighted down it. But the sun burned on the blued steel so that he was blinded. He rubbed soot from a lamp chimney onto the top of the gunbarrel.

Squinting down the barrel of the gun, now, he was able to catch Shelton in his sights. Laurel kept crossing and recrossing his field as she preceded Shelton—but they were coming toward the cabin, having left the trail. There were a long three hundred yards of brushy ground between the horses and the window. Ross had never fired the gun, did not know whether it lobbed high or low, and yet he was certain that this first shot would probably be the most important one he had ever fired. It must cripple without killing.

A hundred yards out, he saw Laurel halt and turn to remonstrate with Shelton. Shadowed by the sun at his back, the rancher's face was masked. But he said something in a low, harsh tone and the girl faced the cabin again and rode on. Ross saw her turn her head to glance briefly northward. There was something viciously cruel about this—to be able to see Laurel and not go to her.

He began to steady down, now, to the shot.

Laurel was in his way; then she moved out of it. He made out her tired features. Her hair had come loose and hung in dark braids down her back. The range was about two hundred feet. A trembling set up in Ross's body. He forced his knee against the wall and pressed the gunbarrel down hard on the windowsill. Laurel's horse moved out of line, angling for the trough in the corral. Thus Lamar Shelton was left as a black horse-and-rider silhouette against a wine-colored sunburst.

With the blinding redness of the sun in his eyes, Ross had only the silhouette for a target. He watched it grow larger, until Shelton's arm, held slightly from his body with a rifle grasped at the breech, was plain enough to draw a bead on. Laurel was within a hundred feet of the cabin. He did not allow himself to look at her. He kept his squinted gaze on that black-clad arm of Shelton's. He began to take up the slack of the trigger. His shoulder set itself against the expected recoil, while the big man on the buckskin horse jogged closer and became an almost certain target.

Then Shelton halted, staring at the cabin. He seemed to stiffen. All at once he rammed his spurs into the horse's flanks. He shouted at Laurel. As the pony jumped forward and to one side, he leveled the carbine at the cabin and fired a shot through the window.

34

ROSS SWAYED out of line, stunned. He realized that Shelton had seen the sun-sparkle on the muzzle of his gun. He heard him loping out of the yard, getting behind the cabin, where there were no windows. Ross did what he had to, then. He leaned into the window, took a bead on the horse and pulled the trigger. He could hear the pop of the bullet as it struck the animal's side.

He heard it fall behind the cabin. Shelton's voice came, strong as a bull's. "Laurel! Come here! They'll kill you!"

Ross saw her halt by the corral. He stood at the window where she could see him, and called:

"In here! Ride to the door!"

She gripped the leaping-head of the saddle and raced for the cabin. A rifle roared behind the shack and out in the pond beyond the girl Ross saw a plume of water toss briefly and fall back. She was at the door, scrambling from the horse as Ross hurried to help her. He caught her in his arms and carried her inside. The horse went buck-jumping across the yard.

Ross put the girl down and said: "In the corner—pull the pallet off the cot and cover yourself."

And he saw her face for just an instant—strained and white, her eyes saying all the things she might never be able to say to him again, and smiling with uncertain lips. He jacked a new shell into the chamber of the gun, and stood by the door, listening to the sounds Shelton was making. But in a moment there was silence. He turned quickly to Laurel. She had not stirred from his side. She seemed shocked. For an instant Ross held her tightly with one arm. "Easy, now," he said softly.

She began to cry. He could feel her tremble as she clung to him. He led her to a corner of the cabin away from any of the wall openings and told her to sit on the floor. "Cover yourself with this," he said, pulling the pallet from a cot. "And stay right here. It'll be all right pretty quick."

197

"Ross!" she said, as he started toward the door. "You're not going outside!"

"I got this far," Ross breathed. "Trust me to go a little farther. Here—"

He pulled Marshal Coles's big Frontier Colt from his holster and slid it to her. Then he slipped through the door and stood for one instant at the right of the stoop, his back against the wall, listening. There was no sound at all from the rancher. The dying horse behind the cabin was trumpeting hoarsely. Laurel's pony stood shuddering near the corral. He knew this ranch yard was sick—sick with death and fear.

After a few seconds Ross moved down the wall to a point ten feet from the door. Then he walked straight out from the cabin and turned to face it. He began backing slowly toward the corral, the carbine held low and steady. As he backed, he began to see more and more of the ground behind the cabin, but Shelton, lurking somewhere close to the rear walls, was out of sight.

Near the corral was a fire ring in which branding irons were heated. A few rusted irons still lay in the ashes. Ross stepped behind it. He went to one knee, keeping his gaze on the cabin and the bare yard running back to a rough hillside. Shelton, out of sight, was still mapping his strategy. One thing he must realize already: Ross could sweat him down from the sanctuary of the cabin. If he meant to take Laurel with him or even things with Ross, he would have to charge one of the windows or the door.

Ross put his palm against the earth and let himself down. The stones of the fire ring were precisely right for a sniper. A blackened granite notch took the barrel of the gun. The other rocks gave moderate shelter. He commenced breathing deeply, the cold air burning his lungs.

He began to question whether he had figured Shelton correctly. A patient man would move straight back from the cabin to the junipers on the hillside, moving behind this screen to a point from which he could fire into the cabin. But Shelton had little time. Ross turned his ear toward the cabin and listened for the slightest sound.

When Shelton's voice came, he started.

"Chance! Listen to me. Keep the damned ranch. But I'm taking my wife."

Ross pressed the butt of the gun against his shoulder.

"Do you hear me? You won't leave that cabin alive if you don't send her out."

Ross withdrew his finger from the trigger-guard, wiped the moisture from it, and curled it around the trigger again.

"I mean that!" Shelton called again. "This is the last chance you'll have. I'll give you one minute."

A moment after his voice died, Ross saw a shadow stir at the east side of the cabin. Then he knew that Shelton was coming to the window through which he had fired before. It was the easier one for a right-handed man. The shadow slipped along until it protruded into the yard. He could tell that Shelton was crouching at the rear edge of the window, timing it, steadying himself. . . . Ross would not be able to see him until he swung out from the wall to fire through the window. He was not afraid for Laurel, for Shelton would not be able to see her in the corner.

Suddenly and surprisingly, without a whisper of sound, Lamar Shelton pivoted into view and thrust the bronze barrel of his saddle gun into the window. His right shoulder and arm were exposed to Ross's view. There was an instant of utter quiet, as the rancher sought his target.

Ross pulled the trigger.

The gun kicked savagely. Black-powder smoke rolled across the yard in a dark smut, and ashes were whipped from the fire ring. Ross heard no sound from Shelton. He made a complete roll to the left, away from the blur of dust and smoke, coming out of it with his legs spread like the trails of a fieldpiece, his elbows jammed against the ground and the butt of the rifle against his shoulder.

Shelton had dropped his rifle and staggered back. He was staring at Ross in a wooden manner, his right arm limp and his left hand clutching the sleeve of his coat near the shoulder. His gun lay near the cabin. Suddenly he leaned down and reached for it with his left hand.

Ross fired again.

Shelton moved back as the bullet struck the stock of the gun. Splinters of walnut and steel flew against his boots. He stood looking down at the broken carbine, stunned by surprise and the shock of his wound. Ross rose quickly and ran toward him. Shelton faced him but seemed to forget his side arm.

As he ran, Ross called, "Laurel—stay where you are!"

Shelton's face was ashen under the mahogany of his skin. His dark hair was rumpled. Blood was trickling now from his fingertips. Ross stopped a few feet from him and looked at this big, injured man with rage and pain in his face.

"Kill me while you can, Chance!" Shelton said. "Be sure I'll kill you both if you don't. Now or later."

Ross took possession of Shelton's Colt. "Walk to the back of the cabin," he said.

Shelton's flat lips smiled. "Where the lady can't see it?"

Ross pointed the rifle at Shelton's thigh. He could see Shelton involuntarily flinch. "Walk back there," he said, "or you'll be coming on one leg when you come after us."

Shelton turned and walked to the rear. Once he collided with the cabin and reeled slightly as he recovered his balance. He stopped beside the rear wall. Ross spoke tersely.

"Walk over behind the water tank."

The rancher moved toward the tank among the leafless cottonwoods. He glanced at Ross's horse in surprise when they came to the west side of the concrete tank. The mud on the ground from leakage was frozen.

"Can you get on the horse?" Ross asked him.

Shelton gazed at him. "What is this, Chance?"

"I'll tell you later what it is. But remember I could have put that shot through your head as well as your arm. . . . Mount the horse and ride over to Laurel's pony."

Shelton followed orders. Ross made him stand by while he changed saddles from Shelton's dead horse behind the cabin to Laurel's pony. He left the sidesaddle on the ground and mounted. "Now we're going to where you crossed the stream."

Shelton looked at him steadily through several seconds; then he turned the horse and rode from the yard. Ross halted at the door of the cabin. He could hear Laurel moving inside.

"I'll be back in an hour," he said. "You'll find things for breakfast in the cooler. I might be hungry."

The girl came into the doorway. She had the Colt in her hand and she gazed at him strangely. "I hope you know what you're doing."

"I think I do. I don't know any other way to do this.—You won't hear any gunfire, if that's what you're thinking."

He rode after Shelton. He was possessed of a great need to finish it all and be through forever with Rancho Pacheco, and Shelton, and Pard Mallet and all his drunken dreams of vengeance and whiskey-wealth. He wanted to scrape all the filth off this coin and find the brightness underneath.

He escorted Shelton five miles into the Mexican mountains on the Chihuahua freight trail. Then he stopped in a pass from which the yellow plains beyond could be seen. Far away, the dust of a wagon train was visible.

"There's a doctor in Villa Hermosa," he said. "If you can't make it, there'll be freighters along soon. They'll help you."

Shelton's skin was drenched with sweat. His eyes had pinched down to pained slits. Now that the shock had worn off, he was being torn apart by the pain of his wound.

"You're a damned fool, Chance," he panted. "I'd kill you right now, if I had a gun."

"You wouldn't have to prod me," said Ross, "if I weren't more afraid of what you can do to me dead than I am alive. I'm going to have her without your blood on my hands. And I hope you hate my guts every night of your life, until the Rurales track you down in some flea-bag of a Mexican hotel."

"I can promise that," Shelton said. "And I can promise that I won't die in a Mexican hotel. If I die, it won't be far from you and Laurel."

"But you don't know where that's going to be," Ross grinned. "Anything that was left for me here, you and Gunlock and Pard Mallet wrecked. Every one of you knocked a little more off it, until now there's nothing left but twenty-five years of tax bills. So we're getting out. I don't know where, and I'll bet you'll never find out before the law finds you first. They're looking for you right now: Henry Lyman's seeing to that. They'll hang you high if they catch you on the American side."

Shelton's face remained hard and gray and expressionless.

"You think you could handle this better, don't you?" Ross said. "But you've been handling things your way all your life, and all you've got left is a bullet through your shoulder. And the wife you never claimed is waiting for me."

He turned his horse abruptly and rode a short distance. Then he looked back, and caught Shelton off-guard: the rancher's face was rutted with desperation. Looking deeply into it, Ross saw something stronger even than pain or hatred. He saw the despair of a strong man who had imagined he was above defeat. Ross knew then that there was very little the law could do to Lamar Shelton which he had not already done to himself.

When he returned to the cabin, a buggy was in the yard. Having forgotten everything but the girl who was waiting for him, he was puzzled. But as he rode in he recognized Henry Lyman's black rig; the head of the appaloosa between the shafts hung dispiritedly. Lyman came into the doorway with a mug of coffee in his hands. His gray stovepipe was on the side of his head; there was something almost jaunty about him.

"Mrs. Shelton," he said, "turns out to be quite a coffeemaker."

"I was meaning to find out," Ross smiled.

He went into the cabin, where plates and some bent silverware had been laid on the table. The fragrance of frying potatoes, salt pork, and raised biscuits filled the room. Laurel, at the stove, did not look around. Ross went to the sink to pump water into a basin. Still Laurel did not glance at him, and he was disturbed. Was she embarrassed, or angry, or what? He washed his hands and face and dried on a flour-sack towel. He raked a comb through his hair, replaced his Stetson on his head, and then looked at the girl, who was pouring coffee at the table.

She walked back to the stove, set the pot down and looked at him with tense, weary eyes. "Everything is all right?" she said.

"Everything that might make trouble," said Ross, "is on its way to Villa Hermosa."

She sat at the table. "I'm glad," she said. Then for the first time she smiled at him.

Henry Lyman turned quietly to the door. "Not going to eat?" Ross asked him.

"In a while," said the lawyer. "I ought to fork up some hay for the horses." He lingered on the doorsill, gazing into the fresh gold of the morning, and Ross moved behind him. He looked with sharp regret at the gold-and-lavender reach of desert hills.

"It was a nice place to grow up, Henry," he murmured. "I'd have liked my own kids to grow up here."

"Well, why not?"

"Why not? Some Mexican will raise his kids here; or else a gringo who comes up with the title to Pacheco ranch after all the smoke clears away."

"That could be you, as well as not," Henry said. He turned, drawing an envelope from his pocket. His seamed face was full of wry joy. "This is the wire I asked you to pick up. Since you didn't, I picked it up myself when I was looking for Mrs. Shelton."

Ross took it, but did not try to read it. "What's the story?"

"Well, we'll just keep everything quiet for a while, until the government works out something with Mexico. But a fraudulent international boundary doesn't seem to be the fault of an ordinary citizen like yourself. Any damages arising from the mixup will have to be stood by the government. And of course, as far as Lamar Shelton goes, he acquired title illegally, and if I know Will Coles, the transfer of title itself is probably as full of holes as a colander. So—if you can be patient, and make out for a while on the Tecolote place—I'll keep this," Lyman said, retrieving the unread telegram.

Laurel was watching him tensely. "But if he should ever come back..."

Ross tried to impart in his smile the sureness he felt. "He won't come back. When I left him, he was finished. I never saw a man more finished. He'd licked himself, finally. And besides that, he's not going to risk hanging trying to find us, when he thinks we've left anyway."

"There's a lot of truth in that," said Lyman. "He licked himself. And I don't think he'll ever be back."

He went outside to tend the horses.

Ross faced Laurel across the cabin. The light seemed fresh and clear in the room, and Laurel regarded him with the provocative face of a woman in love, grave but joyful. He went to her and stood behind her chair, and bending over her he kissed her brow, and her eyes. Her hands reached up to clasp about his neck, and with a whisper softer than a caress she pulled his face down to hers.